WHS McIntyre is a partner in Scotland's oldest law firm Russel + Aitken, specialising in criminal defence. William has been instructed in many interesting and high-profile cases over the years and now turns fact into fiction with his string of legal thrillers, The Best Defence Series, featuring defence lawyer Robbie Munro. William is married with four sons.

STITCH UP

A Best Defence Mystery

William McIntyre

SANDSTONE PRESS

Published in Great Britain by
Sandstone Press Ltd
Dochcarty Road
Dingwall
Ross-shire
IV15 9UG
Scotland

www.sandstonepress.com

The publisher acknowledges support from Creative Scotland
towards publication of this volume.

ISBN: 978-1-912240-28-9
ISBNe: 978-1-912240-29-6

Cover design by Jason Anscombe at Raw Shock
Typeset by Iolaire Typography Ltd, Newtonmore.
Printed and bound by Totem, Poland

Dedicated to the organisers and supporters of Falkirk's annual Mag's Fish Supper Ceilidh, and, of course, Celtic rock band Skerryvore, for their unstinting efforts in support of cancer research.

ACKNOWLEDGEMENTS

With thanks to my wife Gillian and friends Dr Fiona Downs and Lynn Swan for their helpful advice on matters pharmacological.

I hadn't seen Cammy Foster in years. To be honest, I hadn't missed him. Once upon a time we'd played football for the same amateur football club, and I remembered going to his wee sister's funeral along with the rest of the team. I couldn't recall us ever having been particularly close friends. Apparently, Cammy could, and, on the strength of that alleged friendship, enticed me out for a drink.

Wednesday lunchtime I met him in the Red Corner Bar. He had on a worried face he'd not shaved that morning and a crumpled suit he'd not bought yesterday. Since neither face nor suit was making any discernible movement in the direction of the bar, I shouted up a heavy shandy for myself.

'What are you having?' I asked him.

Cammy was having Jack Daniel's and Diet Coke. American whisky was bad enough, but a mixer? The balance of the man's mind was clearly disturbed. The drinks hadn't been poured before I realised this was to be less of an old pals' reunion and more of a request for help.

'I'm not asking you to actually do anything, Robbie. I've just come to pick your brains.' It was what people said when they didn't want to pay for a lawyer's stock in trade: advice. Worse than that, it didn't look like Cammy was keen on paying for the drinks either.

'Let me know if I can do youse any more cocktails,'

Brendan the barman called after us, as we moved to a table next to the fruit machine. I'd drunk most of my shandy, looked at the clock on the wall three times and failed to stifle several yawns, before Cammy had finished filling me in on his predicament.

'Call me old-fashioned, Cammy,' I said, staring into the depths of my pint glass, 'but I usually advise people on how to get off with a crime *after* they've committed it – not before. It's sort of a tradition with us defence lawyers.'

Cammy, who thus far hadn't touched his drink, removed the ironic slice of lemon that Brendan had wedged onto the side of the glass and knocked it back in a oner. *Diet* Coke? Anyone who was worried about the calories in their mixers didn't have a weight problem; they had a drink problem.

'Tell me, Cammy,' I said, 'what do you do for a living these days?'

It turned out he sold electronic gadgets. 'I can get you audio devices to spy on your business competitors,' he said. 'Trackers so that you know where your wife is ...'

'I know where my wife is, thanks. She's ... She's at work, in court or somewhere ...'

Cammy gave me a look of sympathy. 'Are you sure?'

'Yes, I'm sure. I trust her.'

Cammy took a lemon pip from his mouth and set it and his empty glass down on the table between us. 'Okay, okay. You trust your wife. What about your house?' There was a slate loose, but nothing Joanna's dad couldn't sort. 'If you like, I can fix you up with Wi-Fi -capable, domestic appliances. You could control your home using your mobile phone.'

I had difficulty controlling my mobile phone, *using* my

mobile phone. 'Cammy, I didn't ask you what you did for a living because I wanted to hear a sales pitch. I was trying to make the point that you probably don't do much murdering people in your line of work.'

Cammy leaned back in his chair. Trying and failing to look nonchalant, he glanced around the bar to see if anyone might have overheard me. He needn't have worried. There were no Jehovah's Witnesses in the Red Corner Bar, only Jehovah's bystanders. Satisfied no one was listening in to our conversation, he moved his glass to the side and folded his arms on the table top. 'No, I don't, but I'd be happy to start with Ricky Hertz.'

That name. A name everyone in Linlithgow knew and was ashamed of. Ricky Hertz had killed three girls. They'd found the bodies of the first two in a stretch of scrub ground between the lower of the Rugby Club's pitches and the embankment of the Edinburgh to Glasgow railway line. The last time the children had been seen alive they'd been walking a dog not far from the swing park on Mains Road, a mere two hundred metres away. Cammy's sister, Emily, had been Hertz's final victim. Her body had never been found. They'd buried a small, white, empty casket.

Hertz had been tried and convicted, and it was very much hoped he'd die in prison. Indeed, over the years, a few inmates had done their best to see that hope fulfilled, for there is no one more self-righteous than a fellow lifer doing time for a proper murder, and a child killer makes the ideal target. Now, after many years inside, Ricky was outside again, bailed pending an appeal into a possible miscarriage of justice.

'A miscarriage of justice?' Cammy flicked a finger at the lemon pip, sending it sailing across the bar. 'What a lot of shite.'

3

'The Appeal Court wouldn't let him out unless they had some good reason to believe his conviction was unsafe,' I said. 'When was his trial – two thousand?'

'Two thousand and one.'

Enough said. Although by 2001 the European Convention on Human Rights had been adopted by the newly formed Scottish Parliament, it was slow in taking effect.

'There weren't all that many safeguards for accused persons back then,' I told Cammy. 'I'm guessing Hertz's solicitor has raised an Article Six issue.'

Cammy lifted his glass and stood up. 'I don't care what technicality some smart-arsed lawyer has dug up. This is my opportunity; can't you see that? What I need to know is how to do it and not get caught.'

Yes, it was really as simple as that. All Cammy wanted me to tell him was how to commit the perfect crime. I should have felt flattered at being asked.

'And if you did kill him, who do you think would be prime suspect?' I said, guessing I wasn't the first person Cammy had met in a pub and shared what he'd like to do to his sister's killer.

He looked at my depleted pint glass. 'Same again?' I asked for a whisky this time, any single malt. It would be quicker for me to drink, and once I had I was leaving.

'I assumed that you'd tell me to set up an airtight alibi for myself,' Cammy said, on his return from the bar with another JD and Coke for himself and something that smelled distinctly blended for me. 'And get someone else to do the actual . . . you know . . .'

'Murdering?'

He glanced around again. 'Yeah.'

'Good luck with that.'

4

'Actually, that's the main reason I came to see you. I've been asking around. I hear you know people.'

'I don't.'

'But you must do, in your line of work.'

'I'm a defence lawyer. I don't run an agency for hitmen.'

'Is it about money?'

'Have I said anything about money?'

'No, but it's always about money with you lawyers.'

I took a tentative sip and confirmed my worst fears of a cheap blend.

'I might have known it would come down to money,' Cammy muttered, picking up his own glass and taking a slug.

'Look, Cammy, I'm very sorry about what happened to your sister—'

'Then why are you trying to protect that scumbag?'

'I'm not. I'm trying to protect you. Protect you from having to spend the rest of your life in prison with scumbags like Ricky Hertz.'

He shrugged the shrug of a man who just wouldn't be told. 'After what he did to my sister, what would I get for killing him? A couple of years? The jury would probably not even convict.'

'No, Cammy,' I said. 'The jury would be directed to convict, and the sentence would be the same as it always is for murder – life imprisonment.'

'Come off it. For ridding the world of a piece of filth like Ricky Hertz?'

'Up at the High Court they call that taking the law into your own hands,' I said. 'And what the boys and girls in the wigs and red silk jerseys really don't like is folk doing their jobs for them.'

He grunted and rolled his glass between the palms of his hands.

'Cammy, what happened to your sister was terrible. I don't blame you for feeling like you do. If it was me I'd feel the same way, but stop and listen to yourself for a moment. What you're talking about is just plain stupid.'

'Oh, I'm stupid, am I? For wanting justice?' He sniffed. 'Yeah, well, thanks for nothing.'

My turn to shrug. 'You wanted my advice and I'm giving you it. Let it go. Let the law deal with Ricky Hertz. You or anyone else going to prison for him is only ruining another life. If in fact he did kill your sister—'

'If? How can you say if? It was your dad who caught him.'

That was something my dad hadn't allowed me to forget over the years, and I was as proud of his role in the child killer's capture as he was. Well, nearly. 'What I mean is that there may have been some legal problem.'

'I don't understand. How can there have been a problem? What kind of problem, exactly?'

I had no idea. All I knew was that the Appeal Court didn't release convicted child murderers on bail unless a great big problem had come floating to the surface.

Cammy banged the table with a fist. His tall glass toppled. By the time I'd righted it, most of the contents had spilled and were dripping onto the floor. I could see Brendan behind the counter, hands on hips, grubby towel draped over one shoulder, glowering across at us. I lobbed a couple of beer mats into the midst of the small lake that had formed and shouted to him to bring over a cloth.

By this time Cammy was on his feet. 'I'd like to say it's been nice seeing you again, Robbie, but—'

'Cammy . . .'

'No, it's fine. I understand,' he said. 'You're right. I am stupid. Stupid to ask for advice from someone who makes his money defending folk like Ricky Hertz. Maybe it's your dad I should be speaking to.'

Seriously, what had he expected me to say? Here's a list of hitmen I recommend. For more information visit my website, www.hire-a-killer.com? No, this meeting was less about Cammy's warped sense of justice and more about him trying to salve his conscience. The man who killed his wee sister was out, and he thought he should avenge her death. But how was a gadget salesman going to do that? When he'd come to see me, he must have known I'd tell him to take a hike, but, because of my unwillingness, he now had someone to blame for his own inaction. What did I care? I hadn't seen Cammy in more than seventeen years. I could happily wait that long before seeing him again.

Brendan appeared at my side with a damp cloth and a bucket. 'Problem, ladies?' he asked.

'No problem, Brendan,' I said, standing up to let him in and give the table a quick wipe. 'Mr Foster was just wondering if I knew anyone who might kill someone for him. You free tonight?'

'Sorry, I don't kill people on a Wednesday,' Brendan said, wringing the cloth into the bucket. 'Not unless they spill two drinks.'

'It's all a big laugh to you, isn't it, Robbie?' Cammy snarled, after Brendan had sauntered off again. 'Well, my sister never found it very funny.'

'Go home, Cammy,' I said. 'Nothing that happens to Ricky Hertz is going to bring your sister back.'

'No, but at least I'd have the satisfaction of knowing that the evil bastard got what he deserved. If the government had more balls they'd hang folk like him.'

I unhooked my jacket from the back of the chair. Cammy walked over and stood a bit too close. He was tall. I recalled he'd played centre-half. I'd played centre forward, usually when I was supposed to be playing full-back. It had only been a lack of sporting ability that had prevented either of us from playing professionally. He pushed his face at me. 'I won't forget this.'

'Really?' I said. 'What you going to do? Use your mobile phone to turn my houselights on when I'm out?'

There was plenty of room for me to walk past Cammy, and yet he still managed to arrange it so that our shoulders collided. 'It would be different if I had the money,' he shouted after me. 'You'd know people then, wouldn't you?'

I turned. 'Yeah, I would. The sort of people who'd take your money and leave you bleeding up a close. That's the trouble with paid assassins. Very unreliable. You want a job done?' I called back to him. 'Stop trying to blame other people and do it yourself.'

2

'Can I come in?' Kaye Mitchell asked, coming in. 'You'll never guess who's dead.' She thumped her enormous handbag onto my desk, and dropped into the seat opposite to where, late that same Wednesday afternoon, I was busy completing a legal aid mandate. Not easy at the best of times, far less after a couple of drinks. The evil geniuses at the Scottish Legal Aid Board had made the document four pages longer so that I had to spend more time form-filling and less doing actual paid work. Not that there was much work to do these days. No one was being prosecuted. Either the population of Scotland had turned over a new leaf, or it had something to do with the lack of police officers, closed police stations and Crown Office cutbacks.

'Go on,' Kaye said. 'Who do you think no longer shares this earthly plane with us?'

Last time I'd checked, I shared this earthly plane with seven billion other souls. There wasn't time to go through them all before close of business. I ignored her and flipped the form over to page two.

'Okay, I'll narrow it down for you,' she said. 'Who in the world would you most like to have died?'

That still left a lot of prospective candidates.

'Hercule, that's who,' Kaye said eventually, peering around the monitor and over a pile of case files at me, in a what-do-you-think-about-that-then? sort of a way.

Hercule? Was she talking about *the* Hercule?

'Of course, *the* Hercule. Hercule Mercier. How many Hercules do you know? I'm talking about the guy Jill dumped you for.'

'No way. When did he die?'

'Last week.'

'Did Jill call you?'

'No. Jill and I don't talk that much now. After she dumped you—'

'Okay, okay. Just tell me how you know.'

'I happened to see the obit come down the wire.'

Did things still come down the wire? Kaye made it sound like she was editor of the *Chicago Tribune* in the 1920s and not editor of a local newspaper at the end of the second decade of the twenty-first century.

'I wonder how she's taking it,' I said. It was so hard not to feel just the tiniest degree of satisfaction.

'She's bearing up.' The voice came from the doorway. Jill walked into the room wearing a black suit with a thin gold belt that matched the looped links of the chain around her neck, her earrings and bracelet. I didn't know much about fashion; I did know expensive when I saw it. Like a ray of sunshine against an unwashed window, Jill's very presence made my office seem even more dirty and shabby than normal. She had a black and gold handbag to go with her outfit. She set it down on my desk next to Kaye's, and then looked around, a process that pained her.

'I see nothing much has changed about here,' she said. 'Do you never think of giving the place a lick of paint? And why do you insist on allowing that straggly, dried-up old object floor space?'

'What can I do?' I said with a shrug. 'Kaye's office is next door. She keeps popping in.' Those, I realised, were the first words I'd spoken to Jill since the night she'd inexplicably ditched me for Hercule Mercier, the suave, sophisticated, multi-millionaire, pharmaceuticals executive, now, apparently, deceased.

'I'm talking about the umbrella plant, if that's what it is.' Jill plucked at a withered leaf. Humour, mine at any rate, had never fully registered with my former fiancée.

'I'd like a word with you, Robbie.' She looked down at Kaye. 'Alone, if you don't mind.'

Kaye stood and gave Jill's arm a squeeze. 'I'm so sorry for your loss. Let's catch up later over a coffee.'

'Yes, let's,' Jill said, not looking at her.

'Why are you here?' I asked, once Kaye and her big handbag had left the room.

'You were never great on small talk, were you, Robbie?'

I didn't know what to say, which, I suppose, only helped prove her right. Jill was usually right about things.

She sighed. 'I'm here for some legal advice.'

I coughed up a laugh like a TB sufferer coughing up a lung. 'From me? Doesn't Zanetti Biotechnic Inc. have teams of lawyers?'

'Not ones I trust.'

'Oh, yeah, trust,' I said. 'Look that up in a dictionary, did you?'

'Don't, Robbie. Let's not go over old ground.'

Old ground? It was ground I'd never been allowed to so much as step on, far less go over. Hercule Mercier's security personnel had made plenty sure of that by placing a ring of steel around Jill. Now the great man was dead, she seemed to think she could march back into my life as though nothing had happened.

'You know what, Jill? I don't think you coming to me for legal advice is such a great idea. I'm sorry that Hercule is dead, and I agree that what's done is done, but I think you should go see another lawyer. One that knows about wills and dead people and that kind of thing. Try Maggie Sinclair at Caldwell and Craig, she'll make sure you get every penny you're entitled to from the estate. There may even be enough left over for a new handbag once you've settled her fee.'

Jill wandered to the window and looked out at Linlithgow High Street on a bright October afternoon. This was Scotland. There weren't that many sunny days in autumn. Today could be the only one, and I was missing it. 'It's not that kind of advice I'm after,' she said. 'I need a lawyer who knows about crime.'

'Crime?'

'Yes, and you're the best.'

When she put it like that ...

'Or, at least, so you were fond of telling me.' She smiled the smile I'd once loved more than anything in the world. Like our relationship the smile was fleeting. First it started to quiver at the corners, then the whole bottom lip began to wobble. Jill lowered her chin and covered her eyes with a hand.

I couldn't help myself. I came out from behind my desk, walked over and gave her a hug. 'I'm sorry. Yes, I'll help.' Holding her in my arms after all this time felt so unfamiliarly familiar. 'Of course, I'll help.'

Jill looked up into my eyes, blinking away the tears.

It must have been dead on five because Grace-Mary bustled into the room, raincoat draped over one arm. It might be a beautiful day, but this was still Scotland and she was taking no chances. 'That's me off then, I'll see you ... Oh ...'

12

I let go of Jill like she was the smooth side of a toasted bagel. She stepped out of my embrace, tugged a tissue from the box on the corner of my desk and dabbed her eyes with it.

'Is everything okay?' Grace-Mary asked.

Jill nodded, a tissue now pressed against her nose. I bid farewell to my secretary who no longer seemed all that keen to leave. 'Watch your step on the way out,' I said, guiding her to the door.

'It's you who'd better watch your step,' Grace-Mary said, when we'd reached the top of the stairs leading down to the street.

'Me?'

'Yes, you. I saw that just now. You with your arms all over her.'

'Jill's upset. She needed a hug.'

'Yeah, well, needing hugs is how they get you. Keep your paws off. You're a married man. What would Joanna say if she knew the two of you were here all alone? Hugging.'

'But she won't ever know,' I said, 'because no one will ever tell her, and, don't worry, there isn't going to be any more hugging.' I watched her go down the first few steps and then returned to my room where Jill was looking a lot more composed.

'You're right. I shouldn't have come,' she said. 'It's not fair asking you to—'

'Don't be stupid.' I pulled out a chair and gently pressed her into it. 'You know that if you ever need help I'll be here for you. Just tell me what the problem is, and I'll see what I can do. Or maybe you'd rather come back another day. I mean, if Hercule only died . . .'

'It was sudden. Last Friday, in Edinburgh. Hercule's been coming over on business a lot recently. I came to visit him. It was supposed to be a surprise.'

13

'What happened? I mean, how did he die?'

Jill dropped the crumpled tissue in the wastepaper basket and sat down. 'That's what I'd like to find out.'

Scotland doesn't have a coroner system and carries out far fewer routine autopsies than England. Still, if there had been any doubt surrounding the cause of Hercule's death, the Procurator Fiscal would have ordered one to take place.

'If it was a sudden, unexpected death there must have been a post-mortem,' I said.

'There was. I'm still waiting for the results. It's been nearly a week. Hercule's body hasn't been released yet. No one will tell me anything.'

'But, the cops aren't involved, are they? I mean, they don't think there was anything suspicious?'

Jill shook her head. 'No, they don't. That's the problem – because I do.'

'In what way suspicious?'

'I don't know. That's why I'd like you to look into it for me. Find out, exactly, how Hercule died and if you think there is even the remotest chance that he was murdered—'

It was a serious matter. I didn't mean to laugh. 'Why would anyone want to murder him?'

'Hercule was the CEO of Europe's fastest-growing pharmaceutical company. He'd opened four new research and manufacturing centres in the past seven years. Do you know how much it costs to do that?'

I had no idea.

'You're talking ten billion to construct and kit out one such complex. Even then there usually has to be a complete refit every four or five years. The number of contractors involved is huge, the opportunity for corruption immense. Hercule was a tough businessman. He made a lot of people rich, but at the same time others lost out.'

14

'Whoah,' I said. 'This sounds way out of my league.'

'If it's a question of money ...'

Why did people think that with lawyers the sticking point was always money? 'It's got nothing to do with money. I know I said I'd help in any way I can, but I wouldn't know where to start. If you have any grounds at all to think that Hercule was murdered, you need to go to the police.'

'The police aren't interested.'

'How do you know? Tell them what you think might have happened.'

'No, I don't want them involved. Not yet. I could be mistaken, and, if I am, I don't want to go around asking questions and sounding—'

'Delusional. Paranoid?'

'Stupid.'

'But it's okay if I do?'

'You're used to it.'

'Thanks.'

'You know what I mean.'

'No, I'm afraid I don't. My job isn't catching criminals. Criminals come to me so that I can prove they're not criminals. There are lots of other people out there who will help you: the cops, Crown Office, in fact every other branch of the criminal justice system apart from me.' Point well enough made, I thought, I sat back in my chair arms crossed, a sign of my unwillingness to yield to Jill's ridiculous suggestion.

'Robbie, I know it sounds daunting, but all I want are a few questions asked in the right places, and for you to see if anything looks amiss. I trust your judgement. If you need me to give you clearance, I'm a junior vice-president of Zanetti. I'm also listed as Hercule's next-of-kin. I can provide you with any letter of authority you need.'

I really wasn't getting through to her. I tried again. 'If you don't want to use the police, there are agencies that will do this for you. They employ ex-cops who know their way around a murder investigation much better than I do. They'll do it quietly and discreetly.'

'I've already told you. I don't trust anyone. Only you. If there has been some kind of cover-up, you're best placed to recognise it. It's the sort of thing you do, investigating the evidence, looking for loopholes, inventing alternative scenarios.'

'I think you mean establishing defences.'

'If you say so.' Jill picked up her handbag and opened it. 'Okay, how much?'

'How much what?'

'How much will you charge for taking this job on for me? I really don't care how much it costs.'

There is a list of things clients say to lawyers about money. At the bottom is, 'I'll pay you when the case is finished.' Much further up the ladder is, 'I'll pay you upfront,' but right at the top is, 'I don't care how much it costs.'

From her handbag Jill removed a black leather-bound cheque book with her initials etched in gold at one of the corners. She flipped it open.

'It's not just a question of money,' I said.

'Well, what is it a question of?' she asked, pen poised. 'Are you too busy?'

That was one thing I wasn't. While I thought what to say in reply, Jill began writing.

She ripped the cheque from the book and held it out to me. 'Ten thousand do you? Just to get started?'

I thought it over for as long as it took the ink to dry, and decided that ten thousand would do fine. Just to get started.

3

It was hard to believe that my first wedding anniversary had come and gone. I'd married Joanna the year before, after a short engagement. It had been Grace-Mary's opinion, one shared by my dad, and a lot of other people, most of whom hadn't been asked for their opinion, that it was best not to delay things in case my fiancée came to her senses.

It was my brother, Malky, who organised the stag night. I remembered it beginning in the Red Corner Bar. After that things became a little hazy, like a 1970s TV sitcom flashback, all wavy lines, fish-lens faces and blurred images, right up until the point I awoke in an Edinburgh hotel room beside half a kebab, and wearing somebody else's shoes. It had been a night to remember, and one I was happy to forget.

We moved into our cottage on the eastern outskirts of Linlithgow, newly renovated as it was by Joanna's dad's construction company, and settled down to married life. Tina, my daughter, started school in the August and was now in Primary Two. Everything was going fine, until I came home that Wednesday evening to find the kitchen table set for dinner, a bottle of Chianti breathing gently nearby, and my daughter farmed out to my dad's for the night. Even Bouncer the dog appeared to have been told to be on his best behaviour and was lying sleeping on his blanket in a corner.

It was more than enough evidence from which my

finely tuned legal brain could deduce that something was terribly wrong.

'You're leaving me?'

'It's only for three weeks,' Joanna said, pouring me a glass of red.

'Three weeks!'

'Don't say it like that.'

'How would you like me to say it?'

'More calmly. Maybe even with a "congratulations, Joanna" thrown in. It is the International War Crimes Tribunal after all. I put my name down for a stint at The Hague when I first joined the Fiscal Service. How can I refuse? It's a great opportunity.'

'But three weeks!'

'Four, tops. Unless I have to stay on a little longer . . .' Joanna held up her hands. 'Which I won't, of course.' She shoved the glass of wine at me. 'Unless it's absolutely essential.'

'But—'

'I'm only there to cover sick leave. I'm sure it won't last more than the initial three weeks I've been allocated.'

'And if it does . . .?'

'It won't. Probably. Come and sit down. Your food's going to get cold. I made you your favourite, fried cow muscle and chips.'

I sat down and cut into the steak. It was just the way I liked it: rare, but not so rare that a casualty crash team would see it merely as a challenge. I pierced the slice of meat with my fork and lifted it to reveal a nice pink centre with only a slight degree of blood seepage. I could tell by Joanna's face that she was trying not to gag.

'So, when is this all happening?' I asked, smearing on a thick layer of English mustard.

Joanna said something that I didn't quite catch because it was through a mouthful of microwaved macaroni cheese.

'Can you say that again? It sounded like you said Friday.'

She nodded and then swallowed. 'I did say Friday.'

'Not this Friday?'

She nodded some more. 'It'll give me the weekend to read through the papers, pick up the reins and be ready to hit the ground running, first thing Monday morning.'

'This Friday? As in not today, but tomorrow?'

Joanna reached across the table and waggled my cheek. 'You certainly know your days of the week. Has Tina been teaching you?' she said, before digging her fork into the pile of creamy pasta again.

'Talking of Tina,' I said, 'what am I supposed to do with her when you're gone?'

'Well…' Joanna set down her fork and wiped her mouth with a square of kitchen roll. 'I was thinking…' I hated it when she did that. 'It's the school October holidays next week, and there's nothing planned, so why don't you take a week off and spend some quality time with your daughter for a change?'

'Oh, yeah, that's a great idea. I'll put an advert in the paper telling people to stop committing crimes until I'm back at work, shall I?'

'From the way you complain about business, I thought no one did commit crime any more. Anyway, I've made some calls. Grace-Mary is on board with the idea, and Paul Sharp has agreed to cover court for you. I've told him you'll return the favour at Easter. He's taking his kids to Florida.'

That seemingly settled, she picked up her fork again,

and we ate in silence for a while. I didn't want Joanna to think it wasn't without great sacrifice that I'd agree to her terms, but, with the cheque for ten grand from Jill in my hip pocket, I wouldn't starve, and I'd need some free time to make enquiries about Hercule's death. Then I had a thought. 'When did you speak to Grace-Mary?'

'I phoned her at the office, just before she left for the day.'

I hadn't been going to mention Jill's visit. I'd have to now. There was no way Grace-Mary wouldn't have let it slip. I was just grateful the call had been made pre-hug.

'I saw Jill today,' I said, casually spearing a chip.

'Is that so?' Joanna said, trying and failing to sound like she didn't already know. She helped herself to some garlic bread, tearing off a chunk and dipping it into her cheese sauce. 'How is she?'

'Fine,' I said.

'Then why did she come to see you?'

'Well ... She's not that fine.'

'What's the problem?'

'Hercule's the problem. He's dead.'

'Hercule? Her partner? The guy she dumped you for?'

'Yes, that Hercule.'

'When did this happen?'

Malky walked in. 'When did what happen?' he asked, stealing a chip from my plate without breaking stride on his way to the fridge to extract my last bottle of beer.

'Hercule what's-his-name,' Joanna said. 'He's dead.'

'His name's Hercule Mercier,' I said.

Malky cracked open the bottle of lager. 'Hercule? The bloke Jill ditched you for?'

'That's him,' I said.

'Seriously?' Malky laughed. 'He's dead? The millionaire,

skier guy from Switzerland? What happened? Hit a tree? Choke on a Toblerone?'

'Hercule was quite a good skier, but—'

'In the Olympics, wasn't he?' Malky said, as he watched me carve another slice of meat.

'Okay, he was a very good skier, but he was a pharmacist and rich because of pharmaceuticals, not skiing.'

Malky took a slug of beer and burped. 'And now he's dead?'

'That's it. That's all I know.'

Malky shrugged and returned the bottle to his lips, but my answer wasn't enough for Joanna. 'What's Jill saying about it? Why did she come and see you?'

Malky waved a hand to silence her and pulled up a chair. 'Who cares about some dead Swiss farmer? I'm here to find out what you're going to do about Dad,' he said. What to do about my dad had been something I'd been mulling over since adolescence. 'He's not happy about this whole Ricky Hertz thing.'

'Who's Ricky Hertz?' Joanna asked.

Strange, I thought everyone knew who Ricky Hertz was. 'He's a child killer.'

'How many children did he kill?'

'Three.'

'Where?'

'Here. Linlithgow.'

'When was this?'

'Two thousand, two thousand and one. Sometime around then. Have you really never heard of Ricky Hertz?'

Malky, who had remained silent, mainly because he was busy drinking my beer and eating my chips, piped up. 'It was our dad who caught him, you know?'

He sounded just like me, second year at Uni, boasting

to my pals. It had been a proud day when we'd gone along to the High Court to watch Sergeant Alex Munro take the stand and give evidence at the trial. It was an even prouder day when, two weeks later, the jury returned a unanimous guilty verdict and once more the children of Linlithgow could be late home from school without their parents worrying.

At the end of the proceedings the judge had warmly commended my father. The old man's beaming face had been front page, and, for many weeks afterwards, Malky and I had basked in the limelight of the local hero whose DNA we were privileged to share.

'You know that Ricky's out now, don't you?' Malky said, eyeing my plate, preparing for another swoop. 'They think he might have been fitted up.'

'Who does?' Jill asked.

'The judges who let him out,' Malky said. 'Who do you think, the prison janny? I thought you were supposed to be a lawyer? Hertz was sent down for a minimum of thirty-five years and he's only done about half that.'

'How do you know so much?' I asked. My brother wasn't one to keep abreast of the latest Appeal Court decisions unless they were on the back page of the *Daily Record*.

'That cop, you know, the one who doesn't like you.' That didn't narrow it down much. 'He came round to Dad's today when I was there. He's not long away in fact.'

'Which cop?'

'About your height, but heavier. Hairy, but not on his head. The one who thinks Dad's great. That cop.'

It could only be D.I. Dougie Fleming. Living proof that mankind evolved from apes, and that some of us took a little longer than others. He'd been my dad's protégé. The old man had taught him everything he knew about police work. That must have made for an interesting afternoon.

'There's some folk wanting to speak to Dad,' Malky said.

'What kind of folk?'

Malky sighed. 'Police folk, obviously.'

'Police? They don't think Dad had anything to do with—' My words coincided badly with the insertion of another chunk of steak. I began to choke. Joanna slapped my back while I coughed and tried to force down some red wine.

Malky took advantage of my momentary incapacity to nick another chip and then retreated nimbly out of range, showing the sort of fast footwork that had taken him from Linlithgow Rose to Glasgow Rangers aged seventeen, and made him captain of Scotland at twenty-four. 'I suppose they must think that Dad fitted him up.'

I waved my arms about in an attempt both to fend off Joanna's blows and deter Malky from stealing any more of my dinner.

Malky chewed and then stopped as though it had been hindering his thought process. 'Yeah, I'm sure that must be the reason,' he said, normal chewing having resumed.

'How's Dad taking it?' I managed to croak.

Malky stopped chewing again. 'I'm not sure. I only heard a wee bit of the conversation. Tina called me outside because she'd kicked her football into the nettles. Dad didn't seem all that bothered to me. Never really mentioned it after the cop had gone.'

Joanna had heard enough. 'Not all that bothered? He won't know how to express his feelings properly. He's a man. He'll be worried sick and bottling it all up.' To hear Joanna talk was to know she'd never been to a football match with my dad. There were a few under-performing Linlithgow Rose players who wished my dad would bottle up his feelings more often. She gave my back a final thump. 'Go see him, Robbie.'

'All right, all right.'

'On you go, then,' she said.

I stared down at my half-eaten dinner. 'You don't mean now?'

'When do you think I mean?' She pulled my plate away.

'But what about my dinner?'

'I'll put it in the oven. It'll keep till you get back.'

I looked at Malky and very much doubted it.

'Go, Robbie.' Joanna pulled me to my feet. 'He's your father, he's in trouble and he needs your help.'

4

'I don't need your help.' My dad seemed pretty sure about that. He and Tina were in the living room of his cottage, rummaging under the couch for something. The old man hoisted himself to his feet. 'Why don't you go look in your bedroom in case you left it there?' he said to Tina.

'I've already looked.'

'Well, look again,' I told her. 'I want to speak to Gramps.'

'What about?'

'Something that's not for wee girls to hear. Now off you go and ... What are you looking for anyway?'

The missing object turned out to be a bar of chocolate. Since our marriage, Joanna had laid down the law concerning calorie intake, and especially the source of those calories. Ice cream trips to Sandy's café had been curtailed, along with sweets and fried breakfasts which were Saturday mornings only. Now that the finding of a chocolate biscuit, chez Munro, was a job for Interpol, the one confectionery oasis in Tina's sugar desert was my dad's house, where there was always a bar of chocolate with her name on it. But not tonight. There had been a three-pack of Fry's Chocolate Cream earlier in the week, and they'd each had one on Tina's last visit. As was the time-honoured arrangement, the three-pack was to be shared on a two-to-one basis in Tina's favour, but the third chocolate bar was nowhere to be seen.

Chin on her chest, arms folded, Tina stalked out of the living room door. She'd be back any minute, nosy to find out what was going on.

'Why didn't you call me? I'd have been here sooner,' I said.

'I thought you and Joanna were having a special dinner. I didn't think you'd drop everything just to come over and look for a bar of chocolate.'

'You know I'm not talking about that. I'm talking about Ricky Hertz. Why do the cops want to speak to you?'

'I've no idea.'

If he didn't, I was beginning to formulate one. Why had it never crossed my mind until now? It wasn't as though I'd ever trusted a cop to tell the truth before, so why my dad? Had my childhood idolatry of the man who'd caught Linlithgow's only ever serial killer blinded me to the obvious? After all, I knew the old man's reputation. He might have been well respected amongst his peers, but it wasn't for his nuanced approach to police work, nor, I suspected, his genteel interviewing techniques.

Back in the early noughties, not long before my dad had retired after thirty-seven years in the force, and at the time Ricky Hertz had been detained and confessed to the murders, things were very different. No necessity for audio or video recording of police interviews, and no right to have a solicitor present. It would just have been Ricky, two cops, four walls and a locked door. On the other side of that door would have been either a stroll to a warm cell, a packet of fags and a cup of tea, or the police station stairs and the toe of a well-polished boot to help Ricky down them. Which route he took would all have depended on

26

whether he'd been prepared to help the police with their enquiries. I seemed to recall that Ricky had confessed.

My dad lifted a cushion from the sofa and looked under it. 'It's just some routine stuff.'

'It's more than routine if they've let a child murderer out on bail and the cops are looking to speak to you. Malky said Dougie Fleming was here.'

He dropped the cushion and lifted the next, apparently no longer listening. 'And you can stop pretending there's any chance of finding the chocolate,' I said. 'Tina's not here. Just tell me who exactly it is wants to speak to you.'

He plumped up the cushion and threw it back onto the sofa. 'I can't remember what they're calling themselves these days.'

'It wasn't the HMICS, was it?'

'No, I think it was the other mob.'

'The CCU?'

'Ach, it's all letters, and they keep changing them.'

'Dad, if the Counter Corruption Unit want to speak to you, it's serious. What's Big Jock told them?'

Jock Knox was a good friend of my dad's. A great big Highlander who was said to have passed the former police force height requirement test while sitting down. Growing up he'd been like an uncle to Malky and me. It was Big Jock who'd watched my thirteen-year-old brother playing for a boys' club and alerted Linlithgow Rose to a promising centre back. There was many a local hard man who, when Jock had taken them to the car park behind the old police station, had carried out an urgent reappraisal of their durability.

'Jock's saying nothing. Alzheimer's. He can't remember what he was doing five minutes ago, far less two thousand and one.'

'Is anything arranged?'

'They've asked me to go in and answer a few questions.'

'And are you going?'

'Why not? I've done nothing wrong, and, before you say it, I won't be needing you there. I can handle it myself. I've sat through a lot more police interviews than you have.'

'Not when you were being asked the questions, you haven't. Trust me, it's a lot more difficult on my side of the table, and that's where you are right now.' He didn't reply. 'That's why you need me. Don't think of me as your son. Think of me as your lawyer. I don't care what you've done.'

'I haven't done anything wrong.'

'Good.'

'And I don't mind telling them that.'

'No, Dad. You do mind telling them. In fact, you mind so much that you're telling them absolutely nothing. Not a word will you say until I know exactly where they're coming from, and, more importantly, where they see things going. Understand?'

He snorted. 'I understand that for some reason you think I'm going to crack and say something stupid.' Good, he did understand. 'Well, I won't.' He picked up another cushion. Gripping it tightly he shook it in my face. 'You'll not catch Alex Munro letting some jumped-up internal affairs pen-pusher force a confession out of him.' He dropped the cushion again. 'Not that I have anything to confess.'

'Dad, the cops who work with the CCU didn't get the job because they don't know how to interrogate a suspect. They're highly trained. Whoever is dealing with an important case like this will know it inside out. Even the toughest person could crack under the strain. Ricky Hertz's case was a long time ago. You can't be expected to remember every last detail from way back then. Best to say nothing than risk making a mistake that they'll latch onto.'

He put a hand on my shoulder and then used the same hand to give my face a friendly, but not too friendly, slap. 'Thanks, Robbie. But I'm not one of your wee ned clients. I don't make mistakes and it doesn't matter who's asking the questions, you'll not catch me cracking.'

Tina returned to ask whether we'd stopped talking about stuff that wasn't for little girls yet. My dad seemed to think that we had.

'Good,' she said. 'Then have you found my chocolate?'

My dad picked her up in his arms. 'You know what? I think it's disappeared. Maybe Bouncer ate it.'

'But Bouncer's not been here. He's at home.'

'Maybe it was a mouse then.' I thought I saw one side of my dad's moustache twitch. The way it twitched when he said he'd just had the one glass of whisky or he was holding all the doubles in a hand of dominoes.

Tina looked worried. 'You said there wasn't any mouses and that Bouncer had chased them all away. Is that not true?' Eyes wide open now, she glanced around the room. 'Is there a mouse in the house? Is there ... Is there one in my bedroom?' she asked, voice high, tears threatening.

'No, no. Sorry, pet. I don't know what I was thinking. It can't have been a mouse, because the mice are all away now.'

Tina's look of concern vanished in an instant, replaced by something else. Suspicion. She wriggled free and clambered down. 'Then,' she said, staring up at him, hands on hips, head tilted to one side, 'where's my chocolate?'

She scanned the room again, until her eye settled on something.

My dad shuffled closer to his armchair by the fire. From a side table he lifted his glasses from on top of a folded newspaper, popped them into the breast pocket of his shirt and, with a yawn and a stretch, oh-so casually tossed the newspaper onto the armchair. I think it was the stretch and yawn that aroused the most suspicion. Tina leapt across the room and pounced on the newspaper. From underneath, she extracted a familiar navy blue and white item. Without a word she unfolded it and held up to her grandfather one Fry's Chocolate Cream wrapper, neatly folded into a tiny rectangle.

'Looks like the mice here know origami,' I said.

'Did you eat my chocolate, Gramps?' Tina asked. The hand holding up the chocolate wrapper didn't so much as waver.

The old man stared at the chocolate wrapper. '*Fry's Chocolate Cream.*' He screwed up his face in disgust. 'Dark chocolate? Who likes dark chocolate?'

The answer to that, though I didn't say it, was that everybody who tried a Fry's Chocolate Cream liked dark chocolate. Even the people who didn't like dark chocolate.

With an effort, he hunkered down and put his hands on Tina's shoulders. 'Wee girls don't want dark chocolate. Next time we're at the shops I'm going to buy you some—'

Tina shrugged him off. 'Well, did you eat it?'

'You know, I think there was an advert for some nice milk chocolate in the newspaper.' My dad stood up again and started patting himself down. 'Now, where did I put my specs? I could have sworn I had them.'

'Gramps?' Tina said in a low threatening voice.

The old man stopped searching his pockets and looked

down at his granddaughter's serious wee face. 'I'm sorry, pet,' he said, like a deflating balloon. 'I was having a cup of tea this afternoon and there were no biscuits and I saw the chocolate and I was just going to have half and save the rest for you, but it was a big cup and ...'

'You ate it? You ate my chocolate?'

He nodded.

'Is there any more left?'

He shook his head.

Tina rolled her eyes, threw the wrapper in the fire, walked over to the sofa and collapsed into it.

'When's the meeting with the cops?' I asked.

'Monday. Half ten at Livingston.'

'Right then,' I said. 'See you there.'

5

First thing Friday morning, Tina and I waved Joanna off on the plane to Amsterdam. Second thing Friday morning, we hit Sandy's café where I was amazed at the speed at which the proprietor provided us each with a scrambled egg roll. I was doubly amazed because I'd ordered myself the full Scottish, and a Knickerbocker Glory for my daughter.

'What's all this about?'

'Joanna told me to expect you,' Sandy said. 'She also told me that while she's away fried breakfasts and ice cream are off the menu.' He ruffled Tina's hair. Normally she wouldn't have liked that, but she was too busy staring in horror at the roll on egg that sat where a tall glass of ice cream, tinned fruit, raspberry syrup and sprinkles should have been.

'But,' I eventually managed to stammer, 'Jo could be gone three weeks. Maybe longer.'

'Then you're going to be eating a lot of eggs,' Sandy said.

I pushed the plate away. 'Very funny. Almost as funny as your pathetic attempt at scrambling them.'

'What's wrong with my scrambled eggs?'

'They're too runny,' Tina said, lifting the lid off her roll and staring at the slimy yellow gloop. In the Munro household, if you dropped scrambled eggs and they didn't bounce above knee-height, they weren't ready.

'Let's come to an arrangement, Sandy,' I said. I was

a lawyer after all. I was quite prepared to negotiate just so long as I got my own way in the end. 'How about we reach a compromise? Two crispy bacon rolls for me, two scoops of ice cream for Tina...maybe a dash of raspberry sauce...a few sprinkles here and there. Sound reasonable?'

'Perfectly.' Sandy straightened the salt and pepper and the wee vase in the centre of the table. 'But it's not happening. I've got my orders.'

'Okay, I understand that you've been given a set of orders. Now I'm giving you new ones.'

'You can't, you're outranked, and, anyway, scrambled eggs are better for wee girls than ice cream.' He gave one of Tina's biceps a squeeze. 'Makes them big and strong.' From the expression on my daughter's face, and the clenched fists either side of her plate, it looked like she'd be happy to demonstrate how big and strong she was already, if Sandy didn't make it snappy with the ice cream.

'Tina,' I said, 'why don't you go and wash your hands and I'll ask Sandy to make us something nicer?'

Usually, any suggestion I made to Tina involved a discussion before she decided whether to carry it out. Surprisingly, she went off to the Ladies without the need for a debate on the subject of hygiene.

'By the way,' Sandy said, as he watched Tina stomp off in the direction of the toilets, 'you'll never guess who I had in here last week.' He didn't give me any time to take a stab at an answer. 'Cammy Foster. Remember him?' Sandy opened the rolls in turn and studied the runny egg that threatened to drip down the sides and onto the plate. 'Hadn't seen him in years.'

'What was he in here for?'

'Coffee. And he looked like he could use it too. Talk

about rough? He was stinking of booze and was mouthing off about what he was going to do to Ricky Hertz. You know Hertz is out, don't you?'

'I heard.'

'Can't really blame Cammy. Hard to believe that Hertz killed his sister and those other two kids, and they've let him out. How long's he done? Twenty years?'

'Not that long,' I said.

'I suppose one of your lot,' by which Sandy meant defence lawyers in general, 'came up with a cunning plan. What was it? Ricky not getting to watch Sky TV in prison or something?' Resigned to the fact that the egg rolls weren't going to be eaten, he picked up the plates. 'Could have been my sister, she was about the same age. Or that other girl. The one that got away. What's her name now? Used to be Linda Smith, but she's married onto one of the Duffy twins.'

'Linda Duffy?' I ventured.

'Aye, that's it. Which Duffy twin was it she married again?'

The Duffy twins, Phil and Pete, two minds untroubled by a single thought. I hadn't seen them in years. The same age as me, they'd lived around the corner from us when I was a lad, and gone to the Roman Catholic primary that was separated from the state school I attended by a single footpath. Two metres of tarmac between the Proddies and the Papes, neither side entirely sure what the difference was, only that it provided a great excuse for playtime scraps.

Because inter-denominational hostilities tended to cease with the school bell at the end of the day, I used to pal about with the twins sometimes. These days, though I saw them floating around the town now and again, we rarely spoke, communicating by way of smiles, nods and manly grunts when passing in the street.

'I think it was Phil she married,' Sandy said at last. 'Or it could have been Pete.'

'They're twins, Sandy, there are only two of them.'

'Phil, then. Yeah, I'm sure it was the good-looking one.'

The Duffy boys were identical. I let it slide.

'Yeah, Linda was lucky,' Sandy said, scraping both rolls onto the same plate and stacking the dishes. 'And she's got your old man to thank for that. They should have given Alex a medal.'

I didn't say anything about my dad's predicament. If you wanted to spread the word amongst the population of Linlithgow you could take out an ad in a newspaper, post something on Facebook or mention it to Sandy.

Tina returned to find Sandy still at the table, holding the plates on which sat the offending foodstuff.

'Sandy,' I said, 'I've got a bit of business I need to attend to.'

'I thought you were on holiday?'

'That's next week.'

'And I take it you need to attend to this business alone?' he said, looking down at my daughter.

'I'm going to walk Tina to school, but they're finishing at half twelve today. Any chance she could come along here if I'm not back? She could help in the kitchen, do some washing up—'

'Like she did the last time?' Sandy said. 'I'm still finding pieces of broken crockery.'

'Then how about she teaches you how to scramble eggs properly?'

'How long you going to be?'

'Not long.'

'No, really, how long?'

I'll be back by one o'clock at the latest.'

'You'd better be.'

And I would have been, but for the fact that the business I had to attend to was in Edinburgh, and the person I was hoping to do that business with was Professor Edward Bradley who was currently indisposed.

I'd already phoned his office and been told the pathologist was cited to the High Court. No problem there. I assumed I'd corner him in a prosecution witness room, catching up on last year's *Reader's Digest*s; however, no sooner had I arrived than he was called to give evidence in a fatal stabbing.

It was one o'clock before he emerged, mildly flustered and muttering to himself under his breath.

'Oh, great, it's you,' he said, and I followed him down the stairs from court three to the front door. 'What do you want?'

'I've a question I need to ask you.'

'Well, ask it fast.'

'You're grumpy today,' I said. 'Even by your own unusually high standards.'

'You'd be grumpy too if you'd spent the last two hours having some jumped-up little runt in a wig challenging your opinion on defensive wounds.'

'How about I take you to lunch?' I said.

He stopped. 'When you say lunch . . .?'

'Nothing too extravagant.'

'And you're actually going to pay this time?'

I checked my wallet. 'How about a coffee?'

He pushed past me and marched out of the big glass automatic door onto the High Street.

I sprinted after him, dodging tourists on the Royal Mile

and catching up with him after he'd crossed the road onto George IV Bridge. 'It's only one question. What are you expecting, a five-course slap-up?'

It was true that Jill had paid me ten grand to investigate Hercule's death, but there was no point in chucking it away on food for a man who didn't look like he'd skipped any meals recently.

'Robbie, I'm hungry. That sound you hear isn't distant thunder, it's my stomach. I'm walking to my car and I'm going home for lunch.'

'Now you mention it, I am a bit peckish,' I said.

'You're not coming. And if you have a question to ask, send me a letter and I'll send you an opinion *and* an invoice.'

'Oh, I see, it's like that,' I said.

'Yes, it is.'

'How many forensic opinions do I ask you for in the average year?'

'About half as many as you pay for.'

'In that case I hope you won't charge me a fee for asking you for the phone number of your colleague?'

It took a few more strides of his ox-blood brogues for my remark to register. He stopped. Didn't turn around. 'Which colleague?'

'Yasmin Ashmat. Have you got her mobile number or direct dial handy?'

'Ashmat?' He'd turned around now. 'What are you wanting to phone the pipsqueak for?'

'To ask her the question you won't let me ask you.'

Prof. Bradley looked at me confused. 'I don't understand.'

I wasn't sure how I could make things any clearer, but tried. 'Yasmin's a clinical pathologist. I have a question on pathology. If you won't answer it, maybe she will. She sent out flyers a while back saying she was available to give opinions and provide expert evidence, so—'

'You're really going to ask her?'

'Why not? What's the difference if I ask her or you?'

'What's the difference!' Passers-by were now having to treat us as a roundabout in the centre of the pavement. 'The difference is about thirty years of experience. The pipsqueak's twenty-nine. What does she know about anything?'

'You were twenty-nine once,' I said. 'You bought that suit then, didn't you?'

'If I did, the suit could probably give a better forensic opinion than Yasmin Ashmat.'

He started to walk on. I took a hold of the leather elbow patch on his tweed jacket, slowing him to a halt. 'But it's not going to, is it? And neither is the person wearing it, whereas I'm sure Dr Ashmat will be delighted to help. Just as I'm sure she'll do it for free. A loss leader. Good for drumming up business from me in the future. *Paying* business.' I took a step back. 'Anyway, sorry to have bothered you.' I turned around to go back the way we'd come.

This time it was the professor who reached out to me. He put his hand on my shoulder. 'Just one question – you're sure about that?'

'Positive.'

He sighed through his beard at me, simultaneously checking his watch. 'Okay, let's have it.'

'Hercule Mercier. CEO of Zanetti Biotechnic. He died last week. Julie at the City Morgue told me you'd carried out the post-mortem.'

'Robbie, you know I really hate it when people call

them that. It's not a post-mortem. It's a post-mortem examination or, if you prefer, an autopsy. Post-mortem means after death. I don't perform after-deaths. I perform after-death examinations.'

I didn't quibble with him. I supposed members of every profession had their pet hates. Most of mine, with one notable exception, were employed by the Crown Office and Procurator Fiscal Service. Professor Bradley moved out of the way of an oncoming pushchair, stepped on someone's foot and almost knocked over an old lady who'd been trying to squeeze between him and the wall of the National Library.

'Do you want to hear the question or not?' I said, once he'd apologised to various pedestrians.

'Not any more. Not now I know who it relates to.'

'Come on, I only want to know the cause of death.'

'Suicide. I can't say any more.'

'No? Then perhaps the pipsqueak will have more information,' I said. 'She assisted with the after-death examination, didn't she?'

Professor Bradley thought that over for a moment. Unlike defence lawyers, whose legal aid hourly rate was bolted to the floor of Scotland's criminal justice system, expert witnesses could charge the Scottish Legal Aid Board whatever they fancied, and then add a zero on the end. The business I sent Professor Bradley in any year came to a sizeable chunk of legal aid change, to go along with his massive NHS salary and stipend from the University of Edinburgh medical school. He took hold of both my shoulders this time and steered me towards the front door of the library.

'They've got a nice little café in here,' he said. 'And remember, you're paying.'

39

6

Monday morning. The first day of the school October holidays. The first day of my supposed quality time with Tina, and I'd had to leave her in the office with Grace-Mary while I took her grandpa to Livingston Police Station.

There were four of us altogether. Four large men, some larger than others, sharing one small interview room. On one side of the table, my dad and I; on the other, Detective Inspector Dougie Fleming and an officer of similar rank from Police Scotland's Counter Corruption Unit.

The CCU officer introduced himself as Drew Niblo. If he wasn't younger than me, he dressed like it, in a wide-lapelled suit over a pale blue shirt, pink tie around a scrawny neck and smug expression on his face.

'I can assure you, you have nothing to worry about, Sergeant Munro,' he said, smiling serpent-like at my dad as he slipped two blank DVDs into the recorder. 'I'm only here for a chat and to clarify a few things.' His laugh was as fake as a politician's promise. 'Don't go thinking anyone's out to get you.'

'How about you say that again?' I said. 'This time when that thing's recording.'

The remark triggered no response at first. Then Niblo looked slowly up at me, as though he'd tried to be patient, but failed. 'Can I remind you that you're here to observe only?' He turned to my dad again. 'Sergeant Munro, if at any time during the interview you would like to take legal advice, let me know and arrangements will be made for that to happen in a separate room. But ...' he said, glaring at me. 'While you're in here, I expect your solicitor to keep quiet. Understood?'

We were having one of those death match stare-offs, neither wanting to be the first to look away, when the door opened, and a uniformed cop came in with a tray and set four flimsy white plastic cups on the table, a thin grey scum floating over their watery contents. I reached out for one, knocking it over, spilling the thin brown brew across the table. I could be so clumsy at times. Niblo jumped up out of his seat to avoid the murky waterfall, snatching up his paperwork not quickly enough.

'I'll go get some paper towels, sir,' the uniform said, but Niblo was already heading out of the door, taking his dripping notepad with him.

'Careless of you,' Fleming said. A temporary ceasefire had been called in the hostilities that normally raged between myself and D.I. Dougie Fleming. For once, in a police investigation, I could count on him being on the side of the suspect, for that's what I believed my dad truly was, despite Niblo's glib assurances.

'What's this all about?' I asked.

'You heard the man. He just wants to have a chat,' Fleming said.

'Well, why don't you tell that clown when he comes back, that my dad's got nothing to chat to him about?'

'Tell him yourself,' Niblo said. He re-entered the room, wiping coffee from his notes with a previously dry, white handkerchief that was now very damp and very brown. 'Though if your father, I mean, your client, really has nothing to say, then I'd rather he told me himself.'

41

'Can we just get on with this?' my dad said.

Niblo smiled and with the end of a pen typed the details of the interview into the recorder's display. When the machine beeped to signal it was ready to go, we each confirmed who we were, and Niblo proceeded to give my dad a formal police caution.

'I thought this was just a chat?' I said.

'There are certain formalities, as I'm sure you're aware, Mr Munro.'

'Remember, you're here voluntarily, Alex,' Fleming said. 'If you want to leave at any time you're free to do so.'

'But while you are here . . .' Niblo interjected, with a look that said, "This is my case and I'll do the talking." 'What can you tell me about your involvement in the arrest of Richard Hertz in two thousand and one?'

My dad could tell him a lot as it turned out.

'The first time I clapped eyes on Hertz was when me and Jock—'

'That would be Sergeant John Knox?' Niblo said, thumbing through his sodden notes.

'Aye, that's right,' my dad confirmed. 'Me and Jock were driving down Preston Road the day before Emily Foster went missing and we saw a man talking to a wee girl in the play park across the road from the school.'

Niblo curled a lip. 'So?'

'So, a couple of months before that, two weans had been abducted from a swing park in a different part of town and strangled.'

Niblo qualified my dad's statement. 'Not from a swing park. From near to a swing park. I ask you again, so what?'

'So, we thought there was something funny about it.'

'Funny?'

42

'You know? Not quite right.'

'No, I don't know. What was not quite right about it?'

My dad snorted. 'A grown man talking to a bairn in a swing park? What was *right* about it?'

'He could have been the child's father or an uncle,' Niblo said. 'What made you think that something was wrong?'

My dad looked incredulously at Fleming and me as though for affirmation of his interrogator's obtuseness. 'We were cops. It was our job to think things were wrong.'

'And if things weren't wrong?' asked Niblo. 'What then?'

'Then it was our job to make sure they didn't *go* wrong.'

Niblo rubbed his jaw, shaking his head. 'All right. You saw this man. What did you do?'

'We went over to see what was going on and Hertz told us—'

'You knew who he was?'

'Not at first. Only after we'd taken his details, then I remembered him. He was a junkie.'

Niblo disagreed. 'Hertz was a recovered heroin addict. At the time of Emily Foster's disappearance, he had come off heroin and was stable on methadone.'

'Methadone?' My dad snorted. 'That's just the government buying junkies their drugs for them. Once a junkie always a junkie.'

'To be fair to Alex, I mean, Sergeant Munro,' Fleming chipped in, 'after Hertz came off the smack, he was done a few times for possessing various proscribed substances: cannabis, ecstasy, diazepam ... You name it, he took it. He wasn't fussy.'

'You seem very familiar with Hertz's record of past offending, Inspector,' Niblo said. 'Been doing some homework? Are you suggesting that because the man was a drug user we shouldn't care how he was treated?' I had to hand it to Niblo; he was a man who didn't mind ruffling a few feathers to get the job done. Ignoring Fleming's steadily reddening face, he turned to my dad again. 'So, once you'd realised who he was, what did you do?'

'Sent him packing.'

'Before you sent him packing, did he say anything?'

'Ach, he came up with some story about walking past and seeing the girl fall off the roundabout. He said he'd just gone over to make sure she was all right.'

'And?'

'There didn't seem anything wrong with the girl to me.'

'Had she fallen off the roundabout?'

'So Hertz said.'

'What did the girl say?'

My dad coughed.

'For the record, Mr Munro.'

'She said the same thing.'

'And that was it, was it? You told him to leave and had no further dealings with him?'

'Not until Emily Foster went missing.'

'And you put two and two together?' The tone of Niblo's voice seemed to cast doubt on my dad's arithmetic. 'What about the murders of Jennifer Smart and Christine Tomlin?'

'I wasn't involved in the enquiry into the deaths of the first two kids. CID from Edinburgh came through to deal with those.'

'But you were very much involved with the investigation into Emily Foster's disappearance?'

Before my dad could say anything, I leaned across the table at Niblo. 'My client's answering no more questions

44

until you come clean as to what this is all about. If you're accusing him of any wrongdoing, I'd like to know so that I can advise him to say nothing more and terminate this interview.'

Niblo held up his hands in mock surrender. 'Your father is free to leave at any time, Mr Munro. But, believe me, he will be asked these very same questions either now or in a more formal setting.'

'When,' I assured him, 'he'll be refusing to answer.'

'As is his right,' Niblo said, 'but choosing not to answer isn't going to help anyone.'

On the contrary, my years of experience told me that not answering questions was usually very helpful, just not very helpful to the police.

'Sit back, Robbie,' my dad said. 'I'm answering the questions. I've nothing to hide. Emily Foster went missing on the Thursday night. Jock was the senior officer. As soon as he heard she'd been last seen near a swing park—'

'At . . .' Niblo checked his notes. 'Philip Avenue? That's down at the West Port, isn't it?'

'That's right. As soon as he heard, he says to me, "Alex, remember that guy from Preston Road?" And, of course, I did.'

Niblo smiled condescendingly. 'Well, you would, wouldn't you? And so, you brought Hertz in for questioning that same night. Notify CID, did you? This was a homicide case after all, and you were uniformed officers.'

'We were acting on a—'

'On a what? A hunch? Instinct? Your gut?'

My dad breathed in the gut that had been allowed to relax somewhat since its days in the force. 'No, we were acting on seventy years' experience between us, and a reasonable belief,' he said.

45

Niblo was less than satisfied by that answer. 'I still don't understand why you couldn't have lifted the phone to the CID.'

My dad sighed. 'For all we knew Hertz had a watertight alibi. The murders of the first two kids had been across the newspapers and no one had been caught for them. We didn't want to get everyone excited by calling in the CID, only to discover Hertz had been having tea with two nuns in Nairn at the time.'

'So, the pair of you took it upon yourselves?'

'Everything was done by the book. The man was given his rights—'

'Such as they were back then,' Niblo said, peeling apart two soggy sheets of paper. 'For instance, he wasn't allowed a pre-interview consultation with a lawyer?'

'He wasn't entitled to one and never asked.'

'That's how it was back then, sir,' Fleming said. 'Changed days now, eh?'

That was something of an understatement. Scots law's rules of evidence required corroboration. The merest adminicle was usually enough to satisfy most judges, and, in years gone by, this additional evidence had frequently come as a result of police interviewing suspects who'd been given no access to a solicitor. It was surprising how cooperative those suspects often were, even if they later claimed they hadn't been. And, of course, the cops could be relied upon to produce a notebook that tended to settle the issue. According to Dougie Fleming's notebook, he heard more confessions in a week than the average parish priest.

However, the Supreme Court had now confirmed an accused person's right to access to a solicitor before and during interview. 'I know what the old regime was like, thank you, D.I. Fleming,' Niblo said. 'It doesn't mean it was fair.' Eyes still fixed on my dad, he asked, 'Did you enquire as to whether Mr Hertz might need an appropriate adult present?'

'He was thirty years old! Why would he need an adult with him?'

'It's only fair for suspects who may be educationally challenged to have an adult present at interview, especially if they are not legally represented,' Niblo said.

'Educationally challenged?' My dad shifted in a seat that had not been designed in contemplation of his ample dimensions. 'I don't know if I thought about it that much. It was a police investigation into a child abduction, not a quiz show.'

Fleming's face twisted with the effort of controlling a laugh.

'*Was* Hertz educationally challenged?' I asked.

'As a matter of fact, he wasn't,' Niblo conceded, 'but—'

'But nothing,' I said. 'You're making it sound as though he couldn't spell IQ. Why do you keep badgering my client with stupid questions?'

To keep him off balance was the real answer. Niblo had another one. 'I'm merely pointing out certain deficiencies in the interview procedures.'

'No,' I said. 'You're pointing out deficiencies in the *old* interview procedures, the procedures my dad and other cops like him were expected to follow. You can't start criticising him for going by the book, even if it's an old book.' Robbie Munro defending the cops. I felt like a member of the NRA advocating gun control.

Niblo cleared his throat and once more turned his attention to my dad. 'And you brought Hertz in and questioned him for ...' He flicked through his notes. 'Five straight hours. And after that he confessed to killing the first two children. Is that right?'

'That's what happened,' my dad said.

'But he didn't confess to killing Emily Foster? Not the matter for which he'd been detained?' My dad didn't recognise that as a question. Niblo carried on. 'But, of course, you didn't know if Emily Foster had been murdered, did you?' Again my dad remained silent. 'However, when you questioned Hertz, you had the case file on those other children. That's correct, isn't it?'

My dad grunted.

'Could you speak more clearly, Sergeant Munro?'

'Yes, we had certain details.'

'You knew, for instance, that they'd been strangled and where their bodies were found?'

'Yes.'

'But you had nothing like that on Miss Foster. Only that she'd apparently been abducted from Philip Avenue play park? Tell me, do you smoke?' Niblo stared straight ahead at my dad, unblinking. It was a question I hadn't been expecting.

'Nope. Never have,' my dad said. 'Well, maybe the odd cigar at a dinner or something.'

'But not cigarettes?'

My dad shook his head.

'For the tape, please.'

'No, I've never smoked cigarettes.'

'Richard Hertz smoked though, didn't he?'

'I believe so.'

'During the interview – the interview in which he confessed to the murder of Jennifer Smart and Christine Tomlin – you refused to let him smoke. Why was that? There was no smoking ban back in two thousand and one.'

Fleming interrupted. 'I'm not sure how much routine police work you've done, D.I. Niblo, but refusing suspects a smoke is perfectly normal. Helps them to get things over with, and stop wasting everyone's time, doesn't it, Alex?'

'Keep a nicotine junkie rattling and he'll tell you what you want to know. Is that the game you were playing, Sergeant Munro?' Niblo asked, keeping his stare entirely focussed on my dad.

I'd had enough. 'This is getting ridiculous. Are you really suggesting that Hertz's confession was unfairly obtained because my dad didn't crash the fags earlier?'

Niblo's gaze never wavered. 'Do you remember the brand Richard Hertz smoked?'

Why was Niblo even asking this? Everyone knew that Ricky Hertz smoked Benson & Hedges. The local newsagents, where he bought them, had confirmed it. During a search of the play park the police had found a B&H cigarette stub. It had Hertz's fingerprint on it. That, along with the confession and my dad's earlier encounter with him at Preston Road swing park, had allowed the decision on guilt or innocence to go to the jury. At trial, Hertz's legal team had challenged his confession, but it was the cigarette stub at the locus of Emily Foster's disappearance that had sealed the case against him. It was a fine example of the Moorov doctrine in operation. Two sources of evidence were required to prove one crime, but where there were two or more crimes connected closely in time, character and circumstance, they could corroborate each other. The charges Hertz faced had taken place only two or so months apart, and involved the abduction of young girls from around the vicinity of play parks. It ticked all the boxes. At least the jury thought so, and that was all that mattered.

Niblo reached down to his side, picked a brown leather briefcase from the floor and placed it on the table. He popped the lock and produced a clear plastic production bag, sealed at the top with blue tape. Inside was a plastic vial with a white screw top, and, inside that, enough of a cigarette to suggest that someone had only taken a few puffs before discarding it.

'You recognise this particular cigarette, don't you, Sergeant Munro?' he said.

'Not really, but seeing as how you're showing it to me, I'm guessing it's the one the scene-of-crime boys found at Philip Avenue play park, the night young Emily went missing.'

Niblo laid the production bag on the table between us. The paper was yellow, the B&H monogram still just about visible. 'Not the night she went missing, Sergeant Munro, the day after. Which would also make it the day after you interviewed Richard Hertz.' He wasn't going to suggest the cigarette end had been planted, was he? 'Whose idea was it to collect all the cigarette ends from the play park?' Yes, he was.

I put a hand on my dad's arm. 'Don't answer that.'

Niblo sat motionless, like a cobra waiting for its prey to stray into striking range.

'I can't remember,' my dad said.

'Listen, Dad. I'm here as your legal adviser. Now will you listen to my advice and shut up?'

'Can't you, Sergeant Munro?' Niblo said, paying me no heed and flicking through his papers, some of which were drying off and curling up at the edges. 'According to the transcript of your evidence at trial, it was you who took the credit.' He closed the papers and ran his hand along the top of the bundle, flattening it out. 'Did you find the cigarette butt?'

'I was supervising. There was a scene-of-crime team collecting and bagging the stuff.'

'But it was you who instructed the search, wasn't it?'

'Not really. CID were involved by then,' my dad said.

I didn't like where this was going, even though I had no idea where it was going.

'But, whoever instructed or carried out the search, the idea to search for cigarette butts was yours. Am I correct?'

My dad shrugged. 'I suppose.'

'Sounds like a nice piece of police work, if you ask me,' Fleming said.

I could tell Niblo was starting to feel outnumbered. 'D.I. Fleming, out of fairness, I acceded to your request to come along to this interview as a former colleague. That was before the sus . . .I mean, ex-Sergeant Munro, decided to bring a solicitor with him. If there are any more interruptions from anyone, I'm going to end this interview and make some more formal arrangements to reconvene.'

'And just what do you mean by that?' I asked.

'Robbie, Dougie, do what the man says and be quiet,' my dad said. 'I just want to get this over with.'

Fleming and I sat back as though synchronised. Like him, my arms were also tightly folded, and, I guessed, I had a similar scowl on my face.

'Okay,' Niblo said, satisfied that we would now both be on our best behaviour. 'I have to say that I can only agree with D.I. Fleming's uninvited opinion, that this was indeed a very thorough piece of police work. So thorough, in fact, that it managed to unearth a neat piece of evidence that just managed to tip the scales in the prosecution's favour. I mean, without it, what was there against Hertz? Only a somewhat dubious confession.'

It wasn't a question, but my dad answered it anyway.

'The man confessed. What's dubious about that?'

Niblo held up a hand and counted down on his fingers. 'No video recording of the interview.'

'There were no cameras back then,' my dad and Dougie Fleming said in unison.

'And,' Niblo continued, unfazed, 'no audio either. For some reason the tape machine wasn't working. And as for the confession, what was it Mr Hertz is supposed to have said?' He opened his file of papers again, though clearly, he had memorised the words. To be fair, there weren't that many. 'Oh, yes, I remember,' Niblo said. '"*I might as well tell you. It was me who killed the two girls. I choked them and dumped their bodies down at Mains Roads near the burn at the rugby pitches.*" Which, of course, was information already available to the police.' By now Niblo's previously splayed fingers formed a fist with only his thumb protruding. 'And then we have the cigarette stub.' He pushed his thumb down. 'Tell me, did you take part in the search of Philip Avenue play park, Sergeant Munro?'

'Don't answer that,' I said.

My dad stood up and lowered his head at Niblo, their faces inches apart. 'Yes,' he growled.

Niblo couldn't keep the smirk off his face. 'Of course, you did. You've already told me; the search was your idea. Was it you who found the cigarette butt, Sergeant Munro?'

'That's it, we're done here,' I said.

Fleming seemed to agree, because he too was on his feet and making for the door.

Niblo was now the only one sitting down, and the only one not looking the least bit flustered.

'No, it wasn't me who found it,' my dad said, rising to his feet.

Niblo put out a hand, gesturing for him to stay where he was. 'We're almost finished. I have only one more question.'

My dad's narrowed eyes challenged him to ask it.

He did. 'Can you explain then, Sergeant Munro, why your DNA is on that cigarette stub?'

7

'Why didn't you give him an explanation like he asked for, Dad?' The conversation on the way back from Livingston police station to my dad's cottage was a trifle on the fraught side.

'I don't want to talk about it.'

'Oh, now you want to say nothing. Well, it's a bit late for that,' I said.

In reply he scowled and stared out of the window at the West Lothian countryside as it scudded by.

I braked, approaching a tight bend on the Ecclesmachan Road. 'They won't leave it there, you know. If Ricky Hertz is on bail, it means when he goes back to the Appeal Court there's only going to be one decision. In fact, better make that two decisions. After the Appeal Court has decided to quash his convictions, they'll have to decide on how much compensation to give him for spending the last seventeen or so years in the nick on fabricated evidence.'

My dad put his hand on the door lever. 'There's not that far to go. Let me out. I can walk the rest.'

I put my foot down. The only way I was letting him out was if he wanted to jump and roll. 'You can't bury your head in the sand, Dad. We need to assess the damage and see how we're going to fight this thing.'

'Fight what? There's nothing to fight. I've not been accused of anything.'

Not yet he hadn't, not officially, but he couldn't really believe that the Crown wouldn't be looking for a scapegoat.

'How bad is Jock Knox's dementia?'

'I've not been to see him in a while. Last time I was at the home he never recognised me. One night we took him to the pub when the Red River Trio were playing, to see if it jogged his memory. He just sat there. Hardly said a word.'

The Red River Trio was a pub band formed, when the earth was still cooling, by four cops from Lothian & Borders' F Troop. They hadn't thought 'the Red River Quartet' quite catchy enough, and, anyway, whenever they had a gig on at least one of them was working a late shift. Often they were a duo; occasionally a solo artist. Over the years, band members had come and gone. Big Jock Knox had been the original lead singer, a vocalist with more keys than a jailer. I'd been forced to suffer the Red River Trio on many occasions during charity events arranged by my dad, and at which attendance for the Munro boys was compulsory. I usually left feeling I owed the people who dragged fingernails down blackboards an apology.

'We need to go and see him,' I said.

'What for? I've just told you he doesn't remember who *he* is, far less Ricky Hertz.'

I was going to have to paint a picture for him. 'Dad, your DNA is on a cigarette stub that was a strong piece of evidence in the very circumstantial case against Ricky Hertz.'

He turned his face from the window to look at me. 'Thanks for letting me know, but I was at the interview an' all, remember?'

'Then did you miss the part where the man from the CCU practically accused you of planting that evidence, or was he being too subtle about it?'

'They can't prove anything.'

'They can prove you touched that cigarette, and you've kindly given them the proof that although you were at the search you didn't find the cigarette. How else did your DNA get on it if it wasn't planted? Do you want to tell me what did happen?'

He leaned across, his face close to mine. 'I can't remember,' he growled into my ear. 'Now will you let it go?'

'Sorry,' I said, 'I didn't quite catch that. A lorry was going by. But I assume what you said was that you distinctly remember that after the interview, and once back in his cell, Mr Hertz wanted a cigarette and you kindly fetched him one which, in the interests of health and safety, you lit before passing through the hatch in the cell door. That must be how your DNA came to be on it.'

The old man didn't reply. We met the Old Edinburgh Road, where I took a right and then a left. He still hadn't said anything when, after another mile or so, we pulled into the small driveway at the side of his cottage.

'Good,' I said, pulling up the handbrake. 'I'm glad we've got that cleared up.'

'You think you're so smart, don't you?' my dad said, trying to unclip the seat belt that had struggled to circumnavigate his midriff in the first place. 'If I gave him the cigarette in his cell, how did it end up at Philip Avenue play park?'

Had he not been listening? 'It was planted, of course.'

He banged his hands on the dashboard. 'That's what Niblo is saying!'

It wasn't a painting I was going to have to paint him; it was the ceiling of the Sistine Chapel. 'No, Dad, what Niblo is saying is that *you* planted it.'

'Then, if I planted it, why wasn't it me who found it?'

'Dad, everyone knows it's never the person who plants dodgy evidence that finds it. That would look too suspicious.' How naïve was he? This was first day at CID-school stuff. No wonder the old man had never made detective. 'The way it works is that you plant the evidence and let some fresh-faced young uniformed copper find it. They take the credit, and their evidence is highly credible and unshakeable in court because it's the truth. It's just not the whole truth. Who do you think found the piece of circuit board at Lockerbie? The teams of highly trained Police and CIA investigators or just some innocent passer-by?'

'So, smarty, if I didn't plant it, who did?' my dad asked, eventually freeing himself from the seat belt.

Now he was getting the picture. The question was not *if* the cigarette stub was planted, but, rather, *who* planted it? Right now, we needed to take the big fat finger that was pointing straight at my dad and direct it at somebody else. Preferably, someone who couldn't confirm or deny anything.

'You want me to blame Big Jock?'

'Why not? He must have gone back to Hertz's cell and picked up a cigarette butt. You remember that happening, don't you?'

'No, I do not.'

'Then start trying,' I said.

'But I can't blame Jock.'

'Of course you can if it gets you off the hook. Listen, Dad, you're my client now. I don't care what happens to other people. I care what happens to you. If Big Jock's got dementia, he can't stand trial, and so they won't send him to prison.'

'Prison?'

'Yes, prison. Where do you think they send people who pervert the course of justice and cause an innocent man to spend a chunk of his adult life inside – Disneyland?'

'Hertz is guilty. He confessed. I was there.'

'It's not about guilt or innocence, it's about proof, and one big lump of evidence that helped convict Ricky Hertz now has a dirty big rat sitting on top of it. What would a jury have made of the new DNA evidence if it had come out at his trial? How do you think they'd have reacted to Hertz's disputed confession knowing that another important piece of evidence might have been faked? Whether Hertz killed those kids or not is entirely irrelevant.'

'Tell that to their parents,' he said, opening the car door and clambering out.

'That's not the right way to look at it,' I said.

He poked his head in the door. 'Then what is?'

'That if that cigarette butt was planted, there's been a miscarriage of justice and someone's to blame.'

He slammed the car door shut. I rolled down the passenger window. 'And...' I shouted after him as he walked to his front door. 'I say we blame the man who can't defend himself.'

8

Cockleroy is an extinct volcano that sits to the south of Linlithgow overlooking the town. Literally, 'Hat of the King', Cockleroy or Cockleroi, is a grand name for a hill that rises less than one thousand feet, but to a six-year-old it's a mountain.

Monday afternoon, Tina and I were climbing ever upwards. The route to the summit is a wide one, the grass worn short and shiny by the passage of feet. As Tina knew, it was also excellent for rolling down if you didn't mind dodging the occasional ball of sheep dung on the way, which she didn't mind, or, indeed, dodge that well.

On our way to the top we met a man on his way to the bottom. He stopped to pat Bouncer who was well in the lead, with my daughter taking silver position in the race to the summit. For a moment I thought the man looked familiar. It was a feeling I often had and didn't like to act on. It could be an old client, a cop or a witness I'd once given a hard time under cross-examination. He hunkered down and stroked Bouncer's coat. 'Nice dog,' he said to Tina. By this time Bouncer was on his back wriggling about having his tummy tickled. It wasn't like him to be quite so friendly with strangers. The man smiled when he saw me approach. 'I don't know what it is. Dogs just like me,' he said, and, with a final ruffle of Bouncer's furry chest, stood up and continued walking down the hill.

'Was that a strange man, Dad?' Tina asked. 'I thought it was, so I didn't talk to him.'

'That's a good girl. It's all right to talk to people if I'm here, but not if you're by yourself.'

She scampered on, pursuing Bouncer to the top. When I joined them, I put Tina's little pink rucksack, the one I'd been carrying most of the way from the car at Beecraigs Country Park, down on a large rock, opened it and brought out the picnic I'd prepared.

'Peanut butter?' Tina said. 'Where's the jam? You can't have a PB and J with no jam.' Which was technically correct. 'I don't want just peanut butter.' Rather than break the news that we'd run out of jam, I tried to explain that, as everyone knew, peanut butter sarnies were the staple diet of all the world's foremost explorers, who tended to frown on the addition of jam as being for the weak-minded only. She was having none of it. 'I don't like your sandwiches. They're rubbish. I like Joanna's.' Bouncer didn't appear quite so fussy.

'Well, I'm not your mother, and—'

'I know you're not. My mum's dead.'

The introduction of a packet of crisps placated her momentarily and presented the opportunity for a little father-to-daughter chat. I took the hand not holding the crisp bag and walked her over to the trig point. On such a clear day there was a fine view to the north, across the smoking stacks of Grangemouth Oil Refinery, across the Firth of Forth, with all three Bridges clearly visible, and the Ochil Hills beyond. They said on an exceptionally clear day it was possible to see as far as the Bass Rock in the east, and the Isle of Arran in the west. Whoever it was said that, they had better eyesight than me. 'Do you know what you call someone who climbs mountains?' I said, dragging a hand along the distant horizon.

Tina did know. 'A mountain climber.' I'd asked for that. She handed me the packet of crisps to open.

'Mountain climber is one name,' I said, 'but the proper name is mountaineer. Look all around you. See how high up you are. If this is a mountain and you've climbed it then does that not make you a mountaineer too?'

Tina was prepared to concede the point, if warily, not sure where I was going with it. I, on the other hand, knew where I wanted to go, I just didn't know for certain if this was the best route to take.

'Okay,' I said, 'what do you call a woman, like Joanna, who looks after a little girl, like you—'

'I thought I was a mountaineer now?'

'You are a mountaineer, but you're also a little girl. Now will you let me finish?' Tina signalled her agreement with the crunch of salt & vinegar crisps. 'Good. So, if there was this woman who looked after a little girl, went out to work so she could buy the little girl nice things, made good sandwiches, much better than mine, took the little girl places, washed her clothes, washed her face, read her bedtime stories, and was married to the little girl's dad, you'd call that woman a mum, wouldn't you?'

'Mums don't tell bedtime stories, only dads,' was Tina's comeback, the bedtime story being my main contribution to the routine of getting my daughter to sleep every night. I sometimes read from a book. Tina preferred the ones I made up. For a defence lawyer, a good imagination and the gift of storytelling are essential tools of the trade.

'But you would agree that someone who does all those other things is a mum, wouldn't you?'

61

Tina munched a few more crisps in response.

'You see, Tina. Your mum is dead. She was a lovely lady, but it's for Joanna to look after you now that she's gone, and I know your mum would have liked that.' More munching. 'And I know she wouldn't mind you calling Joanna "Mum", because that's really what she is, a mum to you. And Joanna would like it very much too. She loves you.'

Tina stared at me for a moment. What was she thinking? She took another handful of crisps, stuffed them in her face, handed me the packet and ran off laughing with Bouncer hot on her heels.

I'd tried. I didn't know what was the more tiring, my dad's police station interview, a trip up Cockleroy, or trying to talk my daughter into accepting Joanna as her new mum.

After the rigours of the day, later that evening I was relaxing in front of the telly when there was a knock at the door. Tina and Bouncer had answered it before I'd even put down my mug of tea, far less climbed off the sofa.

'I hope you don't mind me springing this visit on you, Robbie.' Jill gave me a kiss on each cheek, continental style. She stared down at Tina and the dog by her side. 'A cottage in the country, a child and a dog. What a picture of domestic bliss. I never thought you had it in you. Where's Mum?'

'There isn't a mum,' Tina said. 'There's just me, Dad, Bouncer and Joanna, and Joanna is in Holland Land.'

Bouncer jumped up at Jill's leg. I dragged him away and told Tina to put him out of the back door.

'Come on through,' I said. 'I'll make you a cup of coffee or would you prefer tea?'

'Tea, please,' Jill said, whisking a colourful silk scarf from around her neck. She folded it and packed it into

62

the pocket of her raincoat before divesting herself of that too. I took it and just about managed to find a space on one of the hooks in the hallway that were festooned with coats and anoraks. 'And don't leave the tea bag in for ages like you used...' She cast me a faint smile. 'Not too strong, please.'

I brought the kettle back to boil, made some tea, that wasn't so much weak as helpless, and brought it through to the living room in the china mug that had the fewest chips.

Jill was sitting down at the opposite end of the sofa from where my mug of coffee was balanced on the arm.

'I just came to see if you'd had a chance to think about what to do about Hercule,' she said, taking the tea from me.

I sat down too. The back door slammed, and Tina came charging into the room and jumped into the space between us.

'What game will we play?' she asked. 'Not dominoes, because Dad cheats sometimes.'

'Surely not,' Jill said. 'Your dad's a lawyer, he'd never break the rules.'

Tina looked at Jill as though she was weighing up that remark. 'Will you be kissing my dad again?' she asked.

'Right,' I said, standing up, coffee in hand. 'I think it's time for your bed. Off you go and brush your teeth.'

There followed a short debate in which Tina argued in favour of the motion that teeth brushing was out of the question until supper had been consumed, and, having won, went off in search of a glass of milk and a biscuit. Toilet or kitchen made no difference to me, just so long as she was out of the way.

'I can see how she takes after her dad,' Jill said.

'Yes, she's a lovely wee thing, isn't she? I think she takes more after her mother.'

'I'm sure she does, when it comes to looks,' Jill said. 'I was thinking more of the stubborn streak and the unshakeable belief that she's always right.'

'I'd always assumed Tina's always-being-right trait came with her extra X chromosome as part of the package,' I said.

'Don't try to out-science a scientist,' Jill replied. 'And, by the way, sex chromosomes are properly called gonosomes.'

'See what I mean about you women always being right?' I said.

Jill took a sip of tea. She wore more make-up now than she ever had when we'd been together, but even the layers of perfectly applied slap couldn't hide the worry lines around her eyes. I decided to move onto the reason she was here.

'I've made some progress,' I said. 'I managed to speak with Professor Edward Bradley today. He's the pathologist who carried out the autopsy on Hercule. I had to buy him lunch before he'd give me any information.' Given the size of my upfront payment, it was important for Jill to know I was incurring overheads. After all, the National Library of Scotland might lend books, but it didn't give away soup and cheese toasties for nothing.

Jill lowered her head and stared into the paleness of her tea. 'What did he say?'

'Hercule's blood sugar was low. I suppose you know he was diabetic?'

Jill nodded. 'He was reckless sometimes. He didn't always look after himself, and drank too much. Alcohol lowers blood sugar, but you're not going to try and tell me he died from hypoglycaemia, are you? He'd had a scare before, but—'

'No, Jill, it wasn't hypoglycaemia. It looks very much as though Hercule took his own life.'

Jill placed her mug beside the handbag at her feet.

I took a hold of her hand. 'Prof. Bradley knows what he's talking about. In fact, there were two pathologists involved in the examination and they both agree on the cause of death.'

Jill pulled away. 'Hercule would not have killed himself. It's ridiculous to even suggest it.'

Tina came through carrying a glass of milk and not spilling all of it. 'There's no biscuits,' she said.

'Then have a piece of cheese instead.'

'Will you cut it for me?'

'Prof. Bradley has years of experience,' I said on my return from the kitchen where I'd left Tina and her chunk of cheddar. 'When it comes to forensic pathology he's the top man. If he says it was suicide, then—'

'Then what? He must be right? Are you telling me you've never challenged the evidence of a forensic expert before?'

I had to admit that criticising the findings of so-called experts was something of a professional pastime for me. Still, the opinion of Prof. Bradley seemed to be soundly based on the evidence. 'Jill, you need to be rational and look at the facts. According to Professor Bradley, Hercule went into a sort of drug-induced coma and slipped away.'

'Slipped away? Is that supposed to be a medical term?'

Tina came through and sat cross-legged on the floor between the sofa and the fireplace, nibbling the tiniest fragments from the chunk of cheese. Supper was something she could spin out indefinitely.

'I had a hamster that died,' she said. 'And a rabbit that ran away. It was really sad, and then I got Bouncer.' It couldn't possibly have heard its name, but the dog started barking and scraping at the back door.

'Tina, bring Bouncer in and put him into his basket. After that go and get ready for bed while I talk to Jill about grown-up stuff. Now off you go.'

'How can I get ready for bed?' Tina said, in a tone of voice that suggested I might temporarily have lost my mind. 'I haven't finished my cheese and we haven't phoned Joanna yet.'

Phoning Joanna was a nightly ritual, and another part of my daughter's do-anything-not-to-go-to-bed routine.

'Sorry about that,' I said to Jill, after I'd told Tina we'd phone Joanna in the morning and my daughter had gone off in a sulk, taking her cheese with her. 'I can't remember word for word what Prof. Bradley said, but the toxicology analysis found evidence of barbiturates and alcohol. It's a classic combination when it comes to suicide. You're a pharmacist, you must know the effect of those kind of drugs. There was a complete shutdown of Hercule's central nervous system. Prof. Bradley says he wouldn't have suffered.'

Jill wasn't listening. 'He must have been poisoned.'

'He *was* poisoned, Jill. He poisoned himself.'

'How can you say that? You didn't know him.'

Tina appeared in the doorway. 'Have you stopped talking about grown-up stuff yet?'

'No!' Jill said. 'Now would you please stay out of the room until we're finished?'

Arms folded, Tina scowled and about-turned.

'You don't have to take it out on her,' I said. 'She's just a wee girl.'

'I know. I'm sorry.' Jill reached down, swapped mug of tea for handbag and delved into the latter. 'Why don't you buy her something nice?'

'Stop it, Jill,' I said, taking hold of her hand, noticing as I did that Tina and Bouncer were lying on the floor, side by side, geographically speaking outside of the room, but watching us through the open door. Anything I said to my daughter would only result in lengthy legal argument on the precise definition of 'out of the room'. It wasn't worth the effort.

Jill removed a small pack of tissues from her handbag and pulled one free. 'You think I'm being irrational, but you don't know what we could be dealing with, Robbie. There are all kinds of industrial espionage going on in the world of pharmaceuticals. Yes, you're a criminal lawyer, but the sort of crime you're used to seeing is assaults, drug busts, housebreakings—'

'And, occasionally, murder,' I said. 'Which is what you seem to prefer over the expert opinion that Hercule...' Aware of Tina's presence I finished the sentence in a whisper, 'took his own life with some heavy-duty barbiturates.'

Jill blew her nose and rammed the hanky back in the handbag. 'Hercule had everything to live for. He had health, he had money. He had me, damn it! There was no reason for him to ...' Jill also spied Tina, elbows on the floor, head propped on the palms of her hands, listening intently. She stood up. 'I'm not ungrateful, Robbie. You've discovered the official line on Hercule's death. Now I need you to dig deeper.'

'And how do I do that? I've absolutely nothing to go on.'

'Then I'm going to have to supply you with more infor-mation,' Jill said.

'What more can you give me than you have already? Hercule was found dead on a hotel bed. He'd taken drink and drugs.'

'No, there has to be more to it than that,' Jill said.

'Why?'

'For a start, he wasn't on any medication. Where would he get his hands on barbiturates?'

'He was CEO of a bleeding—'

'Dad! Are you swearing?'

'No, but I will be in a minute if you don't get to your bed!'

'Who's taking it out on her now?' Jill said.

I waited until Tina had stomped off through to her bedroom, slamming more doors behind her than I knew we had in the house.

'There's only one thing for it,' Jill said. 'We're going to have to stage a reconstruction. The suite is still booked under Hercule's name. I'll meet you there tomorrow night ... No, better make it the day after. Wednesday. We'll walk through everything that happened the day Hercule died.'

'I don't really think that'll be necessary,' I said.

Jill replied with a stare that disagreed with that point of view.

'Then again ...' I said. After all, why shouldn't I humour her? She was paying me enough. 'Being at the actual location, seeing the layout of things, might help give my further investigations a jumping-off point.'

'It had better, Robbie. I want results. Whoever did this to Hercule is going to pay, and I don't mind paying you to make sure of that.'

9

'What are you doing here? Have you no work to go to?'
My dad stepped out of the way as Tina, Bouncer and I,
in no particular order, careered through his front door.
'Oh, no. Hold on right there. It's Tuesday. You know I
have a golf game on a Tuesday.' He also had golf games
on Sundays and most Thursdays. During the golf season
it was more difficult to work out when he didn't have a
golf game. 'So, if you think that you're going to leave me
with little Miss—'

'Calm yourself. I'm on holiday and Tina and I are going
to the play park,' I said. 'I'm not here about today, I'm
here about the Ricky Hertz situation. When are you teeing
off – two o'clock? There's plenty time for a chat about
what we're going to do.'

'Yes ...well ...I've already been giving it some thought.'

'You have? Great.'

'I've been looking into obtaining some legal representation.' I didn't understand. The old man attempted to
clarify. 'Legal representation that's not you.'

'Not me?'

'Try and listen, Robbie ...' By this time Tina and
Bouncer had grown bored and gone off through the
cottage somewhere, leaving us alone in the hallway. 'I'm
going to find a different lawyer. No offence.'

'No offence?'

'Do you have to repeat everything I say? The fact is that I was a member of the Scottish Police Federation for thirty-seven years. I paid my dues faithfully and never once made a claim. I've been in touch with them and they've told me that even though I'm an ex-member they'll consider an application for legal expenses cover.'

'But you've got me.'

'I know. But if I'm really in trouble I want the best.'

'Tina!' I shouted. 'We're going!'

'You're not angry, are you?' he asked.

I wondered where he got that idea from – my clenched teeth or the redness of my face or from the fact I'd spun around and was halfway out of the door.

'It's for the best!' he yelled after me. 'It'll save you all the bother and I'll be able to get a really good lawyer!'

It was only Tina and Bouncer bundling through the door after me that prevented me from going back and throttling the old man.

'What's the matter, Dad?' Tina asked, as I wheel-spinned out of the driveway.

'Gramps is the matter,' I said. 'But let's not talk about him any more. Why don't we phone Joanna and see how she's getting on in Holland?'

Tina took the mobile from my jacket pocket and in seconds Joanna was on the other end on loudspeaker. I'd tried to phone her the previous evening after Jill had gone, and once Tina was in bed, but hadn't managed to get through.

'How's it going?' I called over to the back seat. 'Convicted any war criminals yet?'

'I'm working on it,' she said. 'What are you pair up to?'

'We've just been to my dad's and now we're off to the park.'

'Oh, that's nice. How is your dad? I heard that the Appeal Court want to take evidence on the Hertz case.' News travelled fast. Then again, Joanna did work for the Prosecution Service, and if Ricky Hertz won his appeal it was going to be hugely embarrassing for whoever had been Lord Advocate back in 2001. 'What's the plan? Are you advising him to say nothing?'

'I'm not advising him on anything,' I said. 'He doesn't want me. He's getting a lawyer via the Police Federation.'

'Oh,' was all Joanna said to that news. Like the good court lawyer she was, she knew when not to ask any more questions.

Tina was obviously feeling left out and thought it necessary to pitch in with her own piece of news. 'A lady came to the house and was kissing Dad last night.'

'Sorry?' Joanna said. 'A lady was what?'

'Kissing Dad. And they were holding hands.'

'I'll call you back, Joanna,' I said, stretching an arm over into the back seat, trying to wrest the phone from my daughter. Strapped in though she was, Tina managed to keep it out of my reach.

'Her name was Jill and she was quite pretty, but not as pretty as you, and quite old, but she had a really nice handbag and—'

At my second attempt I managed to flick the phone out of Tina's hand and it landed in the rear footwell next to the nearside door, well out of range of her grubby little mitts.

'What's happening, Robbie? Is everything all right?' Joanna's voice was distant and muffled.

'Yes, everything's fine,' I shouted over my shoulder. 'But it's a terrible line. I'll call you back tonight.'

She said a few more things. I didn't quite catch them

all, and those I did I ignored. Eventually there was silence. Telling Tina not to mention again Jill's visit to Joanna would only have had the opposite effect, and so I said nothing about it and soon we arrived at our destination.

Philip Avenue swing park was how I remembered, but smaller – probably because I hadn't been there since primary school. The park was square, enclosed on three sides by a fence with a 'No Ball Games' sign on it, and on the fourth by a low wall. At one end of the park was a seesaw, at the other two sets of swings. In between those stood a climbing frame and chute, and, in the middle there was a large expanse of grass that was ideal for playing those prohibited ball games.

No sooner had I released Tina from the car than she was racing down the steps, into the park and up the climbing frame. I was left wondering how exactly Hertz would have gone about things. It would have been easy enough, I supposed, for him to have stationed a vehicle within a few yards of the small play park. Emily's mother was a well-known local lush. The wee girl had often been allowed to wander the streets until all hours. It was believed she'd been abducted around ten o'clock at night when, even on a summer's evening, it would have been almost dark. How difficult would it have been to entice a child away, even forcefully remove one, and go unnoticed? From where I stood beneath one of four mature elm trees on the boundary of the park, Bouncer by my side, straining on the leash, I could see that although there were houses overlooking the park, they were set back on the other side of the road, their view of the park obscured by the trees, especially when in full leaf.

Things were slightly different in the cold light of an October afternoon during the school holidays. Already a lone man and his dog on the edge of a children's play area had started to attract attention. I could see a young mum on the far side of the park to my right, pushing a child on one of the baby-swings, all the time watching me out of the corner of her eye. Tina was having great fun clambering over the ironmongery and sliding down again. 'Be careful!' I called to her, more to assert my reason for being there than any real concern that she might fall and hurt herself on the rubber matting.

Yes, I decided, if Hertz had patiently awaited the perfect moment, snatching a child out of the park would have been easy. Mind you, I thought, as I allowed Bouncer to drag me in the direction of one of the trees, not as easy as it would have been for someone, say a police someone, to stroll by and ping a cigarette stub into it.

10

It wasn't called the Newberry Hotel. It was known simply as The Newberry. Located amidst the sweeping crescents, broad boulevards and elegant squares of Edinburgh's New Town, everything about the interior was as stylishly elegant as the Georgian exterior.

'This is very nice,' was my entry for most understated compliment of the year.

'Yes,' Jill agreed. 'Hercule always stayed at The Newberry when he was in Scotland on business. He'd been coming here for years.'

We passed through the lobby without hindrance, only the merest bow of the head from a white-gloved butler who, about to cross our path, stopped to give us right of way.

There was an elevator, but we took the wide, sweeping staircase two flights up until we came to an enormous wooden door we could have walked through side by side. There was no penthouse at The Newberry. Of the nine suites available, each was splendid in its own right, and a memorial to one of Scotland's famous sons or daughters.

The James Clerk Maxwell was named after the renowned nineteenth-century physicist, who'd been born not far from the very spot, in India Street. It had been Hercule's favourite.

'Okay, talk me through it,' I said, taking up position, once Jill had used a large iron key to let us inside.

'Well—'

'No. Leave and come back in again. Let's do this right from the start. Pretend you're carrying your suitcases.'

'Robbie,' Jill said, 'this is The Newberry. You don't carry your own suitcases. You don't even see how your suitcases arrive in the room. They just appear. And I'm not going out and coming in again, that's just stupid. I'll start here from the doorway.'

'Who came in first, you or Hercule?'

'Hercule was already here. He'd been in Edinburgh a week. I came over to surprise him.'

'How was he?'

'Slightly tipsy, actually. He was lying on the bed when I came in.'

'Fully clothed?'

'He was wearing a dressing gown. Obviously, he got up when I arrived. Now let me see…' She strode forward, and I followed her through a large sitting room furnished with easy chairs, bookcases, plush curtains and a chaise longue, onwards down a small hall, past the bathroom to a bedroom with a giant wardrobe, his-and-her dressing tables, wing-back armchairs either side, and a four-poster bed in the centre. Jill walked over to a suitcase stand behind the door. 'I put my handbag down here,' she said. 'The suitcases had already arrived…' She paused to think. 'Yes, that's right, Hercule jumped off the bed and kissed me. I could smell he'd been drinking, though that wasn't entirely unusual for him at the weekends.'

So far so good. 'Okay,' I said, 'continue and don't leave anything out. The slightest detail could be important.' I might as well sound interested. 'Actually…you can leave some of it out. I mean, if you and Hercule…' I jerked my head at the bed. 'You know…?'

75

'We didn't.'

'I wasn't prying.'

'Not everyone takes the bed for a test drive the minute they enter a hotel room, Robbie.'

Perhaps it was just me, then. 'Just tell me what happened next.' And so it went on. The process was like examining a witness in chief, except I was allowed to ask leading questions, something I usually did, anyway, when I could get away with it. 'You must have had a cup of tea.' I walked over to the great oak wardrobe and pulled the door open. 'Where's the kettle hidden?' I imagined The Newberry did a spectacular complimentary shortbread pack. 'And where's the minibar?'

Jill pointed at an ivory dial phone at the side of the bed that looked as though it might have been used to receive the news of Archduke Franz Ferdinand's assassination. 'If you're in need of refreshments you ring down and they're brought up. You don't go to the trouble of making them yourself.'

Perish the thought. 'All right.' I clapped my hands and glanced around. 'No sex, no tea, no minibar raiding. What *did* you do?'

'If you shut up and listen, I'll tell you.' Jill stared down at the suitcase stand. 'I took a few things out. Just what I was going to be wearing later that night, and hung them in the wardrobe over there.' Apparently, she'd managed to do that all by herself, and hadn't needed to ring down for assistance. 'Then I got out my toilet bag, make-up and things, took them through to the bathroom and laid them out.'

'What was Hercule doing?'

'He was back on the bed reading notes for a speech, though I don't know how much he was taking in because he seemed very drowsy.'

'Drowsy.' I tapped my head to let Jill know I was making a mental note of that. 'And then?'

Jill continued. 'There was an empty bottle of champagne on the bedside table. I told him to sleep it off so he'd be fit for dinner.'

'Okay, so meanwhile you're in the toilet, laying out your toothbrush. What then?'

'My mobile rang. I'd left it on top of the suitcases when I came in. It was Harvey Nicks confirming my appointment. I always visit Mark Woolley when I'm here, and he couldn't take me on the Saturday, so I'd had to change to Friday afternoon. That was the main reason I came a day early.'

'Who's Mark Woolley?'

'He cuts hair at Harvey Nichols, Robbie.'

'Expensive?'

'Very. But unlike your barber he doesn't rely solely on power tools and a devil-may-care attitude.'

'You left at that point?'

'Not right away. I went through to the bathroom again, to freshen up, and when I came back through here, straightaway I realised there was something not quite right about Hercule. He was lying on his back. He looked like he was sleeping, but his breathing was shallow and irregular. I recognised the signs.'

'What signs?'

'He was having a hypoglycaemic attack.'

'Did that happen often?'

'Only very occasionally, though I hadn't seen him this bad before, and knew I had to get some sugar into him.'

'A less posh hotel would have had chocolate or some shortbread along with in-room coffee facilities,' I said.

Jill almost agreed. 'Yes, but there would have been a

problem getting him to eat anything given the state he was in.'

'Or a can of Coke from a minibar ...'

'Okay, Robbie, I get it, there should have been a minibar and a kettle with mugs and those horrible little plastic containers of fake milk, but there wasn't. I had to ring down for some orange juice.'

I had visions of a waiter preparing chilled, freshly squeezed orange and sedately bringing it up the stairs on a silver tray to the dying guest.

'I have to admit I was panicking slightly,' Jill said. 'I knew Hercule, like all diabetics, would keep something sweet handy. Zanetti does its own range of glucose gels in little sachets. I thought he might have had some of those stashed away somewhere. I searched the bedroom.' Jill mimed frantically pulling out bedside drawers. 'By this time, he was drifting in and out of consciousness.'

The more Jill spoke, the more she was making it sound like death was due to hypoglycaemic coma and not drug overdose. Maybe Professor Bradley had been wrong, but whether Hercule's death had been down to a reckless disregard for his diabetes or a deliberately self-inflicted drug overdose, he was just as dead, and it wasn't murder.

'I ran back to the bathroom ...'

I followed her down the hall and into the palatial toilet facilities where her voice echoed in the cavernous surroundings. 'I rummaged around and eventually found a supply of glucose tablets in the bottom of Hercule's soap bag. I knew he'd have something like that stashed away. I crumbled a couple of them up and put them in his mouth. Fortunately, the orange juice arrived, and I forced it down him with the glucose. After a few minutes he started to come around. Just to make sure, I asked the hotel to call an ambulance. Paramedics were here in about fifteen minutes, maybe even less. By the time they took over, Hercule was sitting up, looking dozy but a lot better and wondering what all the fuss was about. So ...'

'So?'

'I went to my hair appointment. There was no reason not to. I left him with the paramedics. He kept telling me he was fine and that I should go. I got a taxi the length of George Street and was gone about two hours. When I came back ...'

Jill sat down on a corner of the bed, head bowed, finger and thumb pressed against her forehead.

I waited until she looked up again, a tight smile stretched across her face, tears welling in her eyes. I wasn't good in this kind of situation, and found it best to pretend I didn't notice. 'You said that, when you left to get your hair done, Hercule was lying on the bed. When you came back where was he?'

'He was in the same position, lying on the bed like he was asleep.'

'Any signs of a struggle?'

'There wouldn't be if he was poisoned,' Jill said.

Or if he killed himself, I thought but said instead, 'When do you think the poisoning would have occurred?'

'Obviously it must have been after I'd gone to the hairdresser.' Jill sat up straight. 'You don't think the paramedics slipped him something, do you? I want you to look into that, Robbie. Do we know if they were real paramedics?'

'Jill ...'

'Robbie, it wasn't suicide.'

'I'm only saying—'

79

'I know what you're saying, now would you listen to what *I'm* saying? Hercule did not kill himself.'

I paced up and down the bedroom, head cocked and tapping my upper lip with my index finger, hoping it made me look thoughtful when I wasn't thinking about anything other than the man had obviously topped himself. He ran a pharmaceutical company. Getting his hands on drugs wasn't going to be a problem. There was a window of a couple of hours when he was alone, during which he could easily have ingested the drugs that killed him, especially if he was under the influence of alcohol. I couldn't possibly say it, but he really shouldn't have been left alone.

'Was Hercule depressed or worried about anything?' I asked.

'Robbie, I've told you already.'

'I know, I'm just covering all the bases. You said something about a speech. When was he giving it?'

'He'd already given it that morning. Why?'

'Just that the thought of a speech can make some people very anxious.'

'Not to the extent of suicide.'

I wasn't so sure. I knew a few sheriffs who always looked like they wanted to kill themselves when I stood up to make one.

'Hercule had given dozens, hundreds of speeches all over the world.'

'Still, it's strange, don't you think? That he'd be reading notes of a speech he'd already given when he could have been—'

'Is that all you think about?'

'You don't know what I was going to say.'

'Yes, I do.' Jill stood up off the bed and cracked me on the side of the face with the flat of her hand.

'What was that for?' I thought it only fair to ask.

'For what you were thinking just now.'

It's a gift women have: knowing what men are thinking. A lot of the time men don't know themselves, until they've said it out loud.

Before I could protest, Jill threw herself face down and began to sob into a cream satin bedspread, watering the tiny embroidered pink and red flowers.

My phone buzzed. Joanna. I rejected the call.

'Jill,' I said, 'I think it's best if I go.' Her reply was muffled by the bed covers. 'I've got a call I need to take. Why don't you stay here, and I'll meet you downstairs in a wee while? Take your time.'

I called Joanna back as I walked down the wide stairway to the ground floor, and into an art-deco lounge bar that had groups of high armchairs and low tables, set well apart for privacy.

'Sorry about that, Jo,' I said. 'Bad connection.'

'Where are you?'

'Edinburgh.'

'What are you doing there? Where's Tina?'

'I had to come through and see someone on a piece of important business. Malky is watching Tina.'

'You're supposed to be on holiday. Who did you have to go and see that was more important than your daughter?'

I could have gone down the, 'that's confidential' line, but Joanna would have winkled the information out of me one way or another. 'Jill,' I said, with a light little laugh.

'Jill Green?'

'Yeah, she's upset and asked me to research a legal matter for her.'

'You?'

'Yes, me. I'm a lawyer, remember?'

'Where are you?'

'In a hotel.'

'You're staying at a hotel with your ex!'

'I'm visiting a hotel with a client. I'm in the lounge. It's all to do with Hercule Mercier's death. I can't really talk about it just now, and definitely not over the phone. Hello...? Jo, are you still there?' She wasn't. She still wasn't there when I tried to call back. I placed the mobile phone down on the table with less care than befitted my surroundings.

The white-gloved butler-cum-waiter I'd seen earlier appeared at my side. He had lots of grey hair and was wearing a black suit, a white bow tie and a stiff upper lip. He assessed the situation immediately. 'Can I bring you something, sir? A whisky, perhaps?'

'At ten in the morning?'

'Then, a pot of tea? Or coffee?'

'No, I think I'll have a whisky.'

'Anything in particular?'

'Surprise me.'

He floated off, leaving me wondering what I thought I was playing at? Was I really going to pander to the delusions of a traumatised woman, one who'd not only forced me to set aside my family commitments and professional pride, but had assaulted me? All for the sake of a few thousand pounds? Yes, come to think of it, I was, and, if I wanted to earn any more, I thought I'd better not slacken too much on the pandering.

'Terrible, wasn't it?' I said, when the waiter returned with a cut crystal glass containing half an inch of amber liquid, a small jug of water beside it on a silver tray. 'The thing with Mr Mercier,' I clarified.

'Indeed,' he said, setting the glass and jug down on a small side table by the arm of my chair.

'I was wondering if—'

'I couldn't comment, sir,' he said, straightening to attention. 'Will there be anything else? A newspaper?'

'Just tell me this. You'll be aware of the relationship between Mr Mercier and Miss Green?' Not a twitch of a facial muscle suggested that the waiter knew anything of the sort. 'The day he died. Were you working?'

'I was on duty, sir, yes.'

'Did anyone go up to his room after Miss Green had left for her hairdresser appointment and before she returned?'

I took hold of the sleeve of his jacket to prevent him turning away. 'I know you won't want to breach any confidences about guests, but I also know that you'll have given a statement to the police. I'm a solicitor. Miss Green's legal representative. She's upstairs right now. If you'd like to check with her before you answer, feel free.'

With finger and thumb, the waiter delicately freed his sleeve from my grip and glanced about. The only other occupants were some middle-aged American men, either born with no volume control or with the assumption that the rest of the world was interested in what they had to say, and we were all hard of hearing. Satisfied that our conversation would remain *entre nous*, the waiter cleared his throat.

'As I recall,' he said softly, 'the paramedics stayed for around another ten minutes and then, satisfied that Mr Mercier was on the mend, they departed.'

'Mind if you talk me through the guest register for that weekend?'

'Really, sir, I don't think—'

'I can get a court order, if you'd prefer.' I couldn't, but

he didn't know that. He left and came back with a small notepad on which he'd written details of the bookings for the weekend of Hercule's death. I took it, folded it and put it in my pocket. 'Thanks. One final thing.' I ignored his sigh. 'Did you have any further contact with Mr Mercier after Miss Green had gone to the hairdresser?'

'About a quarter of an hour later Mr Mercier rang down and I took him up some room service. I did not return to the James Clerk Maxwell until after Miss Green had returned, and I heard her cries for help. Now if that will be all ...'

Whether it would be all or not, he left me in as much of a hurry as his waiterly dignity would allow.

I'd all but ruled out the paramedics as a source of poisoning. On the million-to-one chance that it had all been a highly orchestrated assassination, I'd have Grace-Mary check with the ambulance depot and ascertain the identities of the personnel involved. What interested me more was the request for room service after Jill had gone. That was new and possibly relevant. Although the notion that Hercule had been murdered seemed very far-fetched, Jill was my client and if she was paying me to solve the crime, I had to look at all the angles. Could it have been an inside job? Why would anyone in The Newberry want to kill one of their best guests? Perhaps Jill would have a bit more background information on that. I knocked back a whisky that was deserving of a lot more care and attention, and sprinted back up to the room to find no Jill, only a rumpled tear-stained bedspread.

The same butler was waiting for me in the lobby as I walked down the stairs. 'Miss Green asked me to pass on a message, sir. It was that you are to keep digging and that she would be in touch.'

He followed me to the door, where I turned to face him. 'The room service. What was the order?'

'As I recall, sir, it was The Auld Alliance.'

'What's that?'

He came as close to a smile as he'd managed during our brief acquaintance. 'French champagne and a dozen Scottish oysters. Or as some of our American guests would prefer to have it: the lock-and-load.'

11

Thursday morning, I checked into the office to see how Grace-Mary was coping without me. Extremely well was my secretary's take on things. I spent an hour sifting through a few case files that needed feeing-up, while Tina sat in my big, looks-quite-like-leather chair, head peeking over the edge of the desk, drawing pictures on legal aid forms with a yellow highlighter pen.

Grace-Mary put her head around the door at half past twelve to say she was going for lunch. It was going to be a long one. I'd made sure of that by asking her to take Tina along too. I was having to pay, but there was nothing for it. If my dad thought that by giving me my marching orders, I'd simply walk away from his case, he shouldn't have raised such a stubborn son. One phone call from Grace-Mary to the Scottish Police Federation, followed by one five-pound donation from me to the swear box, and I knew which firm of solicitors had been instructed to handle his case. One more call and I knew when and where they'd be consulting. Two o'clock today at Caldwell & Craig's offices in Glasgow.

Caldwell and Craig? Why did it have to be my old firm? Why were they even dabbling in criminal defence work? Not that it had been a dislike of criminal law per se that had caused the distinguished old law firm to dispense with my services several years previously. No, it had been a dislike of my clientele and the paltry sums that legal aid brought in. Back then, the senior partners of C&C decided that only those who could afford to pay handsomely for it should be allowed access to justice.

Things would have been very different had Caldwell & Craig attracted rich criminal clients. As it was, the firm's clients were usually rich enough not to be criminals, and those people who were rich because they were criminals, tended not to instruct dusty old edifices such as my former employers.

So, for the few paying criminal clients who were referred their way, C&C drafted in solicitors with a knowledge of criminal law to cover certain high value cases. It was a role my former assistant, Andy Imray, had filled for a time. Now it was Pearl's turn. I couldn't remember her second name. She was a solid, wide-faced wee woman with a pair of sad eyes that stared out from behind the thick lenses of tortoiseshell spectacles. I'd come across her many times over the years, usually at Glasgow Sheriff Court where she scraped by doing agency work for some of the busier criminal firms. Pearl liked to plead guilty, and, on those rare occasions when she was forced to take a case to trial, she always had about her the air of a boxer looking for a comfortable patch of canvas.

'You can't just come barging in here,' Pearl said, in response to my barging in there. Her words were closely followed by the arrival of the receptionist, who'd obviously thought I hadn't heard her tell me not to go in, even though I'd tried to make it clear that I had heard, but wasn't listening.

'Leave him!' a voice boomed. Pearl and the receptionist ceased their complaints. The former sat down again at the enormous mahogany table in the centre of the consulting room, the latter backed out through the door.

Cameron Crowe Q.C., the source of the voice, didn't look up from his notes. 'I wondered when you'd make an appearance,' he said.

'You?' was all I could come up with at short notice.

'Patently so, me. Why not me?'

And when I paused to think, and get over my heartfelt loathing for the man, why not him? Why not Nosferatu in pinstripes? Okay, he was the most sleekit, back-stabbing, self-important lawyer I knew – and that was saying something – but sometimes sleekit and back-stabbing were the qualities an accused needed most in a legal representative. Better Crowe be for my dad than against him.

'No, really,' Pearl said, having given more thought to the situation, 'you'll have to leave right now.' She rose to her feet again, pointing me to the door in case I'd lost my bearings.

'No, he won't,' Crowe said, with a sigh of extreme patience, wafting a hand and directing me to one of many empty chairs around the table.

I wasn't sure who was more surprised by Crowe's favourable attitude to my gate-crashing the consultation, me or Pearl. Whoever, it was the dumpy wee lawyer who spoke first. 'He can't stay. He has got no business being here, other than to try and steal the client back.' Not only did Pearl look like a frog, she was also good at leaping to conclusions.

My dad decided to enter the debate. 'Do what you're told, Robbie. Leave. I'm not wanting you here.'

'I'll decide who stays and leaves, thank you, Mr Munro senior,' Crowe said. 'And for the moment I say your son stays.' He pointed again to the empty chair next to my dad. 'Sit.'

I sat. My dad twisted in his seat, turning his back on me.

Crowe shuffled his papers, tapped the edges to square them up and looked across the vastness of the table at me. 'Your father seems to be having difficulty remembering what was said at his recent interview with the CCU in Livingston. Unfortunately, I don't have a transcript. You were present. Perhaps your memory of events is clearer than his.'

It was – a lot clearer. I relayed it to Crowe almost word for word, and he noted it down slowly and carefully, raising his eyes from the paper only after I'd finished and he'd added the final full stop as though he were spearing an ant.

'I think I have it now,' he said, placing his pen on top of the pile of papers. Sitting upright in his chair, he clasped his hands on the desk in front of him and tapped his thumbs together. His next remarks were addressed to my dad. 'Mr Munro, may I call you Alex?' He didn't wait for permission. 'Then, Alex, as I think you know, I've been asked to consult with you by Messrs Caldwell & Craig who have themselves received instructions from the Scottish Police Federation. You are no longer a member of the Federation, nor have you been for a many a year. For that reason, I'm to assess whether it would be fitting for the Federation to fund your defence to any charges that may come about as a result of...' He cleared his throat and smiled thinly. 'As a result of what I am sure is a misunderstanding arising out of Mr Hertz's appeal against conviction.'

'I thought the Federation had agreed to cover all my legal costs,' my dad said.

Crowe shook his head. 'Whether your costs are to be

met is at the Federation's discretion, and that very much depends on how I view your case. If I take the view that there is no probablis causa—'

'No what?'

Crowe translated for him. It wasn't a huge help, so I translated further. 'The Federation won't pay your legal bill if Mr Crowe doesn't think there's a good enough chance of you winning,' I said.

'Winning what?'

'Your trial.'

'What trial? I've not been charged with anything.'

'No, Alex, you haven't,' Crowe said, taking over again. 'Not yet, but I fear you are about to face a charge of perverting the course of justice amongst other things. That's why I hope I can help you help yourself.'

Now I understood where Crowe was coming from, and why he'd allowed me to be present. He had some advice to give to my dad that would greatly improve the prospects for success. If that advice was taken, Crowe could recommend the Federation exercise its discretion and he could secure a high-paying trial out of it. He must have thought my dad might balk at his advice, and that I could help persuade my old man to see sense. Clearly, he'd never met my dad before.

My dad still didn't understand. 'How about you speak plainly and lay it on the line for me.'

And that's exactly what Crowe did. 'The Scottish Criminal Case Review Commission is gunning for you. There's nothing they like better than uncovering a crooked cop.'

That was a little plainer than my dad had expected. After a brief, but violent, verbal explosion he stormed off to the toilet. Pearl used the intermission to ring through for some refreshments. I'd hoped for coffee. The receptionist brought through a tray of bottled water and some glasses. She managed to set it down in the centre of the table almost as heavily as her foot on my toes.

'Where were we?' Crowe asked, once my dad had returned, looking no less flustered. 'Ah, yes. The Scottish Criminal Cases Review Commission.'

The SCCRC was the wrongfully accused person's last hope. It had the power to review cases, carry out investigations, and, if there appeared to have been a miscarriage of justice, refer matters back to the Appeal Court for further consideration. The SCCRC had investigated Ricky Hertz's conviction and on the basis of new evidence had sent it back to the Appeal Court. That new evidence had been presented so compellingly that it was enough to persuade the court that Hertz should be liberated on bail meantime, pending a final appeal hearing.

'The evidence that wasn't available at the trial,' Crowe explained, 'was the presence of your DNA on a cigarette stub. A cigarette stub used by the Crown to establish the presence of Mr Hertz at one of the crime scenes.'

'There was other evidence to show he was guilty,' my dad grunted.

Crowe ran a hand over his slicked back hair. 'Yes, there was. Let's have a look at it, shall we?'

When we did, it looked like this: The Crown case, as put to the jury, consisted of Hertz's alleged confession that he'd strangled two children and dumped their bodies. Good, but not sufficient under Scots law. That was where two other adminicles of evidence came in very handy. Firstly, the evidence of my dad and Big Jock Knox that they'd seen Hertz talking to a child in a play park the same day as Emily Foster's disappearance, and, most important of all, the finding of a cigarette stub complete with one of Ricky Hertz's fingerprints at the scene of Emily's abduction.

'The meteorological evidence was important too,' Pearl chipped in.

Crowe agreed. He pulled a single sheet from his bundle of papers. 'The Met Office report showed no record of precipitation—'

'That's rain,' I whispered to my dad.

He swivelled in his chair to face me for the first time. 'Thanks, but I know what precipitation is.'

'Shall I go on?' Crowe asked and, not waiting for a reply, went on. 'To summarise, it had rained heavily the day Emily Foster was abducted, but not on the actual evening. Given that the cigarette stub was dry and intact, it meant that the stub had been discarded between . . .' He checked the sheet of paper again. 'Seven that night and five o'clock the following afternoon, when those conducting the search found it lying by a climbing frame.' Crowe replaced the sheet of paper and straightened his papers again. 'As you'll have gathered, the cigarette stub was a strong piece of evidence that helped shore up an otherwise weak prosecution case.'

My dad reached for one of the bottles of mineral water in the centre of the table, cracked it open and, ignoring the collection of tumblers, took a slug. 'Seems like a pretty strong case to me even without it,' he grumbled.

'Does it?' Crowe helped himself to a bottle of water too. 'What do we have without the stub? A man talking to a different girl, an older girl, in a different play park. Hardly evidence of criminal activity.'

'It might be sufficient taken along with the confession,' I said. For as long as I'd been a defence lawyer, the courts had held that if there was a confession, very little else was required to provide corroboration of guilt.

'Ah, yes, the confession.' Even the glass that was raised to the Q.C.'s lips couldn't hide his smirk.

'What was wrong with it?' my dad asked.

'It's more a question of what was right with it,' Crowe said. 'Every single piece of so-called special knowledge in that confession was information already known to the officers conducting the interview. And it wasn't recorded, merely jotted down in a notebook—'

'That was signed by Hertz,' my dad pointed out.

'Signed in ink but written in pencil,' Crowe replied. 'It's also strange that Hertz didn't confess to the abduction and murder of Emily Foster. Why not if he was making a clean breast of things? Some would say it was because those interviewing him didn't have any details of the case at that time.'

My dad slammed the bottle down onto the table top, face red. 'Are you insinuating—'

'I'm insinuating nothing.' Crowe could play indignant almost as well as my dad. 'What I'm doing is pointing out the obvious weakness of the Crown case. But for the fortuitous finding of that cigarette stub, it wouldn't have mattered if Hertz's confession had been filmed and played back to the jury on the big screen, 3-D, in high definition. By itself it was insufficient. What convicted Mr Hertz of the murder of those three children was this!'

With the skill of a magician, Crowe whisked from his stack of papers an A4 photograph of the plastic vial containing the cigarette stub.

'Okay,' I said. 'So far you've done nothing more than highlight the issues that D.I. Niblo from the CCU raised during the interview on Monday. Let's cut to the part where you help my dad help himself.'

'All right,' Crowe said, 'let's get down to business. As I say, Ricky Hertz is a free man at the moment for one reason . . .' He held up the photograph of the cigarette to us, as though we wouldn't understand what he was saying without recourse to visual aids. 'The SCCRC is basing the appeal on the premise that the verdict of the jury at trial was reached in ignorance of the existence of your DNA being inexplicably present on this vital piece of evidence. They submit that if the jury had known of this relevant piece of evidence it might have taken a different view and as such there has been a miscarriage of justice.'

'We know this already,' I said.

Crowe leaned forward, looking even more pleased with himself than usual. 'Fortunately, we also know the one thing the Appeal Court really hates. Don't we, Alex?'

Alex didn't seem to, but I did. 'Quashing convictions.'

'Precisely. And that's why they won't uphold Hertz's appeal if they are given even the semblance of an innocent explanation for the presence of your father's DNA on that cigarette stub.'

This time it was Pearl who assisted by holding up the photograph.

'Is that it?' I said. 'Is that how you help my dad help himself? In case you weren't listening earlier, I told you my dad was given an opportunity to provide an explanation at the interview with the CCU.' My dad was staring at the polished surface of the table. I gave him a dig in the ribs. 'And what did he do? He decided *that* was the time to make no comment.'

'Doesn't matter.' Crowe's smile was almost natural now. 'I have some good news for you, Alex. The Appeal Court has ruled that your interview with D.I. Niblo was an internal police disciplinary matter and as such should not form part of the SCCRC's investigations or the appeal.'

My dad was looking less flustered and a lot more relaxed. I wanted to know why the court had decided to cut him this break.

'Do you know another thing the High Court really hates?' Crowe asked, this time denying me the chance to reply; otherwise we could have been there a while. 'Convicting cops. Even—'

'Please don't say crooked cops again,' I said.

'Even those police officers alleged to be guilty of procedural irregularities.'

'But won't the SCCRC want to interview him themselves?' I asked. 'They can cite my dad to give a precognition-on-oath, can't they?'

Crowe agreed they could and most probably would.

My dad thought he had the situation covered. 'Okay, okay. This time I'll say nothing. Just like you told me the first time, Robbie.'

At this point Pearl decided to wade in with her considered opinion. 'You can only refuse to answer questions at a precognition-on-oath if you think something you say might incriminate you, Sergeant Munro. It seems to me that if you say nothing and don't come up with an explanation about that DNA, you might as well open the prison gates and let Ricky Hertz out yourself. Don't you agree, Mr Crowe?'

Crowe rocked back in his chair and would have studied the ceiling had his eyes not been closed. He took a deep breath, held it a while and then, righting his chair, stood up. Hands gripping the lapels of his jacket, he walked to the window and let go an enormous sigh. 'Let's cease the charade. The cigarette was planted. Ricky Hertz's appeal is as good as in the bag. Whether that's justice or not, I don't know, nor do I particularly care. What I do know is that when the SCCRC win this one, the Crown will look for someone to blame and that person is in this room.'

I'd no idea why my dad bothered to look at me and Pearl.

'The only way you can avoid spending the rest of your life in prison, Alex—'

'The rest of my life!'

Crowe turned from the window. 'Ricky Hertz spent nearly eighteen years of his in prison. How long do you think the person who fabricated the evidence against him should serve?'

My dad's previously ruddy complexion had taken on a paler hue.

Crowe smiled like he'd spied a nice pulsating carotid. 'Unless, of course, the person who fabricated the evidence is incapax and unable to refute the allegation.'

I understood immediately, and didn't know whether to be reassured or extremely worried that Cameron Crowe shared the same idea as me as to my father's best line of defence.

It took a little longer for dawn to break in the brain of ex-sergeant Alex Munro. He turned to me and asked, 'Is he telling me to blame Jock Knox?' Before I could answer he was on his feet and putting the question direct to the man at the window. 'Are you telling me to—'

Cameron Crowe showed my dad the palm of his hand. 'What I'm telling you is that their Lordships have given you another bite at the cherry. If I were you, I'd make sure my dentures were securely fastened.'

My dad ran a fingernail along his front teeth. 'Do these look like falsers to you?'

'It was merely an expression,' Crowe said.

'I know what it was, and I've a few expressions myself I might use, if there wasn't a lady present,' my dad said. From the corner of my eye I caught a glimpse of Pearl touching up the back of her hair. 'Just let me say this. Jock Knox was the finest police officer I ever worked with and I don't care if he is senile now. I've never hit a man when he's down ...' I didn't doubt it, though I was equally sure he'd hit a fair few when they were standing up. 'And there is no chance, not now, not ever, of me blaming Jock for doing anything improper. Not when he's not able to defend himself.'

My dad manoeuvred his not inconsiderable bulk towards the window where Crowe was standing. The Q.C. was a tall man, but thin. Next to my dad he looked like a long streak of liquorice. He stiffened, tugged the cuffs of his white shirt through the sleeves of his black suit and faced up to the old man. 'Then, Mr Munro ...' It was no longer Alex. 'I'm afraid I must inform the Scottish Police Federation that you have no realistic prospects of a successful defence, and that it would be wasting its members' money by funding it.' He gave my dad a quick up-down look, and clicked his fingers at Pearl who hastily gathered together the bundle of papers and followed him out of the door.

'Well, that didn't go so well,' I said. 'Tell me you've changed your mind and I'm not too proud to run after him.'

'Ach, let him go,' my dad said. 'Who needs him?'

'You do. Cameron Crowe is just the man to get you out of this jam.'

'He's a creep.'

'But he's an excellent lawyer. The best, some would say. I know he would. Isn't that what you wanted? The best? There's no way you can afford to pay privately for senior counsel to represent you.'

'Aye, well...' The old man trundled over to me and laid an arm, like a lead weight, across my shoulders. 'If I can't have the best, maybe I'm just going to have to settle for the cheapest.'

12

Jill phoned on Friday afternoon during a game of hide-and-seek in the garden, and completely giving my hiding place away. Malky was playing too. He was seeking and doing his best not to find Tina, which wasn't easy since she was hiding behind a clothes pole and doing a lot of giggling.

Jill was flying to Switzerland in the morning. Hercule's body had been released and she had to finalise the funeral arrangements.

'I'll be gone about a week,' she said. 'When I come back I expect a full report from you as to what progress you've made with your investigations. Meantime I'll send you a cheque for another five thousand—'

'No, Jill, I don't need any more money,' I heard myself say. As far as I was concerned my investigations were complete. Her deceased partner had committed suicide by means of a large quantity of barbiturates. Case closed.

'And I'll keep the suite at The Newberry booked in your name until I come back,' she continued, ignoring my objection to more money. 'I'm sure you'll want to go back for another look, now that you've had a chance to think things over. Someone got in and poisoned Hercule, I know it. Try and think how one of your clients would have done it. That might help.'

I stuffed the phone back into my pocket. How would

one of my clients have done it? Spiderman hadn't sought legal advice from me recently, and yet he seemed the most likely suspect, given that the James Clerk Maxwell suite was on the second floor. The whole thing was a waste of time. Normally, I wouldn't try and resist someone keen to throw money at me. Providing the cash kept coming I'd have been happy to chase flocks of wild geese bark up a forest of wrong trees, if that's what my client wanted. But this client was different. This client was Jill. So what, if three years earlier she had ripped out my heart and danced on it wearing stilettos? She was emotionally disturbed. It wouldn't be fair to take advantage of her in her present state of mind.

By the time Malky had dragged me from undercover I'd made up my mind to visit The Newberry one more time. That way I could tell Jill I'd done something, before calmly and rationally explaining to her that she was wasting my time and her money.

But that unpleasant task would take place four days later, when Jill returned from the funeral. Four hours later, I was in The Newberry's guest lounge, relaxing amidst a comfortable armchair, swirling ice around what was possibly the world's most expensive glass of ginger beer.

'Dad, why is that lady staring at you?'

It was because Tina had come along that we'd been shown to one of the more secluded corners, at the far end of the room, by a bay window.

'She's not,' Malky assured her, 'she's looking at me.'

I'd asked Malky to babysit Tina while I carried out my further reccy at The Newberry. I'd been surprised when he'd agreed, because he usually went out for a drink with his mates on a Friday night, using a weekly, forty-five-minute game of five-a-sides as an excuse for replacing lost sweat with pints of lager. I wouldn't have bothered asking at all if I'd known that Malky's idea of babysitting was to accompany me and bring the 'baby' along with him. Meanwhile the baby was on her second glass of cola and poking at a bowl of Japanese rice crackers, unhappy that Monster Munchies didn't feature on The Newberry's bar menu.

'You seem very confident about that,' I said. 'Tina, it is me the lady's looking at, isn't it?'

Tina studied the lady, something every man in the place had done already, and nodded emphatically. 'Yep, it's definitely you, Dad.'

Malky picked up my daughter's glass of cola, moved the stripy straw to one side and sniffed the contents. 'What did they put in this?'

'So, Malky,' I said, 'from now on we must assume that whenever a pretty woman looks in our direction, she's interested in you, not me?'

That didn't compute with Malky as a question, more as a bald statement of fact. He leaned back, ran his fingers through his hair and sent a wink and a co-pilot of a boyish grin winging their way across the lounge to where the subject of our conversation was delicately poised on a barstool, sipping from a saucer of champagne. The female in question was a redhead, around thirty, perhaps younger. She was tall and slim, wearing a tight-fitting gold top of fish scale-like material that shimmered under the spotlight of the bar canopy, a wisp of lace around her bare shoulders, and a skirt, the material for which had not been bought by the yard.

'I like her shoes,' Tina said, though it was what lay between those high heels and the strip of material three feet above that was attracting most approval from those present. She crossed her legs. They took a lot of crossing. The raising of a painted fingernail was sufficient for the waiter to sail over and pour more champagne.

Malky straightened the tie he wasn't wearing and got to his feet. 'Don't wait up,' he said out of the corner of his mouth. 'I may be some time.'

Malky made the short walk to the bar like a scud missile homing in on a radar station. As he did, the lady lowered herself from her stool and, without seemingly noticing his approach, floated over to sit in the seat he'd recently vacated. Setting her champagne glass down by my ginger beer, she held out a thin, elegant hand that looked like it might break if gripped too tightly. 'Chiara De Rosa,' she said, in a husky voice with a foreign lilt.

For a moment I forgot my name.

Tina helped me out. 'He's Robbie,' she said. 'He's got a wife already.'

I'd almost forgotten that too. I think it may have had something to do with her eyes. And the legs.

The lady smiled and looked down at Tina. 'And who have we here?'

'I'm Tina and this is my dad and that's my Uncle Malky.' Tina pointed at my brother who was loitering casually at the bar, trying to make it seem like he'd only gone to order a drink, even though the place was strictly table service. 'Uncle Malky thought you were looking at him, but my dad thought you weren't and that you were looking at him.'

The young woman made to pat Tina on the head, thought better of it, and, instead, crooked a finger under my daughter's chin. 'Then you were correct, precious. It was your papa I was looking at. I want to speak to him.

I hope your mamma won't mind too much. It's business.'

'Your mum won't mind, will she, Tina?' I said.

'My mum's dead,' Tina countered. 'But Joanna isn't, and she goes to court and gets people the jail.'

A mild look of concern flitted across Miss De Rosa's exquisite features.

'It's complicated,' I said.

She lifted the champagne glass and wet her lips. 'Sounds it.'

'Is your hair supposed to be that red?' Tina asked.

With a flick of absurdly long eyelashes, the woman glanced down at Tina and then up at me again. It was enough.

'Tina . . .' I handed her the bowl of Japanese crackers. 'Why don't you go over and ask Uncle Malky to get us some more snacks, while I speak to the lady?'

'I'd rather we talked somewhere more private,' De Rosa said, after Tina had gone off, bowl in hand.

There was no one in our immediate vicinity, and, yet there was no doubt that wherever the young lady went there would be prying eyes and ears. Especially eyes. The rain was slapping against the bay window, so we could hardly take our conversation outside.

'You're in the Maxwell suite, aren't you?' She stood. 'Give me a few minutes to powder my nose and I'll meet you there.'

'You're what!' Malky asked, when, glass of whisky in hand, he reclaimed his seat. Tina, gripping a bowl of crispy-coated peanuts, clambered up onto his knee.

'I'll only be gone ten minutes. There's no privacy here. Don't look at me like that. She just wants to chat about something.'

'Oh, I'll bet she does,' Malky said.

'What do you mean?'

'Well ...you saw her. Single, lone female, putting her goods on display in the lounge of an expensive hotel that's full of rich, elderly male guests.'

'Why were you so interested then?'

'I've just realised the true situation. Let me put it this way,' he said, reaching over Tina's shoulder into the bowl of peanuts and stuffing a handful in his mouth. 'If her intentions were honourable it would be me she'd be wanting to take up to the bedroom for ...' He made quotation marks with his fingers, 'a chat.' Malky looked about as he chewed, waving an arm at the other guests. 'Do you see any competition for me here?'

'Okay ...' I said. 'Two things. Firstly, I'm a lawyer.'

'What's that got to do with anything?'

'Lots of people want to talk to me about stuff. Legal stuff.'

'In a hotel room? On a Friday night? With her kind of body? With your kind of body?' Malky rammed home a few more peanuts. 'How does she even know you're a lawyer? It's not like you're wearing a sign.'

'She's just told me she wants to speak to me about business. Tina heard her. Didn't you, Tina?'

But my daughter was too busy licking salt off her fingers.

'Oh, I think you'll find for her it's definitely business,' Malky said.

I reached over to stop Tina licking. 'I'm talking about proper legal business. If it's not, then I'll tell her she's soliciting the wrong solicitor.'

'Did you say you had two things?' Malky asked, tilting his head back and dropping a few more peanuts into his mouth.

'I'm coming to that. Secondly, if she isn't what you think she is, which I'm sure she isn't, and I was interested, which I'm definitely not, being a married man, there would be just as much chance of a good-looking woman like her hitting on me as on you.'

Malky almost choked. 'Tina,' he spluttered. 'If you weren't you and were a grown-up lady, who would you rather have as a boyfriend? Me ...' He beamed a smile at her. 'Or your dad?' he said, screwing his face up.

It was a question aptly put to someone with a six-year-old brain, by someone with the brain of a six-year-old.

I left the two to their peanut-fuelled deliberations, and made my way across the lounge to the lobby, where I was greeted at the reception desk by the same amiable grey-haired old gent who had attended on me during my previous visit. Apparently, the key to the James Clerk Maxwell suite had already been uplifted on my behalf. 'And the champagne will be right up, Mr Munro,' he called after me, as I turned away.

I slammed into reverse. 'Champagne?'

'Yes, sir. The Bollinger 1988.'

I cleared my throat, leaning closer across the high reception desk. 'The eighty-eight. That's quite a ... quite an expensive champagne, I take it?' To my knowledge, there weren't that many cheap champagnes, and I surmised that those that came with a birth certificate were out of my price bracket.

The man behind the reception desk smiled condescendingly. 'The 1988 is one of the finest vintages, sir. Perhaps *the* finest.'

'How much?' I asked.

'Sir?'

'The champagne?'

He gave me a faint smile of incomprehension.

'The nineteen . . .'

'Eighty-eight, sir?'

'Yeah, how much does it cost? You know . . . for a bottle?'

The pale features beneath the mop of grey hair reddened, and the man looked at his feet as though I'd just asked to know the colour of his underpants; which I would have guessed were white and crisply starched.

He reached beneath the counter and produced a Manila envelope. He placed it on the desk and slid it across at me. 'Miss De Rosa asked me to give you this,' he said.

'Oh, did she now?' I snatched up the envelope. 'This Miss De Rosa, what's her game?'

'Her game, sir?'

What was wrong with the man? Did he not understand English? I gritted my teeth. 'Yes, her game. She's not *on* the game, is she?'

The clerk took a step back, horrified. 'Really, sir.'

'Well, who is she and what does she think she's doing? Lounging around, all hair and legs, picking up men in the lounge, taking their room keys and ordering vintage champagne like she owns the place!'

I tore open the envelope and counted ten fifty-pound notes. They were flat and crisp and looked like they'd been printed that morning. I knew about such things – most of the fifty-pound notes I came across in my business *had* been printed that morning. Often not very well.

'Sir,' the clerk said. 'Miss De Rosa can do all these things you've just mentioned, because . . .'

'Because what?'

'Because she *does* own the place.'

106

13

I didn't know what was so special about France in 1988, but it certainly knocked out a fine fermented grape that year. Before I could raise the glass to my lips for a second time, Miss De Rosa, who now insisted I call her Chiara, placed a hand on my arm. We were standing in the plush sitting room of the James Clerk Maxwell suite, the bottle of fizzy French wine bathing in a silver vase of ice water nearby.

'It was Hercule's favourite,' Chiara said. 'Nineteen eighty-eight was a good year. Hercule took bronze in the men's downhill at the Calgary Olympics. And...' She smiled, took another sip and gently wiped the foam from her lips with the stroke of a long, slim finger. 'It was the year I was born.' She raised her glass. 'To Hercule.' I followed in the toast and we both drank.

'You knew Hercule well?' I asked. It seemed rather obvious that she did, but I had to kick off my side of the conversation some way.

'Before I answer that,' Chiara said, 'how well do you know his partner, Jill Green?'

I looked at the bubbles in my glass. The whole world didn't need to know I'd been jilted by Jill, though most of it seemed to already. 'I'm afraid that's my business.'

'So, the reason you are here, it is for business, not pleasure?'

'How about we get to the business you want to discuss?'

She lowered herself into a chaise longue upholstered in a cream fabric with a delicate gold thread running through it, and balanced on four bronze bow legs. 'Jill Green is the business I'd like to discuss.'

'Then I can't help you,' I said.

'Did Findlay give you the envelope?' she asked coyly.

'Yes, he did, and I'm afraid my professional discretion can't be bought,' I said, almost reaching into my pocket and returning the money.

She stirred the champagne in her coupe with a fingernail, bringing the bubbles to life. 'Then you really are here for professional not personal reasons?' I didn't answer. 'You must be, because Miss Green has returned to Berne to make arrangements for Hercule's funeral. Why else would you come? You're a lawyer. I know. I've checked. You defend criminals.'

'I defend alleged criminals,' I said.

'And Miss Green is your client?'

'I've told you. I've nothing to say about Jill.'

'Oh, it's Jill, is it?' Chiara smiled up at me and patted the end of the chaise longue, an invitation for me to join her. 'Will you at least answer one question?' She pouted.

'It depends on what it is?' I said, not sitting.

'I'd like to know who murdered Hercule.'

Another one. The man committed suicide, why couldn't people get it through their heads? No one climbed in through the window and forced a pile of pills down his throat. The man must have been depressed about something, and if anyone had access to the type of drugs required to do the job properly, it was the head of one of Europe's largest pharmaceutical manufacturers.

I finished my drink and looked for somewhere to put my glass down.

Using two fingers, scissor-like, Chiara reached out and took hold of the crease in my right trouser leg, just below the knee. 'Don't go.' She wafted a hand at the ornate, silver ice bucket. 'Pour yourself another drink.'

What was I to do? When it came to beautiful women imploring me not to leave their five-star suites, but, instead, stay and drink champagne with them, there was not exactly a well of experience from which I could draw. I poured another drink, consoling myself with the fact that at least I could include in the final report to Jill that my enquiries had comprised an interview with the hotel's owner. After all, I had to do some work to earn the exorbitant fee that had been foisted upon me, and, if it meant drinking vintage fizz with a gorgeous woman, I'd just have to grin and bear it.

'Hercule's death certificate states that he died from self-administered barbiturate poisoning,' I said, topping up Chiara's glass.

'And because it's on the death certificate I'm supposed to believe it? I don't think so, Mr Munro. I knew Hercule Mercier very well. Better than most.'

'Jill told me he'd been coming here for years.'

'More than that. My father was Swiss. He was a friend of Hercule. He used to come and visit us all the time. My grandmother adored him. When my parents died, my mother first and then Papa, I finished school in Switzerland and came to Scotland to live with her. Not for long though. My grandfather gave me this place for my twenty-first birthday present and I've lived here ever since.'

My dad had given me a bottle of Springbank fifteen-year-old for my twenty-first, and, as I recalled, drunk most of it.

'He must be a rich man, your grandfather,' I said, demonstrating my razor-sharp powers of deduction.

'Very. As is my grandmother. Unfortunately she is extremely ill.'

'I'm sorry to hear that.'

She shrugged and took a drink of champagne. 'She's also very old.'

My phone buzzed. A text from Malky. '*Sorry. Got to bounce.*' The door opened, and Tina walked in.

'How long are you going to be in here with her drinking wine?' she demanded.

'Not long, pet.' I downed the rest of my drink. 'Why don't you go to the toilet and then put on your coat and we'll catch the train home?' This seemed an acceptable agenda to Tina, and she wandered off in search of the loo. 'And don't break anything!' I called after her.

'Mr Munro, I want to know who killed Hercule. As you know, I'm happy to pay for information.'

'I only wish I had some to give you,' I said. 'All I have it what is written on a death certificate.'

'You say that. But somehow I think you know more than you are prepared to tell.' She conjured up a business card and pressed it into my hand. 'If you do have any information. Anything at all. Call me.'

Tina returned from the toilet with a guilty expression on her face.

'Did you have an accident in there?' I asked.

'No,' she said, unconvincingly.

'Have you broken something? I told you not to touch anything.'

I went through to the toilet. Other than it hadn't been flushed, there was nothing untoward that I could see. Jill's and Hercule's toilet bags were still positioned at the either side of the double sinks, and regiments of tiny bottles of shampoos, conditioners and lotions were lined up as though ready for inspection. Albeit there were one or two ornaments scattered about, there was no sign of any breakages. Satisfied, and taking Tina with me, I went through to the sitting room again, only to discover that Chiara had moved to the bedroom.

The place was very much how I'd left it after my visit there with Jill, two days previously. Her suitcases were still on the stand in the corner, even the bedclothes were rumpled. There was no way The Newberry housekeeping was this bad. Obviously, Jill had left orders for the place to remain exactly how it had been on the day of Hercule's death, the better for me to carry out my investigations.

Chiara was standing at the far side of the room by an enormous window, against which the rain was battering. She sighed. 'Mr Munro. Why has Jill Green asked you to come here? If as you say Hercule killed himself, if there is no one to defend for his murder, why has she need of your services?'

'With respect, my dealings with Jill are no concern of yours,' I said.

'If a man is murdered in my hotel, then it is very much my concern.'

'Look, I don't know who you've been speaking to, but Hercule Mercier was not murdered.' I knocked back the last of my champagne. 'He was depressed and killed himself. It's a tragedy, but these things happen.'

'No, Mr Munro, Hercule was not depressed.'

'Who was murdered, Dad?' Tina asked.

I ruffled her hair. 'Nobody. Come on, let's go for the train.'

'Well, I certainly do not believe he killed himself,'

Chiara said, indignantly, turning to gaze out through the rain-spattered window.

'And why's that then?' I asked.

When eventually she turned to face me, there were tears in her eyes. 'Because he had so much to live for.'

'Care to expand?' I asked.

She turned to the window again. 'It is not only you and Miss Green who have secrets, Mr Munro.'

'In that case, you keep yours and I'll keep mine,' I said, and taking my daughter by the hand, left her staring out into the darkness of a rainy Edinburgh night.

14

When it came to an appeal based on the discovery of new evidence, Scotland's criminal Appeal Court had to decide on two things. Firstly, could the evidence have been made available at the trial? If not, then, secondly, if it had been led at trial would the evidence have materially altered the view of the convicting jury? If both boxes were ticked, it was open to the Appeal Court to conclude that there had been a miscarriage of justice and quash the conviction.

In the case of Ricky Hertz, it had only been the new and improved scientific methods developed over the intervening years that had allowed the tiniest strands of my dad's genetic material now to be analysed and his identity established. The question for the Appeal Court was: if at the trial, Hertz's challenge to the finding of the cigarette stub had been supported by this new DNA finding, what would the jury have made of it?

I'd run the scenario past a few colleagues up at the Sheriff Court, and the general consensus was, unsurprisingly, that, unless there was an innocent explanation for my dad's DNA to be on the cigarette stub, the whole thing smacked of a police fit-up. The Appeal Court appeared to have reached a similar view on the matter, which was why Hertz had been granted interim liberation on bail pending the final judgement. In such a serious case, his temporary release was a major indication that the court intended to make the arrangement permanent.

Knowing that my dad had been unable to come up with an explanation, reasonable or otherwise, for the DNA finding when interviewed by D.I Niblo of the CCU, Ricky Hertz's lawyer had cited my dad to provide a precognition-on-oath and he'd been given the minimum forty-eight hours' notice. Ten to ten, Monday morning he was waiting outside Court 6 at Edinburgh Sheriff Court and I was in the agents' room with Fiona Faye QC. Acting on behalf of the Crown, opposing Hertz's appeal, she had been given dispensation to keep a watching brief while counsel for the Scottish Criminal Case Review Commission interrogated my dad.

'In a way your father is lucky.' Fiona took a gold compact from her handbag, opened it and touched up her lippy in the mirror. 'The Appeal Court could have simply left him to be hung out and dried on the strength of his interview with the CCU, which I'm reliably informed didn't go too well.' That was putting it mildly. 'At least he's getting the chance to come up with a story that might get him off the hook.' Lipstick applied, she gave me a wink and turned her attention to her blonde bouffant hair, giving it a flick here and there with the long pointy end of a comb. It was a lot of preparatory work for merely sitting in on a hearing that was going to be held before a sheriff in private.

'What was the wink for?' I asked.

'Come on. You know.'

'No,' I said. 'I don't.'

She cocked her head and tilted the mirror so that it pointed at me. 'Let's not pretend you haven't already been applying your famous imagination to the problem. Not Robbie Munro, author of the Bumper Book of Dodgy

Defences.' She gave her hair a final flick. 'I take it your dad's going to stick his old police buddy in the frame for it? Makes sense.'

'He's not,' I said.

Fiona snapped the compact shut and dropped it and the pointy-ended comb into her handbag. 'You have advised him that keeping schtum won't be enough to prevent a prosecution? No comment simply won't do when that cigarette stub is crying out for an explanation.'

'There is one other option,' I said

'Is there?' Fiona checked the tiny face of her little gold wristwatch. 'Court time. Tell me on the hoof.' She slung her handbag over a shoulder and nodded her head at the file of papers on the coffee table.

'Fiona, I'm not carrying your stuff. Where's the Crown Office solicitor?'

'No idea. Off doing something frightfully important, no doubt.' She looked at me plaintively. 'Be a dear.' And, taking my servility for granted, walked out of the door.

I caught up with her as she made her way downstairs to the ground floor. 'Well, do you want to hear it?'

'Oh, yes, the other option? As in not the one where your dad blames poor old demented Jock Knox or refuses to answer questions? Might as well. Fire away.'

'That my dad gives a perfectly innocent explanation as to why his DNA is on the cigarette stub. One that doesn't leave anyone to blame but Ricky Hertz.'

Fiona stopped midway down the stairs, turned and looked up at me. 'He can do that?'

'No,' I said. She snorted impatiently, and resumed her descent. I trotted after her. 'At least, not yet. But he will . . .eventually. That's why I'd like you to adjourn this hearing.'

By now we'd reached the foot of the first set of stairs and were all set to take the final flight to the lower floor. My dad was waiting at the bottom, pacing the hallway outside Court 6.

'Fiona ...'

'No, Robbie, I am not going to try and stall these proceedings so you can give your imagination some more time.'

'But if you don't, Hertz is going to walk.'

'I'm well aware of that, Robbie. Believe me, there's no one wants to see that little shit Ricky Hertz banged up more than I do. I've seen the police investigation from that other murder, where they found the body of a young girl in the Bathgate Hills. She'd gone missing around about the time of the other three.' I hadn't heard about that one. 'It's the same M.O., but there's not a smidgen of evidence to say it was Hertz.'

'That's why we need to keep the cigarette butt in play,' I said.

'But I don't have a locus to make any kind of request today, far less ask to put this hearing off. I'm lucky to be allowed to sit in and watch.'

'All I want is a few days. A week. No more. If my dad sticks-in Jock Knox or refuses to answer questions, either way Hertz is going free. More time for my dad to provide an explanation is the only way to make sure Hertz goes back inside.'

'Really, Robbie. Is that what you'd like me to say when I get in here? Sorry M'Lord, would you mind putting this hearing off? Mr Munro needs some more time to make up a really good story for his dad to tell you.' She took the first step. I took the first two and turned to face her.

'Come on, Fiona,' I said, arms folded around her court

papers, pressed against my chest. 'Try at least. You know Hertz is guilty.'

Fiona tried to pass by me on the wide staircase. 'I believe he is, Robbie, but I don't know for certain, and so we're just going to have to let the law run its course, no matter how much that upsets you. For who are we, but mere cogs in—'

'Spare me the speech, Fiona. Just ask counsel for the SCCRC to give me a couple of days. Tell him you have a headache.'

'I have,' she said, shoving me aside. 'You're giving me it.' She took the next step. Down below, my dad had spotted us and waved up to me.

'Then at least ask for some time for me to explain things to my dad before he goes into court,' I said, as Fiona walked past me down the stairs. 'I am his legal adviser after all.'

'I'll ask them to give you five minutes,' she called over her shoulder. 'That'll have to do you.'

But five minutes wouldn't do. I took the third step. There was a good many of them still to go, each one manufactured from cold, hard, Italian marble.

'Fine by me,' I said, and with a wave to my dad, folded my legs and, with Crown Office paperwork scattering around me like confetti, fell down every single last one of them.

15

Fiona Faye drove me to hospital faster than any ambulance. Released from his citation temporarily, due to the injury that had befallen his solicitor, my dad went home to collect Tina from school. Malky brought them through with him at visiting time.

'Lucky you landed on your head,' he said, munching on a grape. 'You could have injured something important.'

'Are those for me?' I asked.

'What?'

'The grapes.'

Malky looked down at the brown paper bag in his hands. 'Oh, yeah.' He stuffed another in his mouth and then tossed the bag onto the bed. 'How long are you going to be in here?'

I'd been told I was to be kept in overnight for observations, though I didn't feel it necessary, even though my tumble down the stairs hadn't been a complete success. There hadn't been a lot of time to risk assess the situation, but, immediately before I'd gone into free fall, I'd thought I'd manage to slow my descent sufficiently to come to a controlled landing. All I was looking for was the sort of minimal injury I could exaggerate. Unfortunately, exaggeration was unnecessary. The wrist attached to the hand that I reached out to save myself, had given way and I'd had to deploy my forehead as a brake. The result was a two-inch gash just below the hairline. It had been closed with some neat stitches and was now covered with a sterile dressing. Along with that injury I'd been diagnosed as having a sprained wrist, bruised ribs and a case of mild concussion. Two good things had come of it: I hadn't had to employ any of my limited acting skills, and the precognition-on-oath hearing had been knocked on a week. I hoped my dad would one day be grateful for my efforts. Right at that moment he was less than appreciative.

'You eejit, you could have broken your neck!' He came over and tilted my head back and peeled back a corner of the dressing. 'Hmm. Doesn't look too bad. How's the rest of you?'

'Sore,' I said. 'Almost feels like I've fallen down a flight of stone steps.'

Tina came over and jumped onto the bed. Lying beside me, she raised her left leg in the air. 'I fell too. Look.' She pointed to a tiny graze below the knee. 'We were playing chainy-tig and Jamie Sneddon tripped me up. I'm going to get him back tomorrow,' she said with a determined grimace that made me glad I was in hospital injured and not Jamie tomorrow morning at playtime.

My dad and Malky were drawing chairs around my bed when a nurse approached in a manner something similar to the Wehrmacht approaching the Polish border in September 1939. 'How are you? Drowsy? Nauseous? Headache? You look fine to me,' she said, before I could reply, ticking off things on a clipboard. 'And if you don't need this bed, I'm sure somebody else does. The doctor will be round in a few minutes. If she okays it, you'll be discharged.' She dragged a third chair over, lifted Tina off my bed, plonked her down on it and trundled off.

'Are you coming home tonight, Dad?' Tina asked. She didn't sound very pleased about it.

'Yes,' I said. 'That's great, isn't it?' She hung her head. 'What's wrong?' Silence. 'Is something the matter?' Something had to be very wrong if Tina wasn't going to venture an opinion.

My dad lifted Tina off the chair and sat her on his knee. She turned and buried her face in his chest. 'Your daughter has something to tell you, Robbie.' *Your daughter*? Sounded serious. 'I told her we'd wait until you got home, but now's as good a time as any.'

I stroked Tina's back. 'Have you something you want to tell me?' I asked. 'Have you done something wrong?'

She turned her head to glower at me. 'No, I haven't!' There is no one more indignant than a wrongfully accused six-year-old – unless it's a rightfully accused six-year-old who doesn't want to admit it.

She buried her face in my dad's chest again. He lifted her off his knee and stood her on the floor next to the bed. 'Yes, you have. Go on, tell your dad what you've done.'

'What is it, Tina?' I asked. I looked at Malky. He frowned and looked at his shoes. It was hard to tell if he was upset, angry or just trying very hard not to laugh.

Tina threw herself onto the bed. With no little effort, I swung my legs out of bed, put a hand under her chin and lifted her tear-stained face to mine.

'Gramps says I'm going to jail,' she wailed.

I pulled her to me and gave her a hug. 'No, you're not. There's only one person here in danger of going to jail, and it's not you. Just tell me what you've done. It doesn't matter how bad it is, I'm on your side. Okay?'

My dad stood up and drew the curtain all around the bed, cutting us off from the other patients. Then from his jacket pocket he produced a tiny, silver box. He handed it to me. Small and thin, it was heavy for its size, with some

120

fancy engraving on the lid. 'Tina stole it the other night, when you took her through to Edinburgh. Tell your dad what you did, Tina.'

Through much sobbing and tears and with some prodding from my dad, Tina confessed that on Friday night, when she had gone to use the bathroom at The Newberry, she'd been nosing around, found the silver box and helped herself to it. My dad had found it in a clothes drawer when he'd taken her home after school to get changed before coming to hospital.

I gave it a shake. Something inside rattled. I tried to open it, but it had some type of intricate but delicate clasp I couldn't work out. I didn't want to try and force it open, break it and make things worse. I returned the box back to my dad for safekeeping, and was trying to gauge how angry I should be, when the curtains were drawn back and a large woman in a white coat appeared, stethoscope slung over one shoulder, clipboard in hand, leaving me with no option other than to defer sentence upon my daughter until later.

'Right,' the doctor said, in a loud friendly voice, 'Mr Munro, you stay right where you are, the rest of you scoot.' Smiling, she held the curtain open and shooed my visitors out. Once they'd gone she took a peek under the dressing and shone a pen torch in my eyes. 'Got a headache? I'd be amazed if you didn't. Take a couple of paracetamol every four hours, that should help.' She glanced at the clinical notes. 'Says here, no nausea, no drowsiness, blood pressure normal. And so . . .' She tucked the clipboard under her arm. 'I'm going to release you back into the bosom of your family, and give your bed to a sick person.'

There were more instructions about having someone keep an eye on me when I got home and on keeping the dressing dry. I was to visit the practice nurse at my local surgery to have it changed, and the stitches would come out in ten days' time.

'Happy with that?' she enquired in a manner which suggested it didn't really matter if I was or not – I was leaving. From the clipboard she extracted a head injury advice sheet and went over it with me. 'Any questions?'

'Just one,' I said. 'Doctor, do you think that by looking at them, you could tell the difference between someone who had overdosed on barbiturates and someone suffering from hypoglycaemia?'

'Are you diabetic?' She checked the clipboard. 'There's nothing in your notes about that.'

'No ...'

'Then what a strange question. Though, I suppose you have had a bump on the head. Maybe we should keep you in a little longer.'

'No, really, I'm fine. It's ...research for a book I'm writing.'

'I thought you were a lawyer?'

'I am. I'm writing a crime fiction novel.' I laughed. 'We've all got one in us.'

'We've all got an appendix too. Sometimes it's safer not to remove them.' She tucked the clipboard back under her arm. 'Okay. Hit me with your scenario.'

'Man has symptoms of hypoglycaemia—'

'Or barbiturate poisoning. You said that already. Hurry up, please, there are some actual sick people in here I have to see.'

'He's given glucose, becomes a lot better. Seems fine in fact, but two hours later is dead. Post-mortem says he overdosed on barbiturates. Oh, and he'd had quite a lot to drink.'

'Not exactly John le Carré, is it?' She sighed. 'Alcohol would definitely drive down the blood sugar levels.'

'Wouldn't he notice?'

The doctor wrinkled her nose. 'Maybe not. Some people, especially those who've had diabetes for a long time, develop a condition known as hypoglycaemia unawareness, and don't get the warning signs that signal a drop in blood sugar, especially if they've been careless with how much they've been drinking.'

'But glucose would bring them round again, wouldn't it?'

'Diabetic coma is a serious condition, but caught in time, once the blood sugar level is raised back to normal, I wouldn't see a problem.'

'How long would it take someone to die from barbiturate overdose?'

'Are you sure you're a writer and not a serial killer?' She laughed. 'Look, I've got to get going and your family is waiting.'

'Please?' I said.

She sighed. 'All right. The most common barbiturates used by drug addicts are the short-acting variety prescribed as sedatives and sleeping pills. They act within about half an hour of being swallowed, and their effects usually last six hours or so. There are others that would take a much longer time to kick in, perhaps a couple of hours depending on various things, like how much of the drug has been taken. That do you?' She pointed to the name tag pinned to the lapel of her white coat. 'Remember to give me an acknowledgement.' And with a swish of curtain she was gone, leaving me sitting there, backside hanging out of my hospital gown, wondering how I was going to make Jill finally accept that her partner had killed himself, and, just as importantly, what punishment I should impose on my sticky-fingered daughter.

16

The head injury advice sheet recommended that someone keep an eye on me in case I began to display symptoms of bleeding on the brain. My dad kindly volunteered for the job. This involved him coming back to my place, putting Tina to bed with a story, drinking substantial quantities of my whisky and dozing off in front of the European football roundup, before crawling off to sleep on the fold-down in the spare room. For all the interest he paid to me, I could have had the West Lothian Pipe Band round for rehearsals and he'd never have noticed.

In the morning he woke me with a mug of tea. 'How are you feeling?'

'Not dead,' was the most positive description I could come up with. The slightest muscle movement was agony. I tried sitting and felt a shooting pain in my side.

'How's your head?'

'A wee bit nippy. It's my ribs that are the sorest.'

To test out that theory Tina, who'd come in eating toast and ready for school in her grey and black uniform, jumped onto the bed beside me and gave my forehead a kiss. She was trying to be nice, I knew, but the stab of pain in my side was so severe that even my dad noticed and lifted her off the bed.

'Right, you, little Miss Raffles,' I said after I'd got my breath back. 'I've been thinking what to do with you.

You can't go around taking things that don't belong to you.' I'd wondered about a deferment of sentence for good behaviour, but that was only asking for trouble. The chances of Tina remaining trouble-free for any length of time were remote and would only compound matters. 'When your mum gets back—'

'She's not my mum. She's Joanna. My mum's dead.'

'Well, when Joanna gets back, you can help her weed the garden.'

'What are you going to do?' Tina asked huffily.

'Nothing. I'm injured, and I haven't stolen anybody's stuff.'

Tina considered that for a minute. For once she couldn't come back with a response.

'You want anything else, toast or porridge or something?' my dad asked, after Tina stomped out of the room in a trail of indignation and toast crumbs.

I told him I was fine. I'd try to get up and go to the office. The stiffness in my side would hopefully wear off, and I was supposed to get the dressing on my forehead changed.

My dad came over for a closer look. I'd washed my face before going to bed and some water had got onto the dressing so that the edge of it had lifted. With one swift flick of the wrist, he ripped the whole thing off.

'You're not needing a dressing. It's just a few stitches.' He crumpled the dressing and dropped it into the small wicker wastepaper basket in the corner of the room. 'Best to let the air at it.'

'The air's full of bugs,' I said. 'That's what the dressing's for. To stop the bugs getting in.'

'Away. That's nonsense. This is the countryside, there's only good bugs out here. It's hospital bugs you've got to worry about. Do you know how many people die in those places?'

I was about to protest, but Dr Alex Munro had moved on. 'It's your own fault anyway. Clumsy galoot. You'd trip over your shadow. If you hadn't fallen down those stairs the court hearing would have been over and done with. Now I've got to go all the way back through to Edinburgh again next week.'

Was he oblivious to the fact that my stairway plunge and resulting injury had all been for the purpose of having the hearing put off and giving him a stay of execution?

'Dad, can I ask you a couple of questions?'

'Make it quick, then. I've got to get Tina to the school.'

I could make it quick all right. 'How sure are you that Ricky Hertz was guilty of murdering those kids?'

'Very sure. Next question.'

'Are there any circumstances under which you'd blame Jock Knox for fitting up Hertz?'

'None.'

'Why not?'

'Why not? If I told you all the reasons why not, we'd be here all day.'

'Give me one then,' I said.

'All right. I'll give you an example. Years ago, you were just a boy, there was this man I didn't get on with. He was a loud mouth and a bully. I'd had to warn him a few times for slapping his wife about. He wouldn't take a telling and we'd had several disagreements in the past. One night he was waiting for me when I came off duty. He attacked me.'

'Sounds like self-defence to me,' I said.

'It was. For about five seconds. After that, less so. I got a wee bit carried away.'

'How carried away?'

Sufficiently carried away, apparently, that the individual had received a spot of non-surgical facial rearrangement. I still couldn't work out Big Jock Knox's role in it all.

My dad riffled his moustache with a finger. 'I knew how it would look. One man badly injured and going to hospital in an ambulance, the other totally unscathed and going home for his tea. Who was going to believe it was me who'd been attacked?'

'I get it, Dad. Big Jock stuck up for you, said he'd witnessed the whole thing. He lied for you, but—'

'He never lied.'

'What did he do, then?'

'He gave me a corker of a black eye. You should have seen the thing. It was away out here. *Now* it looked like self-defence. Except the man never made a complaint. He left town and never came back, so it was a bit unnecessary. Still it's the thought that counts, eh?'

'Dad, are you seriously telling me that you want to protect the reputation of Jock Knox because thirty years ago he punched you in the face?'

'That's right, and I'd have done the same for him. Ach, maybe there are better examples. The point is he always had my back and now I'm not going to stick the knife in his.'

He made to leave.

'One last thing,' I said.

'You've asked your two questions,' he said, his back to me.

'This isn't a question,' I said. 'It's a fact. You don't realise how serious this all is. You're in a state of denial about the whole thing.'

'No, I'm . . .' He turned around, grim-faced. 'Very funny.'

'Listen to me,' I said. 'I'm not trying to be funny. You can't refuse to give a precognition because it might incriminate your old pal. The only reason you can give is that you're scared you will incriminate yourself.'

'I've done nothing wrong!'

'That's not how it looks. Say nothing and the only inference that can be drawn is that you planted Ricky Hertz's cigarette stub.' I struggled to sit up straighter. 'That means you're going to jail and Ricky Hertz is staying out.' He made to protest, but I didn't let him. 'Trust me on this, Dad. I'm a lawyer. This is my job, and it's not an idle threat like telling a wee girl she's going to prison for stealing a pretty box, so she'll not do it again. This is real. You won't get another chance. Your chance is now.'

'So, I should blame Jock? Why? Hertz will still win his appeal.'

'Yeah, that's right, Hertz will not go to jail, but neither will you, and neither will Jock because he's too ill. How many times do I have to tell you?'

He didn't give it nearly enough thought. 'No. It's not happening.' He called to Tina to fetch her schoolbag. 'I'll take the bairn to school, but mind, it's Tuesday and I've a game of golf this afternoon, so you'll need to pick her up at three.'

'There are no golf courses in prison!' I called after him. 'If you want Hertz to go to jail and for you to stay out, you've got a week to come up with an innocent explanation why your DNA is on that cigarette butt!'

But the only sounds I heard in reply were Tina's incessant chattering and the front door slamming shut.

17

I hobbled into the office at the back of eleven, having phoned to say I'd be late.

Grace-Mary came into my room as I was taking off my jacket and hanging it on the hook behind the door. She took hold of my tie and brought my head level with hers. 'You want to put a dressing on that,' she said, letting go again, suddenly. 'I'll phone down to Dr Beattie and see if he can squeeze you in. Your diary's pretty much free all day.'

I waved her away. 'It's fine. I'm letting the air at it.'

She went through to reception and returned with *The Scotsman* newspaper. 'You know you made the headlines, don't you?' She dropped it on my desk open at page 7: *High-Flying Lawyer Crash-Lands.*

'High-flying? Not bad, eh,' I said, not reading further.

Grace-Mary was less impressed. 'The papers always describe you solicitors as "top lawyer" or "legal eagle" or something,' she said. 'What was wrong with: "Clumsy Lawyer Trips Over His Fat Feet and Falls"?'

'Accurate, but not snappy enough,' Kaye Mitchell said, arriving, as she usually did, unannounced and not particularly welcome. 'That banner was one of mine.' She shoved a pile of case files out of the way to clear a space on my desk and set down her enormous handbag. 'Will you look at the state of this place? You're needing to get

129

him organised, Grace-Mary. How do you expect him to find anything amongst all this?'

My secretary collected some of the scattered case files and made a pile of them. 'I keep telling him to tidy up, but with Robbie a clean desk is merely a sign of a cluttered desk drawer.'

Kaye picked up the newspaper. 'Making up hooky headlines is really an art form. One our new boy hasn't quite mastered yet. I sent him through to cover your dad's story. He was going to use, "Did Local Cop Frame Killer?" until you crash-landed. It was a nice wee scoop for him, you nose-diving like that. I'm sure it more than outweighed the fact that you nearly flattened him. Just a shame it was too early in the week for the *Gazette*.'

'In future, I'll try and time my accidents to meet your weekly print run,' I said.

'No need,' Kaye said. 'Edinburgh was grateful enough when I sent it through to them.'

'Yeah, thanks for that,' I said.

'Well, you know what they say?'

'That no publicity is bad publicity?' Grace-Mary ventured.

Kaye screwed up her face. 'I was thinking more along the lines of it's an ill wind that blows nobody any good.'

Grace-Mary clearly didn't understand. I didn't really want her to. 'Robbie fell and nearly killed himself. What good came of that?'

'The *nearly* part?' I suggested, hoping to derail Grace-Mary's train of thought.

'I'm talking about the court hearing being put off for a week because of it,' Kaye said. 'Alex Munro lives to fight another day. How very convenient. All because of Robbie's poor sense of balance. How are you, anyway?' She pouted in fake sympathy.

'Sore,' I said.

Grace-Mary barged in between us. 'Tell me you didn't throw yourself down those stairs on purpose, Robbie. No, don't smile like that, you'll split your stitches. What were you thinking of? How do you think Joanna would have liked it if she came back and found you in a wheelchair?'

'Was it that obvious?' I asked Kaye after my secretary had picked the bundle of case files off my desk and closed the door firmly behind her.

'Only to everyone who knows you,' Kaye said. 'And a few who don't. Still, it has made a great story even greater.'

'Do you really have to report my dad's case? I'm not trying to obstruct the freedom of the press or anything, but—'

'Yes, you are.'

'Okay, I am. What'll it take?'

'I'm sorry, Robbie . . .' She didn't look it. 'But Linlithgow doesn't get that many serial killers. Chuck in a corrupt cop and it's what we in the wonderful world of journalism call a sizzler of a story.'

'He's not corrupt,' I said. 'He's covering for a friend.'

'Big Jock Knox? Surely your dad's not going to say it was him who planted Hertz's cigarette stub?'

'Why not? One bent cop is as good as another for your sizzling story, isn't it? Why's that a problem? All he has to do is say that it must have been Jock who planted it and—'

'He'll be done for perjury.'

'What?'

'Have you done any research into this case at all, Robbie?'

Research? Why would I need to do research on a case I'd grown up with? My dad's finest moment?

131

'If you had,' Kaye continued, reaching down into the depths of her handbag and extracting a spiral notepad, 'you'd know that according to the police station rota, Jock Knox went off duty immediately after the interview with Ricky Hertz. He went on holiday for a fortnight and left your dad to take care of the case and to take all the glory. Jock Knox was most likely in the Highlands or somewhere up north visiting relatives when that cigarette butt was being planted.'

Slowly and carefully I sat down, placed my elbows on the desk in front of me and dropped my head into my hands. Then I quickly removed it again.

'You've burst your stitches,' Kaye said. 'Why haven't you got a dressing on that thing? Typical NHS cuts. If you get an infection in that wound, you'll know all about it. Just be glad it's a good three feet from your brain.'

She snatched a tissue from the box and handed it to me. I dabbed gingerly at my forehead and checked the result. It wasn't so bad that I felt the need to sit in a GP surgery all afternoon.

'What was Jill wanting to see you about the other day?' Kaye asked, returning her notebook to her handbag. 'I've not heard from her.'

'If I give you another story – one that you never officially got from me, understand?' Kaye zipped her lips. 'How about you lay off my dad? No big splashes in the newspaper. No corrupt cop stuff.'

'No can do, Robbie. However ...' She came around my side of the desk and looked at my head. 'Tell me what you've got on Jill and I'll have someone bring round the first aid kit.'

I could feel a drop of blood gathering in my eyebrow. 'Have you heard of The Newberry? It's a hotel in—'

132

'I know what and where The Newberry is, Robbie. I've just never had enough money to stay there. I don't even know anyone with enough money to stay there, except . . . Jill. This is about her, isn't it? Jill and her dead partner. The one she dumped you for.'

'What do you know about the owner, Chiara De Rosa?' I asked.

'Absolutely nothing,' she said, 'but I soon will.' Once more Kaye delved into her handbag, this time removing her mobile phone. 'What are you doing?' she asked whoever was unfortunate enough to have taken her call. 'Well, stop it. I'm trying to run a newspaper here. What have we got on Chiara De Rosa? No, he's not a footballer, she's the owner of The Newberry. Yes, that's what I said, The Newberry. It's a posh hotel in Edinburgh. Well, get off your backside and find out – fast – and bring what you have next door to the lawyer's.' She killed the call and let the phone fall back into her bag. 'That's the trouble with these young reporters. They think there's time to sit around drinking coffee. What they don't seem to realise is that the news never takes a break.' Kaye went to the door, poked her head out, shouted down the corridor for Grace-Mary to stick the kettle on and then took up the seat opposite me. 'My new boy will be here with the gen in a moment.'

'What about the first aid kit?' I asked.

Kaye tugged another tissue from the box on the corner of my desk and handed it to me. 'Probably best just to let the air get in about it.'

18

Chiara De Rosa was Swiss. Swiss/Italian to be precise. To be even more precise Swiss/Italian with a little American thrown in.

'Chiara's grandfather is loaded.' Kaye finished the last of her coffee, kicked off her shoes, crossed her feet at the ankles and rested them on my desk. 'He retired years ago, bought up a large chunk of Scotland and has lived here ever since. Chiara's parents both died when she was young. The grandparents became the boy's guardian until—'

'What do you mean, the boy's?'

'When Chiara was twelve she was a boy. Charlie.'

No way. And yet, she had been very tall and there was a lot of make-up.

'You look surprised. Let me guess. You've met her?'

'We had a drink together.'

'Good, was he? I mean, she?'

'Very. Exceptional. Malky tried to hit on her.'

'Yeah, well, from what I hear, one doesn't have to be too terribly exceptional for that to happen.' Kaye turned the page of the notebook that had been delivered a few minutes before by an out of breath young man, whose shoes I did vaguely recall meeting briefly at the bottom of the stairs at Edinburgh Sheriff Court. 'Can I continue? Good. Charlie stayed in Switzerland until he was twenty, had all the nips and tucks and chops … Stop wincing, Robbie. And then Chiara came to live with his …her grandparents, who gave over The Newberry to her.'

Kaye snapped the notebook shut. 'Now are you going to tell me why you wanted to know all that?'

Grace-Mary came through. 'The surgery has offered to see you at three o'clock, but you've got Tina to pick up from the school then, so I've asked them to squeeze you in before your two o'clock appointment.'

'What two o'clock appointment?'

'Do you never check your email? I sent you a message ten minutes ago. A Mr Foster called. He needs to see you urgently. He says you'll want to see him too. You've to meet him in the pub. He says you'll know which one.'

'Phone him back and tell him I'm busy.'

'But you're not. And he never left a phone number.' She placed a basket of mail in front of me for signing, and retreated. It had gone twelve o'clock, and there were a few case files I thought I'd better look over before court tomorrow.

'I'll need to get going,' I told Kaye.

'Not before you tell me why you wanted to know all that stuff about Chiara De Rosa. Obviously, it's not a coincidence that she just happens to own the hotel where Jill's boyfriend died, or that Jill came to see you, so spill.'

'Love to,' I said, 'but it would be wrong for me to help out a journalist who was hell-bent on ruining my own father's reputation.'

The wound on my forehead was starting to nip. The blood had congealed in the stitches and felt hard and lumpy. I needed to have it cleaned and dressed, then have a quick word with Cammy Foster, and collect Tina from school. Before any of that I had some case files to check over. There was no time to explain to Kaye about my investigations into Jill's death, and yet I was beginning to wonder if my ex-fiancée was as paranoid as she'd first seemed. The more I thought about it, Kaye did have certain attributes that might come in handy.

'I suppose I could ease off a little on your old man,' she said. 'If what you give me on this Newberry thing is any good.'

'Oh, it's good,' I said. 'Potentially, at any rate.'

'Potentially?'

'It's really a case of what you make of it.'

She looked away, playing hard to get, but not, I suspected, as hard to get as a short notice table for two at the Burberry – for someone who didn't have my contacts. 'Kaye,' I said, 'you'd agree with me if I said you were a highly suspicious individual with a twisted mind, a warped sense of morality and a tendency to see the worst in people vis-a-vis any given situation?'

'I'm a journalist,' she conceded, 'if that's what you mean.'

'And you want to know what Jill came to see me about and where Hercule, Chiara De Rosa and The Newberry all fit into the picture?'

'I do.'

'Then,' I said, 'meet me at The Newberry tomorrow at eight o'clock for dinner and maybe we can work it out together.'

19

'I'll need to make this quick, Cammy,' I said, pulling up a bar stool alongside him. He was different today, more smartly dressed, fresher looking.

Brendan, the barman, floated over and slid a glass of whisky in front of me. He nodded at the dressing on my forehead. 'Do you think it will catch on? Stair-diving? The Olympic committee are always on the lookout for new sports. You could be a front runner. Team GBH.'

He'd probably been working on that line all day. I ignored him. I didn't have to come to dumps like the Red Corner Bar to be made a fool of. I sniffed my drink and was pleasantly surprised. 'Laphroaig?'

I lifted my glass to Cammy who was clutching a glass of his usual Jack and Coke. He raised his drink and we clinked.

'I just wanted to say sorry, Robbie. All that talk last time. I think it was the shock of hearing that Hertz was out. It got to me.' He finished the drink and pointed at mine. 'Another?'

I was about to refuse, and then thought, where was the harm in one more? I had two hours before I had to collect Tina. I could walk along to the school and take a taxi home from there. Anyway, Cammy owed me for all the snash he'd given me the last time, not to mention the cheap whisky. He seemed to know he'd been a right prat, and if he wanted to make amends by buying me a couple of Islay malts, it would have been churlish to refuse.

I think I was on my seventh, or it could have been the eighth, dram when I decided Cammy was less of a prat and more of a pal, and also a great listener, hanging onto my every word. Which was good because after a few drinks I did generally have quite a lot of words for people to hang on to. The conversation ranged far and wide, from football and families to old friends and acquaintances. We touched momentarily on Ricky Hertz being on bail and the conditions that would attach. I assured Cammy that in addition to the standard conditions of bail, Hertz's order would have a few bolt-ons such as a curfew, an obligation to report to the local police station daily and a prohibition against contacting any witnesses from his trial, especially the relatives of victims. He could easily find out all the information for himself. Bail orders were a matter of public record. After that we'd moved on to tales from the court. I had a million.

'...so that's why, Cammy, no one should ever take their mobile to a murder,' I said, having regaled him with one of my best war stories. I found my mouth with the rim of the glass, tipped the contents in and set it down on the bar counter. 'That's how they get you.'

Cammy shoved my glass to the side. He was making his drink last. 'Same again?' he asked, rhetorically, I assumed. As a form of apology, Cammy was really grovelling for his past misdemeanours and sparing no expense. From Laphroaig, I'd headed up the east coast of Islay, stopping off briefly at Lagavulin and was now sampling the delights of Ardbeg. The ten-year-old was one of my favourite Islay malts, but was it the best? There were so many others and no point in forming a rushed opinion.

'See if Brendan's got a Bowmore tucked away some-where,' I said, deciding to go cross-country. 'The twelve-year-old, if he's got it.'

'He's not got it,' said a horribly familiar voice from behind me. 'Will a six-year-old do?'

I turned around to see my dad standing there.

'Do you know what time it is?'

I didn't, but I could read his face like a clock face and knew the school day was long over. I jumped to my feet.

'That wee lassie had to walk along from the school to your office all by herself. Anything could have happened.'

'She's six years old, nearly seven, Dad. It's only a five-minute walk from the school. She knows the way,' I said.

He slammed his hand on the bar top. 'She's a wee girl, and, in case you're forgetting, there's a child murderer walking the streets of this town!' He helped me off the bar stool by the scruff of my neck. 'Come on. You're leaving.'

'If you're talking about Ricky Hertz, Mr Munro, he might not be a murderer after all.' Cammy Foster let his statement sink in for a moment. 'Ask Robbie. He says that if the Appeal Court has let him out there must be a good reason. He thinks there might have been a miscarriage of justice. Don't you, Robbie?'

My dad turned and looked through narrowed eyes at Cammy. 'Do I know you?'

'It's Cammy Foster, Dad,' I said. 'It was his wee sister who Ricky Hertz—'

'Oh, you're Cammy Foster, are you?' My dad let me go and walked over to him. They were about equal in height if not in mass. 'It was a shame what happened to your sister, son,' he said, 'but let's get this straight. You'd be as big an eejit as your father was to think that Hertz

139

wasn't a cold-blooded killer that would have hanged if I'd had my way.'

Oh, great. What an objective standpoint from the man alleged to have framed Hertz, and thus caused the miscarriage of justice investigation that Cammy had so unhelpfully mentioned.

Cammy held up his hands. 'No offence, Mr Munro.' He was surprisingly calm, and, unlike me, showing no effects from our afternoon drinking session. It was almost as though he'd been drinking straight cola. I, on the other hand, felt nicely woozy.

I pulled my dad away and walked him to the door, where he barged out into the glare of a late afternoon, almost knocking over a couple of Brendan's regulars who were standing on the High Street having a smoke. They were the kind of guys who'd once been told hard work never killed anyone, but saw no sense in taking risks.

One of them stepped into his way, a snarl on his face and a cigarette in his mouth.

My dad ripped the cigarette from the man's mouth and threw it into the street. He pushed his face at the man. 'You want to start something or were you planning on keeping your teeth?'

I pulled him away and together we set off up the street towards my office. 'Listen, Dad, I'm really sorry for forgetting to go for Tina, but there's no need for you to start picking fights with everyone. What was all that about calling Cammy Foster's dad an eejit?'

'The man I was telling you about. The one Big Jock helped me out with?'

'When he kindly punched you in the eye?'

'That was Dan Foster, Cammy's dad. I suppose it's not Cammy's fault. He never had much of a chance not to be an eejit. He wasn't brought up, he was dragged up. Best thing I ever did running his old man out of town. And as for that useless specimen he called his mother . . .'

'What about her?'

We had reached the Cross Well. He stopped and looked at me. 'You're bad enough letting your six-year-old daughter walk home from the school in broad daylight.'

'Dad, you used to let me walk home from school when I was six, and it was a lot further.'

'That was different. You were a boy. And ugly. Anyway, I'm not talking about someone letting their child walk home from school – that's bad enough. I'm talking about the kind of mother who'd let a girl of four stay out till whenever. No wonder she was stolen. The number of times me and Jock found that bairn filthy and wandering the streets at all hours of the night, and had to take her home. The woman shouldn't have been allowed to bring up a budgie. When I think about how she let that wee lassie go down to that swing park herself and then when the wean got abducted she was on telly crying her beads out. Made me sick just to watch it.'

He started walking again at speed. 'And that guy whose cigarette you snatched back there? What had he done?'

My dad had no answer to that. He just kept on walking, until suddenly he stopped and stared straight ahead into the distance. 'That's it,' he said, softly. Then louder. 'That's it!'

'What's it?'

He seized hold of my shoulders in a sudden eureka moment. His formerly frosty expression thawed into a smile. 'I know how my DNA got on that fag end!'

20

My dad drove Tina and me home. The old man was in a much better mood now. We both were. He agreed to babysit while I went through to Edinburgh to keep my dinner reservation at The Newberry. He even agreed to run me to the train station.

Booking the Blue Room at The Newberry for dinner wasn't something one normally did on the same day as one hoped to dine. Not the same week or even month. For some it was never possible. For others, namely, representatives of Zanetti Biotechnic Inc., such as myself, it just took one phone call and less than three hours' notice.

Not that I was feeling too much like an evening out, as opposed to collapsing on the couch in front of the telly. Even after a cold shower and a change of clothes, I was still feeling mildly woozy.

I gave Kaye a call. 'Really sorry about tonight, Kaye, something's cropped up. How about we do dinner at The Newberry some other time?'

'Like when?'

'I don't know. Sometime.'

'But I've done my hair and make-up.'

'I'm sure Alan will appreciate it.'

'Alan won't even notice. When he heard I was going

out, he arranged for some of his mates to come round and play poker. And what about Jill? You were going to tell me all about Hercule and—'

'I know, I'm sorry.'

'Sorry? Is that all I get?'

'Got to go, Kaye. That thing I was telling you about . . .'

'The cropping up thing?'

'Yeah, that's the one. It really can't wait. See you later.'

I hung up and punched some more buttons. I might be feeling rougher than the outside of a rhino, but there was still work to be done.

'You'd like to take me to dinner, Robbie?' Fiona Faye Q.C. was doing a fine job of concealing her excitement. 'Why ever would you want to do that? It wouldn't be so you can ear-bash me about your dad's case, would it?'

Of course, I did. I also had another reason. Fiona might not have the suspicious and twisted mind of a journalist, but she did have the mind of a woman, which was much the same thing, and, more importantly, the mind of a woman who had dealt with a lot more murder cases in her career than I had. A visit to The Newberry could kill two birds with the one expense account – Jill's.

'And so,' Fiona continued, rather haughtily, I thought, 'not satisfied with your homage to aviation disasters, you want to try and pervert the course of justice. Like father, like son. Is that it?'

'What do you mean?'

'What I mean is that, although at the moment I'm acting for the Crown in opposing Ricky Hertz's appeal against conviction, if he is successful it's your father I'll be coming after next.'

'Dinner's on me,' I said.

'We-ell, why didn't you say? I didn't know Pizza

Express had a two-for-one on this week. Sorry, Robbie, but no tha—'

'At The Newberry.'

There was a pause, and then, '*The* Newberry?'

'Yes, the one in the New Town just off Charlotte Square. Do you know it?'

Another short pause was followed by the clearing of Fiona's throat. 'What time's our table booked for?'

Our table was booked for eight. I suggested we meet at seven for drinks, and at seven fifteen we were sitting in the guest lounge, drinking aperitifs and studying the menu. I had already ordered a bottle of Beaune 1st Cru 'Champs Pimont' mainly because I liked the name, but also because it was ninety-nine quid a bottle and I wasn't paying. The sommelier suggested he decant the bottle so that it had time to breathe before we sat down to eat. Seemed like a good idea to me.

'Listen to you, ordering wine like you know what you're doing,' Fiona said, after he'd gone. 'You even read the wine list and didn't do what men usually do and order the second cheapest on the menu so as not to look like a cheapskate.'

To start, Fiona decided on the ravioli of brown crab from Fingal's Cave, served in its own bisque, followed by red legged partridge, seared foie gras, braised red cabbage and celeriac and lemon confit. She closed the menu and looked up. 'How's the head, by the way?'

I touched my new dressing. 'Fine.'

'Good, then get this through it. I know why I'm here and until din-dins arrives you have my undivided attention. After that all shop talk stops.'

Seemed fair enough to me. I still had more than half an hour to get my view across. 'It's like this, Fiona. I'm not one to normally assist the Crown ...'

'You can say that again.'

'And, while I do appreciate the good work of the Scottish Criminal Case Review Commission, it's just that in my dad's case I think the SCCRC may have been a tad ... careless.'

I could tell that Fiona was fighting back the urge to yawn, but, no doubt, the thought of crab, partridge, and all the forced-feeding that poor goose had had to go through, was keeping her mouth closed and smiling, thinly, but smiling nonetheless. 'Careless, Robbie? There was a team of three investigators working on the Hertz case for the best part of two years. Hertz has always protested his innocence and now with the new DNA findings ... If anyone was careless, it was your dad.'

'Yes, how exactly did they manage to find his DNA now and not before the original trial?' I waved to the waiter to bring Fiona over another gin and tonic. After my earlier visit to the Red Corner Bar, I was making do with sparkling water. Fortunately, the soreness in my ribs had subsided. Every breath was no longer a painful experience, and I was combating the discomfort in my side as well as an encroaching alcohol-induced headache with the help of a couple of paracetamol.

'A lot has happened in the world of forensic DNA analysis since two thousand and one, Robbie. They can look for all sorts of new kinds of genetic markers these days, based on VNTRs. That's variable number tandem repeats, to you.'

Variable number tandem repeats weren't anything to me. I'd never heard of them. 'So, it's definitely new evidence that was unavailable at trial. I get that. Who's so interested in setting Hertz free?'

'Would it be too corny for me to say, justice?' Fiona

took her fresh gin and a small bottle of Indian tonic from the silver tray that was brought to her. She'd asked for one of the new craft gins and it came with a raspberry bobbing about in the glass, rather than the usual citrus slice. She poured in the tonic and waited for the fizz to die down. 'Let's face it; Hertz's conviction has always stunk. If he'd been one of your clients we'd never have heard the end of it.'

'But it all boils down to one thing, doesn't it?' I said.

Fiona raised her glass to me. 'It does indeed. The planted cigarette butt. It's what our American friends would call ...' She paused to take a sip and glance around. There were a lot of Americans in the lounge, all doing their best to talk louder than each other. Most were succeeding. 'A doozy. Even Lord Galloway thought so, and it's usually a case of abandon all hope when he's on the bench in an appeal.' She took a long drink and smacked her lips. 'And that is why Ricky-boy is out and about.'

'We don't know if my dad planted it,' I said.

Fiona nodded sagely and took another sip. 'We're definitely going to stop talking about this when it's time to eat, aren't we?'

'I mean it, Fiona. He remembers what happened. Something jogged his memory earlier today.'

'The toe end of your shoe up his rear end, perhaps?' Fiona said.

'No, seriously. It all came flooding back to him.'

Fiona set down her drink, placed an index finger on each temple and closed her eyes. 'Got it!' she said, opening them again quickly. 'He remembers now that poor old demented Jim—'

'Jock.'

'Jock Knox told him that he'd planted the cigarette,

146

but, unfortunately, Jock is unavailable for comment on account of being mentally incapacitated.' She fished out the raspberry and popped it into her mouth. 'Amazing how a little gin can enhance one's psychic powers.'

'Then you'd better have another because you're way off the mark.' I said. Fiona stopped chewing the better to listen. 'The cigarette wasn't planted. Hertz is going back to prison and my dad will expect a formal apology. Nothing too gushing. Just something clearing his name and perhaps praising him for preventing those well-intentioned souls at the SCCRC from allowing a child killer once more to roam our streets. You can take the credit if you like. I'm sure the Lord Advocate won't mind.'

'Oh, you can be a right little drama queen when you try, can't you, Robbie?' She sat back, hands resting on the arms of the chair. 'Okay then, let's hear it. How did your dad's DNA come to be innocently upon that cigarette butt?'

'Linda Smith,' I said.

'Who's she?'

'She's now Mrs Linda Duffy, but eighteen years ago, when she was nine years of age, she was playing in a swing park and was approached by Ricky Hertz.'

'Is this the one that got away? The little girl from the play park at ... Where was it?'

'Preston Road. My dad and Jock Knox went over to ask Hertz what he was doing, and he came away with some story about how he'd gone over to help Linda because she'd fallen off the roundabout.' I took a gulp of gin and tonic before I continued. I couldn't see the big fuss about all the different types of gin that were around these days. Stick in a bottle of tonic and they all tasted the same to me. 'When my dad was talking to him, Hertz lit up a cigarette. My dad thought he was being cheeky, so he snatched the cigarette out of Hertz's mouth and threw it away.'

Fiona seemed thoroughly unimpressed by this late-breaking news. 'You do realise you're in the wrong play park? Philip Avenue, where Emily Foster was last seen, is a mile away.'

'My dad remembers Hertz bending down, picking the cigarette up, nipping it and putting it back in the packet. After that they told him to get lost and didn't see him again until he was detained in relation to Emily Foster's disappearance. The cigarette with traces of my dad's DNA was in the pack. Unless he was a very heavy smoker it could easily still have been in the pack the next day. Hertz must have been smoking it when he abducted Emily Foster. He dropped it in the process and that's why it was found at Philip Avenue.'

Fiona's expression of great indifference hadn't changed any. She finished her drink and looked about for sign of a waiter to take us through to dinner.

'What's wrong with that?' I said. 'It's a decent enough explanation.'

'It is certainly an explanation, Robbie, How decent, I wouldn't like to say. Your dad could have taken the cigarette out of the pack when he detained Hertz and planted it during the search.'

I thought I should remind senior counsel that she was supposed to be challenging Ricky Hertz's appeal, not cheerleading it.

'I know what my role in the appeal is, thanks,' Fiona said. 'Unlike you, I occasionally feel obliged to consider my opponent's side of things, and right now there's a pretty strong argument in favour of thinking that had the

148

jury heard that the all-important cigarette butt didn't only bear the accused's fingerprint, but also the interviewing cop's DNA, they might have come back with a different verdict.'

The waiter drifted over to show us through to the dining room. I didn't have much time.

'Even if they'd been given an innocent explanation as to how the DNA got there? Remember the appeal is not what an *actual* jury makes of my dad's explanation. It's what the Appeal Court would like to *think* a jury would have made of it. When was the last time a High Court judge disbelieved a police officer?'

We both stood and followed the waiter to our table. He pulled out a chair for Fiona. She sat down, and he whisked a starched white napkin across her lap. After I'd had the same treatment, he gave us a little bow and retreated to allow the sommelier in so that we could sample the wine. I let Fiona do the honours.

'You know I'm only doing my job, Robbie,' she said as, having approved, she was poured a glass, 'but I will take on board what you've told me. I can see how it might help your dad; it's just a shame there was no independent evidence.'

I put a hand over my own wine glass. The sommelier sniffed dryly, set the decanter down in the middle of the table and withdrew. Seemingly satisfied that all shop talk was finished, Fiona sat back and took another sip of wine. 'Good choice. I'll have to take back everything I've ever said about you. You do know how to show a girl a good time.'

'You think this is good? Wait until after dinner,' I said.

'Why, what's happening then?'

'Then, Fiona, I'm going to show you the bedroom.'

21

It was testimony to the quality of The Newberry mattresses that the one on to which Fiona dropped her ample posterior only released a gentle sigh.

'So, it was all an elaborate ruse to get me into bed, was it, Robbie?' she said, jokingly I hoped.

'If it was, it was an expensive one,' I said.

'Don't kid me, Robbie. I may be worth it, but there is no danger of you ever having footed the bill for that little lot.' Fiona bounced up and down a few times. 'So, you've given me the news about your dad. What's the other reason for me being here?'

'The bed you're sitting on,' I said. 'That's where Hercule Mercier died a couple of weeks ago.'

Fiona bounced her backside off the bed and stood up, brushing the hem of her skirt. 'Nothing contagious, I hope?'

'Alcohol and barbiturates, according to Professor Bradley.'

'Suicide? There's a lot of it going about. Especially amongst you men.'

'I've a client who thinks it might have been something else.'

'The client who paid for tonight?'

'She's asked me to make some discreet enquiries.'

'Discreet? That'll be a first for you. Still, where on earth did you find a client who could afford to stay here?'

'She's a good friend. So good I nearly married her once.'

'The girl who dumped you? Jill, wasn't it? You should have kept a better grip on her if she can afford a suite at The Newberry.'

'That's sort of the point,' I said. 'If I had kept a better grip on her she wouldn't.'

'Traded up, did she? I'm afraid that's us women for you. Men go for youth and looks. They'd rather have a brand new flashy sports car or souped-up hatchback. Women prefer a vintage Rolls-Royce.' Fiona stumbled and put a hand on the bed to steady herself. 'Do you know, I think I may be a little bit tiddly.'

She wasn't tiddly. She was drunk. So she should have been after two gin and tonics, a bottle of red, two glasses of pudding wine and a couple of cognac digestifs.

'What are you talking about? What have sports cars got to do with anything? You drive a Maserati.'

'I'm talking fig ...' She made a few bold attempts at figuratively, but they didn't go too well. 'It's an ... an ...analo ...It's an example, Robbie. Men like the young and beautiful things, women like the rich and ...well, rich is usually enough. Take you and what's-her-name.'

'Jill?'

'No, the other one. That dinky wee PF.'

'Joanna? My wife? Mrs Munro?'

'Yeah, her. There's got to be a good age difference there.'

'Seven years.'

'There you are, then. Can't say it came as a huge surprise when I heard the news. I saw that ship steaming along the horizon way back.' Fiona expressed just how far back with a wide flourish of the arm. She looked down at the bed, thought about sitting on it again and decided not to. Instead she walked over to an armchair in the corner of the room and flopped into it.

'I think I'll ring down for some coffee,' I said.

'Take my Tim, for instance,' Fiona continued, having raised no objection to the coffee suggestion, if she'd even heard me make it. 'Now that's a relationship that works. I'm twelve years younger than him, so he likes that, and he's stinking rich so that's fine by me. It's a win-win.'

Tim, Fiona's present husband, was a quiet man with a dry sense of humour. He was an expert in timepieces and worked for a major auction house, though I suspected he had no need to and that there was old money in the background.

'How is Tim?' I asked, when I came off the phone to room service.

'At home, refurbishing a carriage clock he found in a junk shop. It's in an awful condition, and he's terribly excited about it.'

'Fiona ...?' I said, wondering if I should bother asking at all. 'Could you give me your expert opinion on what you think might have happened in this room?'

'Happened to who? Oh, the dead guy. What's his name? Hercules?'

'Hercule,' I corrected, starting to wish I'd brought Kaye after all. If I my own brain hadn't been so fuzzy following my virtual tour of Islay courtesy of Cammy that afternoon, I would never have let Fiona have so much to drink. There was little mileage in asking the Q.C., in her current state, to speculate as to how the CEO of Zanetti Biotechnic had met his end. Had he been poisoned? The barbiturates might have taken hours to kick in, and their effect been disguised by the attack of hypoglycaemia. Or else could Hercule, not in a fit state of mind, have taken the drugs after Jill had gone to the hairdresser? Those were the only real possibilities so far as I could see.

'Sho whadja wanna know?' Fiona asked. She was getting worse.

'It doesn't matter,' I said. 'I think we need to get some coffee down you and then I'll call a cab.'

'No, no, you've brought me all the way up here.' Her words were now punctuated by hiccups. 'Whadja wanna know? Go on. Ask me. Anything. I'll tell you. I'm senior counshel. I know everything.'

'My client—'

'You mean Jill?'

'Yes, Jill.'

'The one that dumped you?'

'That's the one. She thinks Hercule was poisoned.'

'And you want to know who dunnit, is that it?'

Actually, that was it.

'Simple.'

'But you don't know any of the circumstances.'

Fiona flapped a hand at me. 'I don't need to. It's all about the holy trinity of murder: means, motive and opportunity. Find all three and you'll find the killer. You should know that.' She stood up and gave me a shove. 'Now wheresh the loo?'

I directed her down the hall, steered her into the bathroom and closed the door just as coffee arrived.

'Will there be anything else, sir?' the waiter asked.

'Yes, there will be,' I replied. 'A taxi.'

22

Jill flew in from Berne on one of Zanetti Biotechnic's private jets to find me in Sandy's café, mid-week, mid-morning and mid the bacon roll Sandy had allowed me – he was keeping a record for Joanna.

'Have a good time at The Newberry last night?' she asked. Hercule's funeral had taken place the day before. Jill couldn't expect me to be in mourning for Hercule, but from her view I could see why my junketing at her expense on the very day her ex-partner was being interred might seem heartless. I thought I'd throw her some news to make it look like I was doing something.

'I took one of Scotland's top criminal Q.C.s there for dinner to give me a line on my inquiries into Hercule's death,' I said.

'Quite a bar bill the pair of you ran up.'

'It was a lot cheaper than paying for a private consultation.'

Jill sat down at the table. Sandy came over and she ordered a flat white and a Danish.

'It's been lying beside other pastries that have nuts on them,' Sandy said, when he returned with Jill's coffee and a cinnamon swirl. 'I've got to tell you that in case you're allergic. Can't have folk going into shock on the premises, rolling about on the floor and all that, it's not good for business.'

Allergies? I wondered. 'I don't suppose—'

'No, Hercule had no allergies. I'm a pharmacist, don't you think I've thought about that already?'

Jill then went on to tell me about someone who'd died using oil for removing earwax, not realising that the ingredients included oil from aragan nuts. I knew a lot of nuts. I'd defended a few. Aragan wasn't one I recognised.

'So,' she said, slicing the pastry into four, 'what did you learn at this consultation with senior counsel? I assume it was with Fiona Faye? I was told by the concierge—'

'You mean the butler guy? Tall, grey hair, always sniffing like someone's farted?'

'Charming as ever, Robbie, but yes, that's Findlay. He told me that you and a blousy, blonde lady, who'd had far too much to drink, ate a meal in the Blue Room before adjourning to the bedroom.'

'All with a view of considering the many different avenues open to someone intent on murdering Hercule,' I assured her.

'And?'

'You want to know what we came up with?'

'It's what I'm paying you for.'

Over the next several bites of bacon roll – they're not so good if left to get cold – I considered how best to set out the full results of my fact-finding mission with Fiona. I decided to provide a summary. There wasn't really a longer version.

'Means, motive, opportunity,' I said, popping the final morsel into my mouth.

'Means, motive, opportunity? You run up a two-hundred-and-fifty-pound drinks bill, not to mention a total of ten cordon bleu courses between you, and all the combination of your great legal minds can come up with is that whoever killed Hercule must have had the means, motive and opportunity? I could have got that advice watching any third-rate cop show on TV!'

I wiped my fingers and mouth with a paper napkin. 'It's a sound base to start from.'

'To start from! You've had fifteen thousand pounds and two weeks to do something and you're telling me you're only just starting?'

I waited until she'd calmed down slightly, and taken a bite of cinnamon swirl. There was less chance of my being interrupted when her mouth was full of flaky pastry. 'I'm not just starting. Here's what my inquiries have uncovered so far. One: Hercule died from barbiturate poisoning. Two: if not self-administered, someone poisoned him.' I ignored the rolling of Jill's eyes and went onto number three. 'According to the medical advice I've obtained, the drugs would have taken anything between half an hour to four hours to kill him. Most likely one or two. Which means, four: either Hercule was given the drugs immediately before you arrived on your surprise visit, or, five, immediately after you left for the hairdresser.'

'Let me add a sixth,' Jill said. 'All of that is entirely obvious.'

'True,' I had to agree, 'but fundamentals are important. For instance, we now have a time frame. We can use it as part of a process of elimination. All we need to do is identify those people who might have been in contact with Hercule for any reason during that period, and eliminate them from our inquiries one at a time. Whoever is left is—'

'The murderer.' Jill bit savagely into another quarter of pastry.

'Jill,' I said softly, 'you have to keep in mind that it's very possible we can eliminate everyone. There may not have been a murder.'

'There was,' she said.

'Okay,' I said, 'let's eliminate the easy ones first of all. Grace-Mary has checked out the paramedics. There is no reason to suspect them. They responded to a 999 call and were properly logged out. They dealt with Hercule immediately after attending someone who'd fainted in Jenners, probably at the prices, and before being called away to help a cyclist whose front wheel had got trapped in a tram track and taken a header.'

'What happened to your own head?'

'It's nothing. I tripped at court and fell down some stairs. Back to Hercule. The paramedics are in the clear so far as I can see. They didn't even give out any medication because Hercule was already coming round after you'd boosted his sugar levels. Then there's the guests. There are eleven suites at The Newberry, and, of them, only eight were occupied that weekend. I've checked with Findlay the butler guy, and three of the suites were booked by Americans who were over here to play golf. They left for Muirfield right after breakfast and didn't return until around six.'

Jill was listening intently now. 'One of the rooms was Hercule's, that still leaves four,' she said.

'That's correct. And, of those remaining, one was taken by long-time guest, Mrs Hammerstein. She's ninety-one. Another by Rod Stewart's tour manager who was sounding the place out for Rod prior to a series of gigs at Murrayfield next year. One suite, The Lulu, is permanently occupied by Chiara De Rosa. I take it you know who that it is?' I said.

Jill did. 'She's the owner. She was at the funeral. I think we can rule her out. Hercule was probably her best customer after Mrs Hammerstein.'

'Which leaves only one possible contender,' I continued.

157

'The occupant of the John Logie Baird suite. Someone by the name of Braxton Cobb.'

'Braxton Cobb?' Jill laughed, scornfully. 'Who told you that?'

'Findlay.'

She shook her head. 'Sorry, but there is no way Braxton Cobb was responsible.'

'Why not? Think means, motive and opportunity,' I said.

'Okay, Robbie, I'll grant you Braxton Cobb is extremely wealthy and he does know Hercule quite well.'

'There's the opportunity, then,' I said. 'No need for this Cobb guy to sneak into Hercule's suite. It would be easy for someone who knew him to visit his suite and slip him the poison.'

Deep in thought, Jill chewed on another piece of pastry. 'Are you absolutely sure Cobb was there that weekend? I never saw him.'

'I got a list of guests from Findlay by pretending if he didn't give it to me I'd get a court order. Braxton Cobb's name is definitely on it,' I said.

Jill washed the pastry down and set her coffee mug on the table with an air of finality and a steely look in her eye. 'Then, by your process of elimination, it must have been him. Who else could it have been? And don't say nobody, or I'll pour the rest of my coffee over your head.'

'I did have another idea as to the culprit,' I said. 'If someone *must* be to blame for killing Hercule, which I am still highly dubious about, it could have been one of the staff at the hotel. Findlay pretty much has the run of the place, doesn't he? Pass keys, access to the kitchen, the bar. No one would have thought it suspicious him going into Hercule's room. They call it hiding in plain sight.'

I'd like to say Jill was listening carefully; it was more like incredulously. 'The butler done it? Really, Robbie? That's your alternative scenario?' Jill rose to her feet, planted her hands on the table and leaned over at me. 'This is not an Agatha Christie plot,' she hissed. 'This is my ex-partner; the CEO of a multi-national corporation being assassinated. Do you know who Braxton Cobb is?'

I didn't.

'Braxton Cobb is Chiara De Rosa's grandfather. Not only that, he also happens to be married to Luciana Zanetti, founder of Zanetti Biotechnic. He's a major shareholder with money to burn. He used to own The Newberry, along with a lot of other property in Edinburgh and a large chunk of Perthshire.'

'Then he must have come down to visit his granddaughter.'

Jill waved Sandy over and ordered more coffee. 'No. Cobb never leaves his home. Hasn't for years. He's a recluse. I think you're right. It was definitely him. We need to take this to the police.'

Having spun her the means, motive, opportunity crap to try and justify my fee, I thought it was time to start reeling her in again before she did anything rash and I got the blame. I took hold of her hand. 'Jill...try and look at things rationally, and not like a conspiracy theorist. My process of elimination is all very well. It's given you a possible suspect, but nothing more. Before you make allegations against someone, especially a rich someone who could take us both to the cleaners for defamation of character, you need hard evidence.'

She pulled her hand away. 'Then find me some.'

'Can I go back to the start of this conversation and the result of my consultation with Fiona Faye?' I said. 'Cobb may have the means, he may have had the opportunity, but where's the motive?'

After her fresh coffee arrived, Jill filled me in on some background information on Chiara's grandparents.

Chiara De Rosa's maternal grandmother, Luciana Zanetti, had been a research chemist in the 1970s. She'd helped develop a range of new drugs that later formed the basis of a treatment for AIDS. She'd worked for a time in America and Canada. It was there she met and married Braxton Cobb, a businessman with a line in indigestion tablets and haemorrhoid creams. Together they formed Zanetti Biotechnic Inc. Luciana brought the expertise and had been the driving force. Cobb was more of a salesman and a figurehead, whose use to the company had dwindled over time. When many years later Luciana had been diagnosed and given the bad news, she'd left the business in the hands of Hercule Mercier. Braxton Cobb hadn't liked it. If it wasn't to be him, Cobb had wanted his daughter, Natalie, who also worked for the company, to take charge, and keep it in the family. Then one day, when Hercule was due to fly off on a business trip, at the last moment he was replaced by Natalie. The plane had gone down in the Italian Alps with no survivors. There had been rumours that Hercule had arranged for the plane to be sabotaged to get rid of the competition. The other rumour was that Cobb had tried to kill Hercule and the plan had backfired. Neither rumour was ever substantiated, but the death of his only child had not endeared Hercule to Cobb.

'How long ago was the plane crash?' I asked. The answer was that it had been ten or more years before. 'And Cobb waited until now to do something about it? And why would he want to kill the CEO of the company he's retired from? A company in which he has a large shareholding, and which was doing so well under Hercule's management? I still don't see a motive.'

Jill sipped her coffee, eyes as glazed as her cinnamon swirl. I could tell for her the mystery of Hercule's death was solved. She delved into her handbag and brought out a silver box, almost identical to the one Tina had stolen. I'd been meaning to break that news to Jill. Now wasn't the right time.

Jill pressed one corner of the box down while at the same time pushing the little clasp sideways and then up with her thumb. The lid sprung open. Inside Jill's silver box was a small stack of business cards. She flicked through them, removed one and handed it to me. 'You need to go and see this person. If Cobb had a motive to kill Hercule, she'll know.'

I looked at the name of the card: Dr Emanuela Zanetti, the address Rome. There are many towns in Scotland that share their names with cities all over the world: Perth in Australia, Aberdeen and Houston in the U.S. I wondered if Rome was one of those. It wasn't. It was the Italian Rome.

'I'd go,' Jill said, 'but if Braxton Cobb found out he'd know I was onto him.'

'I can't just drop everything and go to Rome,' I said. 'I've a business to run and a daughter to look after.'

'Spent all my money already, have you?' I hadn't. Not nearly. Jill produced her chequebook. 'Would another five thousand cover it?'

'Okay,' I said. 'I'll go, but I don't want any more of your money ...'

Jill looked at me sideways. 'I sense a but.'

'But what are the chances of using the Zanetti private jet?'

'You're going by jet,' Jill said, 'but not private. Easy.'

23

The Ospedale Fatebenefratelli sits on an island on the River Tiber. The hospital specialises in gynaecology and obstetrics and is reached by the Ponte Fabricio, the city of Rome's oldest bridge, built around 62BC. I'd arranged to meet Emanuela Zanetti there at three o'clock on Thursday afternoon. She was a busy woman, but could give me an hour of her time.

I caught an early flight, landing in Rome at ten thirty, and by noon had booked into a city centre hotel. There really should have been no difficulty in my making the appointment on time. The problem was that I set off way too early, and when in Rome it was hard not to sightsee: everywhere I turned there was a historic landmark of some sort.

With a couple of hours to spare, and armed with a free map of the city, I walked the short distance from the terminus to the Basilica Papale di Santa Maria Maggiore, the largest church in Rome dedicated to the Virgin Mary. Its other, more common name was Our Lady of the Snows because it was the spot where miraculously snow once fell during the Italian summer. Not such a miracle in a Scottish summer. Inside, the architecture and decoration were breathtaking. Exquisite marble sculptures, oil paintings, frescos, intricate mosaics, gold-lacquered icons, and, above it all, a Masonic-like all-seeing eye set in a crimson triangle. In one of the transepts there was even a dead pope in a glass box. The place had everything. From there I made my way in a loop, down to the Coliseum, past the Circus Maximus and on to the Tiber Waterfront, with Roman villas and enclosed gardens on one side of a wide roadway, and, on the other, the river and an endless row of sycamore trees, their bark a flaky patchwork of green, white and brown.

It was a walk that brought me to the Ponte Fabricio, one hour early. So, I continued up the Aventine Hill, to take in the Dominican Church of Sabina. And I still would have made it back in plenty of time had I not stood in the queue outside the great green door to the headquarters of the Knights of Malta waiting in line to peer through the Aventine Keyhole at the perfectly framed dome of St Peter's in the distance.

As it was, I arrived ten minutes late and met Emanuela, not inside the building as planned, but on the narrow cobbled bridge.

She seemed to recognise me. Maybe it was because I was white, sweaty and looking faintly lost. 'Mr Munro?' It wasn't really a question. 'You are late.' Her English was excellent, her manner a trifle brusque.

Emanuela was an elderly woman. Deep wrinkles gouged furrows in her thin, suntanned face. She had on a plain, black, below-the-knee dress with a round white collar and a silver cross above the left breast. A length of black cloth, held in place by a white hairband, hung from the back of her head and draped over her grey hair onto her shoulders. What should I call her? Mother? She answered that question for me.

'Doctor Emanuela Zanetti,' she said, taking my hand. 'You had an hour, you now have forty-five minutes.' She

163

sounded serious. Somehow, I could tell this was her being friendly. 'Come.' She turned on a stout walking shoe and led me back the way she had come, across a similar cobbled bridge to the other side of the river and into the Trastevere. Five minutes later we were sitting outside at a table in front of the Bar San Calisto. To be honest, it wasn't the sort of place I thought you'd find a nun. Then again, a nun had never taken me out for a drink before.

Without asking what I'd like, she ordered for me, calling out to a waiter who, arms folded, cigarette dangling, was propping up the doorway.

'You like?' she asked when the waiter brought us two small glasses packed with crushed ice, a swirl of dark coffee caught inside, topped with a ludicrous amount of whipped cream and with a tubular wafer biscuit sticking out of it at an angle. It was the house speciality. To go along with this unusual beverage was a small plate of the most knobbly biscuits I'd ever seen.

'Ugly but good,' Emanuela said. I'd been called worse. 'You understand? The biscuits. *Brutti ma buoni*.' She picked one off the plate and crunched into it. 'Ugly but good.'

And so they were. Extremely good. For some reason they'd served five biscuits between the two of us. After we'd shared the first four, I was ready to arm-wrestle the elderly nun for the fifth.

'Your head,' she said. 'Before you go, come back to the hospital and I will give you a fresh covering.' Her wrinkles creased into a smile. 'Now, for what reason have you come all this way to see an old woman?'

I wasn't sure what to say. I didn't have much time to say it in, and she was a nun, so I thought I'd have a go at the truth. 'Jill Green asked me to come. Jill is the—'

'I know who Miss Green is, and I know her relationship to Hercule Mercier.'

'Then you'll know that Hercule is dead. The doctors say it was down to a combination of alcohol and barbiturates. They seem to think it was suicide—'

'And you do not?'

'No, I do. Miss Green does not.'

'If Miss Green does not think Hercule took his own life, what then? Murder?'

The old bird was quick on the uptake when it came to talk of foul play. It must have been all that Old Testament reading. I glanced around at the other tables, where customers were busy setting in about their own iced coffees, and thought that those near enough to hear probably didn't speak English, while those that did were unlikely to understand a West Lothian accent. Already Emanuela had asked me to speak slowly, when I thought I was.

'Who does she blame for this?' she asked.

'Braxton Cobb,' I said.

The nun nodded as though she could understand why that was. 'I thought this might have something to do with my brother-in-law.'

'Jill sent me to see you because she thought you might have some more information as to why Mr Cobb would want to kill the CEO of the company he started,' I said.

'You have heard the rumour of how his daughter was killed?'

I had.

'Have you met Mr Cobb?'

I hadn't.

'Then you should know that he is a very charming and sincere man. You should also know that he is a very stupid man.' She didn't say it as an insult, more by way of a medical diagnosis. 'When he met my sister many years ago, he was a drugs salesman for his own small company. Perhaps Luciana felt sorry for the handsome young man with the bad leg. I don't know.' Using her biscuit as a spoon, she scooped cream into her mouth. 'They fell in love, got married—'

'And made a lot of money,' I said. 'How did that happen?'

She smiled. 'Do you know what orphan drugs are, Mr Munro?'

It turned out they weren't drugs that had tragically lost their mums and dads. Emanuela explained. 'Orphan drugs are the ones the big companies don't want because they cure the diseases only a few people have. That means there is not enough money to be made on them. In America if you take on the development of orphan drugs there are government incentives. Braxton Cobb's company made over-the-counter medications. It was doing reasonably well. He persuaded Luciana to work for him, ostensibly to research orphan drugs. I believe he was more interested in the tax breaks available than anything else. Then, when Luciana was working on a drug that had been intended as a cure for one particularly rare ailment, she discovered what came to be the precursor of an anti-retroviral drug that could fight HIV.' The rest, according to Emanuela was history. 'Luciana saved many lives by her discovery. Now Zanetti Biotechnic's range of drugs is unending. That is the problem.'

I couldn't see what was so wrong with that.

'I am a Roman Catholic, Mr Munro.' If not, the nun costume was a great disguise. I nodded for her to continue, retaining eye contact while casually palming the last ugly biscuit. 'I believe in the sanctity of human life. That is the only thing I have in common with Braxton Cobb. At the Ospedale Fatebenefratelli I help women who are pregnant with unwanted children. I tell them that in God's eyes no child is unwanted.'

'It's good work,' I said.

'I do what I can. It is not easy.'

Impressed though I was, I really didn't know what all this had to do with Hercule's death and told her so, aware the clock was counting down.

She sighed as though what she was about to tell me sorrowed her. 'Braxton Cobb is a man from South Carolina. He's a Christian man, so he says, but he has many strange unscientific beliefs concerning the age of the earth, the truth of evolution; those kinds of things.'

'I seem to remember that at one time the Roman Catholic Church killed a lot of people who didn't share the same views as Mr Cobb.'

'The point I am making,' she said, patiently, 'is that Braxton Cobb greatly disapproved of the direction in which Hercule was taking the company, even though many others on the Board saw the commercial sense in it. Running abortion clinics, manufacturing morning after pills, building clinics for assisted deaths, researching drugs to ease transitioning between sexes ... Braxton wanted to put a stop to it all.'

Somehow the old nun managed to manoeuvre her small glass tumbler skilfully enough to take a sip of iced coffee from beneath the mountain of cream.

'Okay,' I said. 'Cobb has unenlightened views on some things. A lot of people do. Like Islam and the Roman Catholic Church. All the things you have mentioned are legal in most western countries, except, perhaps, assisted suicide, and I don't expect someone in your position would go along with that either.'

The old nun shrugged. 'For those of us who care for the suffering, it is possible to see things from both sides of the argument. Good health, after all, is merely the slowest possible rate at which one can die. A good death when the time comes is also important.'

'But if Braxton Cobb is the boss, why didn't he just tell Hercule to stop and change direction?'

Emanuela took another drink and set down her glass again, wiping whipped cream from the tip of her nose. 'There is a very good reason why the company is called Zanetti Biotechnic and not Cobb Biotechnic. Braxton has had no say in matters for many years. Oh, yes, he could control and influence Luciana, but in reality he was never anything more than a front man, a handshaker. Luciana is not only a fine chemist, she was also the ... How do you say it? The brains behind the company. Until her illness became too much, what she said was final. It has been a long illness. She knew it was coming and that eventually she would waste away. She did not want to see that happen to her precious company. She handpicked Hercule Mercier to run the business when she was no longer able. She trusted him implicitly and treated him like the child she'd lost. Whenever Hercule was in Scotland, or anywhere in the UK, on business he'd visit.'

'You seem very different, you and your sister,' I said.

Emanuela dug into the cream again, this time with a teaspoon. 'I chose my path in life. My sister chose hers. She thinks religion and science do not mix. I say, look around, how can they not? Luciana knew her husband's views when she married him. Don't they say that opposites attract? Please don't get me wrong. I think Braxton tries to be a good man, but as we say, *Dio mi guardi da chi studia un libro solo*. Fear the man who reads only one book.'

'With certain books, law books in particular, it's not the reading, it's the interpretation of what they say that's the problem,' I said.

She nodded. 'And there you have summed up Christianity's difficulties in one sentence, Mr Munro. If everyone correctly interpreted scripture, everyone would be a Roman Catholic.'

I wasn't so sure. I'd not read a lot of Bible, but I knew there was stuff in there about helping the poor. I had some difficulty relating the rich splendours of the cathedral I'd visited only a few hours earlier to the beggars I'd seen on the streets of Rome.

The good thing about iced coffee is it never grows cold; however, the cream on mine was on the slide, and it took some fancy spoon work to restore order. It gave me a little time to think. Given his religious beliefs I could understand Braxton Cobb's disapproval of Hercule's approach to business; nonetheless, it was a big jump from disapproval to poisoning someone. 'If, as you say, Mr Cobb is a Christian man, surely he wouldn't condone murder? That can't be what you're suggesting?'

'I am suggesting nothing, Mr Munro. I am only stating facts. It is for others to determine the truth. But if I am asked, do I think Braxton Cobb would see killing one man, Hercule Mercier, as a means to save many as yet unborn or the elderly and unwanted? My answer is yes. There are many in my own church who would see things the same way. Many governments too.'

When I'd done my law degree, utilitarianism had been a philosophical topic covered by both jurisprudence and criminology, excellent subjects for those who could write pages of waffle, and none of the hassle of having to come up with a correct answer. I'd done well in the exams.

'Even if Cobb was responsible for Hercule's death, surely the next CEO would simply take over where Hercule left off?' I said, thinking I could see a flaw in her theory, even though she denied having devised one.

'Possibly.' The old nun was a fast worker with a teaspoon. She had the rest of the whipped cream scoffed in no time at all, and drained the last of the dark liquid from the crushed ice. She wiped her mouth daintily with a paper napkin. 'But then he may simply be buying time.'

'For what?'

'My sister is very ill. She will not live much longer. I visit from time to time, but though I am a doctor, it is very upsetting for those of us who knew Luciana in her prime to see her that way. I hate to say it, but sometimes I wish God would take her.' With the twitch of a hand she crossed herself and touched the cross pinned to her dress.

'What happens when she dies?'

'I assume Luciana's controlling interest in Zanetti Biotechnic will pass to her husband. I don't know for certain.'

'Then why doesn't Cobb kill his wife?' If the guy was into religious utilitarianism, surely killing a dying woman was preferable to, and a lot easier than, taking the risk of smuggling drugs into a top-class hotel, creeping into someone's room and poisoning them?

'No, Mr Munro, killing my sister is something my brother-in-law would never do, even were it not for his religious views on assisted suicide. For all his failings, Braxton has loved Luciana since the very first day they met. His wealth has made him attractive to many women, but he has remained faithful and made my sister very happy over the years. Even before her illness, he always cared for her as though she were made of glass. Over these past few years I do not think Braxton has left Luciana alone for a single day. He has all the money in the world and yet lives the life of a recluse on his estate in Scotland, just to be by her side.' She laughed drily. '*Quello è amore.*'

'What about Chiara? Doesn't she have a say in anything? And if Cobb's so dogmatic why does he have a transgender granddaughter?'

'Braxton does not approve of Chiara.'

'He gave her a hotel for her twenty-first birthday. I wish I had a grandfather who disapproved of me that much,' I said.

'That wasn't a birthday present, Mr Munro. That was a go away and stay away present. And I am sure it would have been my sister's idea that Chiara be given the hotel, not his.'

I finished my own coffee, which was, without doubt, the most difficult I'd ever tried to drink, and then I asked the obvious question, 'Why does Cobb keep in touch with her?'

'He doesn't,' was the answer. 'As far as I know the two have not talked since Charlie ...' Emanuela made the universal sign for scissors with the first two fingers of her right hand, 'became Chiara.'

Then why had Cobb, the recluse, the man who never left his sick wife's side, gone to stay at the hotel run by the granddaughter he didn't speak to, on the very weekend Hercule Mercier had died? Cobb, it seemed, had means, opportunity and now here I was being presented with the motive. Was Jill so crazy after all? My brain was reeling.

Emanuela stood. 'Come with me,' she said. 'Let me bandage your head.'

24

'Are we all in, then?' Phil Duffy asked.

I returned home Friday early afternoon, having left behind instructions for my dad to look after Tina and for Grace-Mary to find me Linda Duffy née Smith.

Both had accomplished their missions. Tina was in one piece and my secretary had tracked down Linda, formerly the wee girl from Preston Road play park, via her husband's Facebook page. Following directions from a particularly busy newsfeed, I came across Phil Duffy standing beneath a tall tree, a length of chain in one hand and a large padlock in the other.

'Look, we've talked about it for weeks, we either do this thing now or never. What's it to be?' he asked, to a tsunami of apathy from those gathered, namely, his wife, twin brother Pete, a man in a woollen tammy and a woman out walking her dog. They had all assembled at Beechwood, a one-hundred-metre strip of woodland on the south-most boundary of Linlithgow. Between it and the next town of Bathgate lay several miles of West Lothian wilderness, hills and Neolithic burial sites. Some said it wasn't enough.

Phil's twin was first to speak. 'Is the whole thing not kind of . . .?'

'Oh, here it comes, Mr Negativity,' Phil said. 'Kind of what, Pete? Kind of risky? Of course it is. But it's worth it.'

'No, I mean, is it not ...?'

'Dangerous? Possibly.'

'No, what I mean is ...is it not kind of ...?'

'Stupid.' Linda said. 'Pete means, isn't it really, really stupid? You don't even know when the bulldozers are coming in. You could be tied up here for days, weeks.' Whoever the dog-walker was, I could see by the look on her face that she tended to agree.

Linda went over to her husband and put a consoling arm around his waist. 'You've got to admit, Phil, it is a lot of fuss to make over a few trees.'

'Probably against the law too,' the dog-walker muttered.

Phil detached himself from his wife's arm. 'Oh, I see, it's stupid, it's a fuss over nothing and it's illegal. Are those the best arguments you can all come up with?'

'What's the problem?' I asked.

Everyone turned to see who the newcomer was. Dog included.

'Robbie?' Phil said. 'Robbie Munro? Are you here to protest too? We could do with a lawyer. We've got to stop the new development. This is our heritage. We grew up around here, we played amongst these trees ...'

'I remembered there being more of them,' I said.

Pete agreed. 'Me too. Hardly enough wood here for a barbecue.'

But there was to be no reasoning with Phil. 'That's not the point. Think of all the times we played Robin Hood and his Merry Men here.' He turned to the man in the woolly hat. 'Geordie, how can you forget your role as my right-hand man, Little John?'

'I was Friar Tuck,' the woolly hat said.

'Were you?'

'Aye. You used to make me nick packets of crisps from

my dad's shop and then you'd fight me for them. You hit me over the head with a stick once 'cos I never had any smoky bacon.'

Phil turned to his brother. 'Of course, Pete, you were little John. What say you?'

'You made me be the sheriff of Nottingham, because my hair was longer than yours. I spent the whole time running away because you had a big stick. All I had was a wee plastic sword.'

Phil dropped the chains and padlock and walked over to the woman with the dog. 'Katie – the fair Maid Marian – you see it my way, don't you?'

'Maid Marian? Little John, you mean. I was bigger than all of you back then. I've still got a bump on my head where you—'

'Great times,' said Phil.

'Bloody big stick,' said the woman with the dog.

'I moved closer. 'I hate to break this up, Phil, but I was wondering if I could have a word with Linda about something important?'

'You're not here about the trees?'

'To be honest, first I heard of it was on your Facebook page half an hour ago. Have you thought of handing a petition in to the Council?'

'Yeah,' Pete said. 'Do one of those online ones. Get enough signatures and they have to debate it in the Scottish Parliament.'

This suggestion elicited some grudging consideration by Phil, and so while the two brothers tried to add up how many people they could rely on to sign, I guided Linda to a secluded spot near to a dry-stane dyke that separated the wood from the nearby housing estate that was looking to expand.

'Are you here about Ricky Hertz?' she asked.

'How did you know?'

'I had the cops round at my house yesterday asking me questions.'

It had to have been Fiona's doing. Great brains think alike. Hers had recovered from its hangover a lot faster than I thought it would. 'What did they want?'

Linda leaned against the wall and picked at a piece of moss as she spoke. 'They wanted to know about that time I met Ricky Hertz. They took a statement, and I've got to go and see a lawyer in Edinburgh about swearing an oath or something.'

'Did they say you were to give a precognition-on-oath?'

'No, it was something else.'

'An affidavit?'

'That's right. You really are a lawyer, aren't you?'

I certainly was and by now an extremely excited one. 'What did you tell them?'

'The same, as before. I've told the story hundreds of time. I'm the girl who got away. All thanks to your dad.'

'Did they ask you about my dad?'

'Yeah, I've never been able to remember which one he was. I just know that they were both very big.'

Like me, Phil would have been around eighteen or nineteen when Ricky Hertz was convicted. Linda, the wee girl from Preston Road play park, would have been a good nine or ten years younger.

'When the cops came to see you yesterday, did they ask you anything about a cigarette?'

She looked up at me frowning. 'How did you know that? Yes, they asked if Ricky Hertz was smoking when he spoke to me.'

'What did you tell them?'

'I told them he was smoking, but one of the cops, I can't remember which one, it's too long ago, he took the cigarette out of his mouth and threw it away.'

I took a deep breath in. 'Did you see what happened after that?'

She smiled. 'Yeah. Ricky Hertz bent over and picked up the cigarette.' She laughed. 'That's when one of the policemen kicked him up the arse and told him to beat it and not to come back.'

'And you told the cops that yesterday?'

'Yes. Why? Was there something wrong with that?'

'No,' I said, grabbing her head in my hands and planting a kiss on her forehead. 'There was something extremely right about it.'

25

After my trip to Beechwood, I went straight round to my dad's house to bring him the good news. He was sitting at the kitchen table with Tina, chomping his way through the biggest bowl of rice pudding the world had ever seen. Tina's helping was only slightly smaller with slices of tinned peaches smiling up at her.

Before I had a chance to say anything, my dad reached a hand into the fruit bowl and slapped a selection of red, blue and green paper rectangles on the table. 'What do you think of these then?'

'Not a lot,' was the answer that sprung most readily to mind. I had got over the heady excitement of different-coloured paper when I was around three years old.

'It's tickets for the fish supper thingy,' Tina said.

'The Fish Supper Ceilidh,' my dad clarified, with a great deal of satisfaction.

The Ceilidh was held annually, nine miles away in Falkirk Town Hall. There was dancing, drink, an auction, a raffle, games, drink, a fish supper at half-time, more drink and great music. The event was always a sell-out, and with so many returning guests who claimed first dibs on tickets, my dad had tried for years to buy some, always without success.

I hated to break it to him. 'The Fish Supper Ceilidh is held in January. This is October.'

He drew a hand across the small pile of coloured paper, spreading the tickets across the table like a card sharp. 'Diane has talked them into doing one for St Michael's Hospice.' The relationship between my dad and the late-fifties but foxy Dr Diane Prentice was one shrouded in mystery. Ex facie it centred around the arranging of charity events for the local hospice where she'd been a consultant for many years. Although they didn't seem to organise all that many, they certainly had plenty of meetings. Beyond which I didn't like to pry.

'Thanks to me and my connections we were first in the queue,' my dad said, swiping the tickets off the table, tapping the pack square and dropping it in beside a hand of bananas and an ancient apple.

'We?'

'Aye, we're all going. It's tomorrow,' he said, through a mouthful of rice pudding. 'Mind, you'll need to get yourself a kilt.'

'Dad doesn't like kilts,' Tina said, who'd had to live through the arguments about my choice of wedding attire, scarcely twelve months previously. I wasn't getting into the kilt argument again. Be it by domicile or blood, I didn't know anyone more Scottish than me. I had a great respect for the Highland dress, just so long as I didn't have to wear it.

'Never mind that,' I said. 'I've got even better news.'

My dad looked up at me, face full of rice pudding, mouth tilted in a fixed expression of incredulity as to how there could be any better news than that he'd just imparted.

'I think you're off the hook,' I said.

'What do you mean?'

'Your explanation about Ricky Hertz's cigarette butt. I ran it past the Advocate depute on Tuesday night.'

'Who?'

'The Q.C. who's acting for the Crown to oppose Hertz's appeal. She's already made some enquiries, as have I, and your story checks out.'

He finished chewing and set his milky spoon down on the table, not looking as thrilled as I thought he might.

I continued. 'You'll still be asked to give a precognition-on-oath next Monday, but that along with the affidavit from Linda Smith—'

'Who?'

'I mean, Linda Duffy ... You remember, the wee girl from Preston Road play park? She backs up your story. Once the Appeal Court sees the statements from you two they'll have to ask themselves whether that evidence neutralises the new DNA evidence.'

Tina finished her pudding and peaches, jumped down from the table and went into the living room to watch TV.

My dad picked up his spoon and started in on the bowl again.

'Dad, do you know what this means? This is the Appeal Court. If there is even a straw of evidence that helps uphold a conviction, they'll clutch at it. You and Linda Duffy are handing them a couple of tree branches. Trust me. Ricky Hertz is going back to jail and you're going to the Fish Supper Ceilidh.'

He said no more until he had finished his rice pudding, then rose from the table and dropped his bowl into the big Belfast sink. 'It's no big surprise. I always knew that the truth would prevail.'

'You're welcome,' I said. He was impervious to my sarcasm.

'And here's the man I have to thank, right here,' he said, staring out of the window. There was a knock on the back door. Without waiting for it to be answered, D.I. Dougie Fleming walked in to meet my dad whose face was now wreathed in smiles. 'Come away in, Dougie,' my dad said, and the two of them shook hands warmly and slapped each other on the back. 'Will you have a cup of tea or coffee, or ...' He gave Fleming a nudge. 'Would you like something a wee bit stronger to celebrate?'

Fleming declined alcohol and accepted coffee. He took off his jacket, hung it on the back of the chair my dad had pulled out from the table, and sat down.

My dad put the kettle under the tap. 'Great idea of yours, Dougie, to go and speak with the wee lassie, Duffy.'

Fleming tried to look modest and failed, even though the only reason there could be for him making further inquiries, was because of my consultation with Fiona Faye the night before. The state she was in I was surprised she'd remembered.

My phoned buzzed. I didn't recognise the number.

'Hi, Robbie. It's Cammy.' His voice was weak and strained. 'I need to speak to you urgently. Can you come and see me?'

There were so many ways to say no that I hadn't chosen one before another, stronger voice said, 'Do what he says.'

'Please, Robbie,' Cammy said.

'Who was that who spoke just now?' I asked.

'Just come, Robbie.'

'Where are you?' I don't know why I bothered to ask because I had no intention of going.

'The Moorings, in Falkirk,' Cammy said.

I recognised it as the name of a homeless men's hostel. 'What are you doing there?'

'I'll explain when you get here.'

'Cammy, I'm busy and I don't even know where The Moorings is. It'll take me ages to find it.'

'It won't. Phone this number if you get lost. Please. It's very important.'

Before I could say anything he was gone.

'What was that about The Moorings?' Fleming asked. 'You know that's Ricky Hertz's bail address, don't you?'

I didn't. I had expected him to have been bailed to an address outside Linlithgow, but had no idea where. Had Cammy gone round to see him? He must have. How did he even know the address? I thought back through a hazy mist of Islay malts to our discussions in the Red Corner Bar the day before. I'd told Cammy all about bail orders, how they were a matter of public record. All he would have had to do was contact the Clerk's office to discover where Hertz was living.

Fleming got up off his chair and climbed back into his jacket. 'Problem?' he asked.

'Quite possibly,' I said.

26

By the time I arrived at The Moorings, word of Cammy's situation had spread amongst the other residents and out onto the street where a small crowd had gathered.

'I'm not sure what's going on exactly, but it looks like a hostage situation,' Fleming told me, after he'd had a brief chat with a group of local cops who were standing at the entrance door to the block of flats, talking into their lapel-mounted radios. 'Hertz has got Foster in there and will only negotiate through you. Take this.' He pressed something into my hand. It was about the size of a fifty-pence piece and twice as thick. It had double-sided tape on the reverse. 'Stick it somewhere inconspicuous and we'll be able to hear everything that's going on. If anything gets too hairy, we'll come crashing in. The Fast Action Response Team are on their way.'

The Fast Action Response Team clearly didn't go in for acronyms, but if they'd been alerted it meant only one thing. 'Hold on a minute. Has Hertz got a gun?'

Fleming winced. 'We think so. No idea where he got it from, but one of the other inmates—'

'It's a hostel not a prison,' I said.

'Okay, one of the other . . .guests, that do you? He says he heard Hertz shouting something about a gun.'

I didn't like the sound of that. Ricky Hertz might be, for the moment at any rate, a convicted child murderer, but I didn't want to give him the chance of moving up an age bracket, starting with me. As for Cammy, he was fine when he was buying me whisky, but risk my life for him? Not likely.

'Of course, you don't have to assist,' Fleming said. A van pulled up and a small TV crew emerged and began to assemble their apparatus. 'Not sure how that'll look on the six o'clock news, though.'

Hertz was living in a room and kitchen on the second floor. He was keeping in touch via a mobile phone, and, as instructed, I had to go up myself, strictly no police.

They'd given me a bulletproof vest. It meant that I had to stick the microphone just under the collar of my shirt and hope Hertz wouldn't notice. I knocked on the door. It opened. A hand reached out, took hold of my vest and yanked me inside. The door slammed shut again, and I was shoved, cold metal jammed in the back of my neck, down a short hallway into a sparsely furnished room that stank of weed. Cammy was sitting rigid on a grubby, velour sofa, eyes wide, shirt sticking to him, dark rings of sweat at the armpits.

Ricky Hertz was a lot less ugly than the mugshot that flashed up on the screen every time his name was mentioned on the news. He was now in his late forties, short black hair streaked with grey, medium height and of a slim, wiry build. That he looked older than his police photograph was to be expected. What was not expected was that I recognised him as the man who'd stopped and spoken to my daughter as we made the ascent of Cockleroy hill nearly two weeks before.

'Take your clothes off,' he said. He was agitated, head twitching, turning this way and that, not making eye contact.

'What?'

'You heard.'

'Look, it's not necessary.'

The gun disagreed. It was a cheap ex-target pistol. The sort of gun someone like Cammy Foster would have bought on the street for an outrageously large sum of money. It was old, the metal chipped and scarred. One side of the grip was missing. The chances of it being capable of firing were highly remote, not that the people who sold those sorts of things did refunds.

'Now!' The gun was now in my face allowing an even closer inspection. I was convinced it was a replica, just not sufficiently convinced so as to disobey Hertz's command. I removed the Kevlar vest and then my shirt. Hertz saw the black disc near my collar bone and peeled it off.

'And the rest of them,' Hertz said with a wave of the pistol.

'Why? You've got the bug,' I said.

'I want to make sure there's not any more.' Once he was sure there wasn't, Hertz searched through my clothes, jeans, shirt and socks and then told me to put them on again, which I did, quickly. It clearly wasn't warmth of his surroundings that was causing Cammy to sweat so much. There was either no central heating in the place or Hertz was keen on maintaining a low carbon footprint

'Okay, sit down and let's talk,' Hertz said, still looking everywhere except at me.

I sat down next to Cammy whose deodorant wasn't quite cutting it. Hertz handed me the button bug. 'Tell them everything's fine and that you'll be out of here in ten minutes so long as no one bursts in here or tries to shoot me through a window.'

I did as I was told. Dougie Fleming must have told his

men to stand down because after a cautious peek through the blinds, Hertz came over to the centre of the room and stood in front of a three bar electric fire that didn't look like it had seen much action lately.

He took the bug from me, closed his fingers around it and held it tightly in his hand, the pistol held just as firmly in the other.

'What's going on?' I asked, tying a shoelace.

'You tell me,' Hertz said. 'I was sitting watching telly when your man breaks in and starts pointing this at me.'

He didn't go into further detail. He didn't need to. It was obvious. Cammy, intent on revenge, had paid Ricky Hertz a visit. Cammy was a big man, but a gadget salesman who drank too much. Hertz was a lot smaller, but someone who'd spent over seventeen years in prison with nothing to do except visit the gym. He'd already avoided several attempts on his life by people who knew a lot better than Cammy Foster how to commit murder.

'How about Cammy gives you an apology and we both leave?' I suggested.

It was a suggestion Hertz chose to ignore. 'You're the son of the cop that fitted me up, aren't you? Not your fault,' he said, entirely reasonably, I thought. 'I've read about you. You're a defence lawyer. Maybe if I'd had you acting for me back in two thousand and one I wouldn't have been sent down. Anyway, I've done my time. Now those lying, cop bastards are going to do theirs.'

It wasn't the moment to tell him about the latest evidence that was about to send him back to prison for the rest of his life.

He came over to where I was sitting on the couch. 'If you know anything about my case, you know that I never killed nobody. I want you to tell him,' he pointed the gun at Cammy, 'that I didn't kill his sister. And then ...' He handed me first the button bug and then the pistol. 'You take him out of here and tell everyone else I just want to be left alone.'

27

The gun turned out to be a replica. Cammy would have found that out if he'd tried to shoot Ricky Hertz. As it was, the opportunity had never presented itself. I doubt if he would have availed himself of it if it had.

Cammy was taken away by the police. Far from being accused of anything, Hertz was treated as a victim and a statement taken from him to use against his attacker.

Cammy needed a lawyer. Reluctantly, I went with him to the police station. The cops didn't even bother to question him. What he'd tried to do was obvious. He was processed in the usual way: fingerprinted, photographed, DNA'd and then, thanks to his lack of prior offending, and a very reasonable duty inspector, released on a bail undertaking to attend Falkirk Sheriff Court in three weeks' time. A report would be sent to the Procurator Fiscal who would have to decide what to charge him with. There was a whole range of possibilities, each one with a prison cell at the end of it.

By the time I'd picked up Tina and a doner kebab and returned home, it was nearly nine o'clock on a Friday night. It had been a busy day and I was all set to collapse in front of the telly. My phone buzzed. I shouldn't have answered it.

'Hi, Robbie.' It was Kaye Mitchell. 'Where are you?'

'I'm at home.'

'Who with?'

'A kebab and a bottle of lager.'

'That's great. Don't move.' She hung up, which saved me the bother of pretending my phone battery was running out. Half a kebab later, there was a knock at the door and bright lights outside my window.

When I answered the door, one of those bright lights was shone straight in my eyes and a microphone shoved in my face.

'Hi, Robbie, any chance of a quick word?' a vaguely familiar female voice asked.

I blinked a few times to recover my vision and looked out to see Cherry Lovell, presenter of *Night News*. Apart from the occasional glimpse on TV, I hadn't seen Cherry since the case of helicopter sabotage I'd had a year or so back involving the death of playboy Jerry Thorn and his girlfriend.

Cherry, looking as blonde and beautiful as ever, was standing on the doorstep, a cameraman on one side, a sound man and a girl in a Parka carrying a clipboard on the other. I could just about make out Kaye Mitchell hovering in the background.

Tina, who'd been sent to put on her pyjamas, arrived wanting to know what all the fuss was.

Cherry handed her microphone to the woman with the clipboard and lifted Tina up into one of her arms, put the other around my neck and hugged us tightly.

'Your dad's an old friend of mine, sweetheart. Did you know he was a hero?' Tina did. 'Well, would you like the whole world to know?' Tina would. It was all very nice. What wasn't quite so nice was that my daughter's remarks were taken by Cherry's camera crew as an invitation to enter, walk past me and progress down the hall.

Cherry released her grip on me and, still carrying Tina in her arms, followed them with Kaye tagging along. When I eventually made it to the living room, the crew were setting up their equipment. Cherry divested herself of her raincoat and Tina, and turned to me.

'Okay,' she said, 'how about we sit you in that armchair, Robbie? That's it, the master of the house. No, wait, even better, let's have you on the sofa with your daughter looking up adoringly.' She walked over to Tina, guided her towards the couch and hunkered down beside her. 'You can do adoringly, can't you, precious?'

After it had been explained to Tina what adoringly was, my daughter thought it might be just about doable, and father and daughter took up position as directed, my initial protests assuaged by the thought of my heroic deed of the day being made known to the wider public, or at least the few who bothered to tune into *Night News*.

Clipboard-girl handed Cherry a single sheet of paper. She scanned it quickly and gave it back.

'I'm rolling,' the cameraman said. Kaye backed into a corner on the far side of the room, well out of shot, smiling encouragingly at me. There was something about that smile I found unsettling.

'We'll do the intro later,' Cherry said, and swung the microphone at me. 'Robbie Munro, what was it like when the police sent you into that block of flats to meet a convicted serial killer who, it's said, was armed with a gun?'

I explained that there was an ongoing police inquiry and I couldn't go into detail about what had taken place in Hertz's apartment, but managed to give a version of events that emphasised my bravery while trying to sound modest. It wasn't easy.

It all went very smoothly. Cherry was highly comple-mentary, and, yet, I had the strangest feeling ... I looked over at Kaye again. Her smile was more encouraging than ever which only served to unsettle me further.

'You've been a criminal defence lawyer for many years, Mr Munro,' Cherry continued, camera rolling. 'Can you tell us your views on corrupt police officers who fabricate evidence?'

Kaye was no longer smiling encouragingly. In fact, she was no longer looking in my direction, instead she was studying a painted stone that Tina had made during handiwork at school and we kept on the mantelpiece.

'Obviously, I don't approve of anyone fabricating evidence,' I croaked a small laugh. 'In the witness box it should always be the truth, the whole truth and nothing but the truth. Now, if you'll excuse me ...'

I made to rise from the sofa. Cherry put a hand on my shoulder. 'What do you think should happen to your father if he's found to have fabricated the evidence that convicted Ricky Hertz?'

This time I did stand, despite Cherry's efforts to keep me remained seated.

'That's it,' I said. 'Out.'

To drive home the point, I walked towards the living room door. Nobody else seemed inclined to follow. 'I mean it,' I said, opening the door.

Cherry came over, microphone held out to me at arm's length. The cameraman followed, clipboard-carrying girl bringing up the rear with Kaye doing her best to remain invisible.

'Surely you must have something to say?' Cherry said.

'I *have* something to say,' I said. 'You're leaving.'

At my command for them to go, no one budged an

190

inch. I stepped into the hallway. The only movement was the camera swivelling to keep me in frame. Cherry was not for letting up. 'Don't you think it a little hypocritical, that you, a defence lawyer who spends so much of his time accusing police officers of lying, should now try and defend one accused of perverting the course of justice, just because you're related?'

I didn't reply.

'What's the matter?' Cherry said. 'Is your father so obviously guilty of lying that even you can't stick up for him? The Court of Appeal must think so. Why else release Ricky Hertz on bail?'

I was going to have to say something or else prove wrong the adage that there's no such thing as bad publicity. I took a deep breath. 'I'll stick up for my father the same way I always stick up for truth and justice.'

I could recognise Kaye's snigger even if I couldn't see her.

Cherry gave a light little laugh of her own. 'Most legal experts say it's only a matter of time before the Court of Appeal squash the conviction.'

'Listen to this legal expert,' I said. 'Firstly, this is Scotland, so it's not the Court of Appeal it's the Appeal Court, secondly, convictions are quashed not squashed, and, thirdly, I am certain Ricky Hertz will be going back to prison where he belongs.'

Cherry's beautiful blue contact lenses sparkled. 'Is that an opinion you'd like to stake your career on?'

I heard the front door open. Malky came in, five-a-side kit bag slung over his shoulder. 'You got any beers in, Robbie?' he called down the hallway to me.

I had to make this quick before Malky entered stage left and started mouthing off.

'Tell you what,' I said, walking through from the hall into the living room again, closing the door behind me and causing the posse of TV news people to back away and give me room. 'Why don't you, Miss Lovell ...' I put a hand on each of her shoulders and gently about-turned her to face the camera lens. 'Look into that camera and call my father a liar one more time, and then after Ricky Hertz's next appeal hearing we'll see who still has a career.'

28

Falkirk Town Hall was set out with three sides of the vast room lined with trestle tables, leaving a large area in the centre reserved for the dancers. On stage, Skerryvore, Scotland's foremost Celtic rock group, named after a lighthouse off the coast of the Hebridean island of Tiree from whence hailed two of its members, the blonde-haired and bekilted Gillespie brothers. Especially for the occasion, the eight-piece band was going back to their Ceilidh roots in support of St Michael's Hospice, mainly thanks to the persuasiveness of my dad's date for the evening, Dr Diane Prentice. My date was Tina, which meant I had to stay off alcohol, and the lack of whisky, highland garb and facial hair, set me apart from most of the male guests and some of the women.

From the start of the night bagpipes, accordion, guitar, fiddle, drum and vocals, blasted out a fusion of traditional and rock music, and the dance floor was packed with people performing such mainstays as the Gay Gordon, the Eightsome Reel and the Military Two-Step. Some of the dancers even seemed to know what they were doing; those who didn't had just as much fun.

For a man who was more used to listening to the Red River Trio trying to find a key, like a drunk man at his front door, I could have happily sat back and listened to the music. That wasn't going to happen, not with Tina there. My daughter scarcely missed a dance, and although I did now and again manage to offload her onto Malky or my dad, the half-time break for auction, raffle, and fish supper, gave me time to breathe. After that I was raring to go again. It was great to see my dad looking so relaxed and, all in all, it was shaping up to be a most enjoyable evening, until, that is, the last set dance of the evening.

Like all Scots schoolboys, I had been forced to engage in 'social dancing' classes during my formative years. These were arranged during P.E. lessons as end-of-year dances loomed, and accordingly I did have a grasp of some of the less complicated moves. For instance, I knew from bitter experience never to volunteer to be centre-dancer in a Dashing White Sergeant set, and just to say no to the Hooligan Jig; however, there should have been some kind of health warning given to those uninitiated, like myself, in the Orcadian Strip the Willow.

The basic Strip the Willow is a fairly innocuous dance, involving eight consenting adults, who perform a few birls and whirls in a dance reminiscent of children's parties of yesteryear and the Grand Old Duke of York. The version to which the Orkney Islands lend their name is very different. For one thing the number of participants is predicated by the number of people who can be crammed into two parallel lines the length of a dance floor. The dance floor at Falkirk Town Hall was the length of a football pitch.

As I discovered, the Orcadian Strip the Willow was the dance equivalent of running the gauntlet. When my turn came, holding her two hands, I spun Tina around for a count of eight and then set off whirling my way down between the two ranks, men and women either side, taking each female in turn as I went, birling her around, before returning to Tina for another birl and then so on down the never-ending line. Things had progressed without mishap until, towards the middle of the avenue, I was presented to a small, sturdy lady, thick of thew, and wearing a cream blouse, tartan skirt and a determined expression. Hooking my arm in hers, she semi-squatted, taking upon herself the centre of gravity of a dying star and the spin-cycle of an industrial centrifuge. Hurled back towards the centre, I spun around with Tina once more before my momentum hurtled me off to meet the next female in line. That's when the problems started. In my state of extreme dizziness, and accustomed as I was to the rough treatment from seconds before, I seized hold of her, not realising how thin and weak she was, and sent her flying off across the floor, crashing into her partner who was gently spinning Tina around.

It's funny, isn't it, how the smallest, weakest women always seem to marry the biggest, strongest men? This big strong man wasn't happy at my manhandling of his wife. For a moment I thought he was going to take a swing at me, and, as it happened, I was right. He did. It would have been an excellent shot too, had it hit me. It didn't. He was big and strong all right, but about as fast as the approach of a Scottish summer. I dodged. He missed, and staggered forward, colliding with the next set of dancers who were whirling their way up the line. All three ended up on the floor. One of those dancers was my dad. The other was Linda Duffy. Linda was dressed in a loose-fitting black trouser suit, with a plunging neckline, the whole outfit held together by a combination of double-sided sticky tape and a degree of optimism. I helped her up. Phil, her husband, was nowhere to be seen. When my dad eventually struggled to his feet again, I saw he had brought with him, under one arm, the head of the large man who had tried to punch me and who was now extremely red in the face and clearly having some difficulty breathing. It took a few other dancers to step in and defuse the situation, which was eventually resolved with some handshaking and talk of conciliatory drams.

'Home to Donegal' was Skerryvore's signature tune, and the band, seeing the commotion, smoothly transitioned into this final slow number of the evening.

The dance floor flooded. I looked around for Tina and saw that she was dancing with Malky, standing on his feet and being chauffeured around. I was going to return to my seat when I was taken a hold of by Linda Duffy.

'Your dad's great, isn't he?' she said in my ear as we embarked on what I called a slow waltz, or a shuffle, but which Linda saw more as a way of keeping my podiatrist in business. 'Saved my life, you know?' she said, face close to mine, breathing alcohol fumes up my nose. 'If it hadn't been for your dad, that Ricky Hertz would have had me away and strangled like those other poor wee lassies.' She trod on my foot again then laid a head on my shoulder, not out of affection, more because it had grown too heavy to hold up. I saw Tina watching me as she and Malky sailed by. The song was a good one under normal circumstances, but on this occasion seemed to go on forever. When at last the music stopped, I roused Linda, who I had been dragging around the dance floor for the past few minutes, and led her back to her table where her husband was deep in conversation with a ginger-headed man about tree preservation orders.

'Thanks, Robbie,' she said, as I guided her to the vacant seat by Phil's side. 'And tell your dad thanks for the tickets.' She kissed me on the cheek. 'He's a great guy. I'd say anything for that man.'

196

Had I heard her correctly? 'You'd *say* anything?'

'I mean, do anything,' she slurred, with a shake of her head as she collapsed into the chair. 'I'd do anything, I mean, say anything, at all.'

29

Sunday morning, I was in bed, wondering how long a lie-in I might sneak before Tina came bouncing through. Not long was the answer. The phone woke her. It was Braxton Cobb's personal assistant.

By midday my daughter and I were occupying two of four large wicker chairs on the lawn of a walled garden to the rear of a country mansion, set amidst the rolling hills of Perthshire. In a distant corner, a gardener was busy raking leaves and feeding a small crackling bonfire, while in the trees nearby, a squadron of starlings pecked at the last of the crab apples.

The weather was about as good as October gets in Scotland. Bright and clear, any wind there might have been not penetrating the ivy-covered walls that surrounded us.

I took a long drink from a tall glass, reclined and studied the old man who, with the aid of a silver-topped cane, was hobbling towards us. By his side walked a younger man, dressed in a grey suit with an open-necked white shirt. He seemed anxious lest the old man should stumble, while at the same time equally anxious not to lend support unless absolutely essential: like some worried dad teaching his child to ride a bike. I stood up as they neared.

'Braxton Cobb,' the older man said, smiling like a piano. He was tall and stout with a good head of unconvincingly black hair and a goatee to match. He tucked the silver-topped cane under one arm and shot out a hand. 'Kind of you to come, Mr Munro. Is it all right if I call you Robbie?' He spoke slow and easy with a profound Southern drawl.

'I don't see why not, it's my name,' I said, and he laughed politely while lowering himself onto one of the unoccupied wicker chairs, his right leg sticking out straight in front, parallel to the ground. He rapped it with his cane. The leg made a dull hollow sound. 'Vietnam, 1970. I dodged the draft, moved to Canada and got my damn leg caught in a bear trap.' He chuckled as though he enjoyed the memory. He struck me as one of those if-you're-happy-and-you-know-it kind of people who are tiring to be around for any length of time. Hopefully, like the drugs his company manufactured, he'd be okay in small doses.

Using both hands he adjusted something at his knee and bent the leg into a more natural position.

'Now then, Robbie, it was kind of you to come all this way. And you too, little lady,' he said to Tina, who was sitting in her own wicker chair, uninterested in the new arrival and more intent on sucking on an ice cube. 'Would you like some more lemonade?'

Tina decided she would. At the merest inclination of the old man's head his aide turned, looked towards the house and nodded. His gesture brought a young lady who had attended to us earlier, scurrying from the shadows carrying a jug. She took Tina's glass and poured, ice cubes clinking, holding slices of lemon at bay with the paddle of a large wooden spatula. With a slight curtsey, she left as speedily as she had arrived.

'Is she your slave?' Tina asked.

Cobb smiled and reached out a chunky hand to ruffle

my daughter's hair. 'They abolished slavery, don't you know, darling?' He laughed. 'Even where I come from.'

'Your sister-in-law says hello,' I said, thinking I might as well come right out with the reason I assumed I'd been invited. It couldn't be a coincidence that so recently returned from Rome I had been summoned to meet one of Zanetti Biotechnic's founders.

'How is Emanuela? Still making the Pope happy by bringing lots of little Catholics into the world?' he asked, his smiley face less smiley now.

'It's difficult not to when you're an obstetrician and a nun.'

'The last thing this world needs is more Roman idolaters. Still, I suppose I should let the old worry bag worship God in her own way, while I worship Him in His.'

'She speaks very highly of you too,' I said, 'and for what it's worth she seems happy enough. It's good that she can keep busy at her age.'

'Keep busy and then what? Die?'

Were there other options? 'It's good to keep busy,' I said.

'By busy you mean work?'

I looked around. 'Are you telling me you won the lottery or inherited this place?'

The smile returned to his face. He leaned forward and let his aide rearrange the cushions at his back. 'I remember a story my daddy told me when I was a boy. It was about a rich man who saw a poor man sitting on a stump by the side of the road in the sun, drinking beer. The rich man stopped his Rolls-Royce, got out and said to the poor man, "You know if you gathered all the wood lying here around, you could sell it for firewood. Pretty soon you'd have enough money for a cart so you could collect even more. After that, maybe you could get yourself a mule. Collect enough wood and you could buy a truck. Who knows? One day you might own the biggest firewood company in the whole state. Then, after forty years or so you could retire, sit back in the sun and have a beer." And the poor man said, "That's what I'm doing right now!"'

I laughed, though I'd heard something similar before.

'I don't get it,' Tina said, stopping sucking juice through a straw for a moment. 'And my dad doesn't drink beer. He likes special lemonade. And why was the man collecting wood?'

'Maybe you'll like this other story better,' Cobb said, smiling down at Tina. 'There was once a poor old man and he lived by the side of a lake. One day a fairy came—'

'I don't believe in fairies,' Tina said, qualifying that rather bald statement with an 'Except for the tooth fairy, obviously' which was directed at me, in what I thought was an overly patronising manner.

'Well, you can believe in fairies when they're in a story,' Cobb said. 'This fairy gave the man a magic leather pouch and told him that every time he put his hand in he would pull out a gold coin.'

Cobb paused to stare at Tina, eyes wide as though she'd be impressed by this.

She wasn't unduly so. 'I got gold coins at Christmas. They were in a wee net and had chocolate inside. They were in my stocking.'

'So, you don't believe in fairies, but you believe in Santa Claus?' Cobb said, treading on what for a parent is treacherous ground.

'Who do you think brought the coins?' Tina asked, with the look on her face I'd seen a million times. It was the one that said, 'Are you senile or have you always been this stupid?' She then went on to identify what she saw as a design flaw and the difficulties in extracting chocolate from tight-fitting tinfoil; something I couldn't say I'd noticed on Christmas morning.

Cobb tickled her under the chin with a stubby fore-finger. 'The coins I'm talking about weren't chocolate coins, gorgeous, these were real gold coins. And the fairy said to the man, "You can take as many gold coins as you like, but you can't spend them until you throw the pouch back into the lake and then it will be gone forever." And do you know what happened?' He didn't give Tina a chance to reply, not that it looked like she would, too busy poking a stray slice of lemon at the bottom of her glass with the straw. 'When the fairy came back many years later she found a pile of bones lying on an even bigger pile of gold coins. And do you want to know why?'

Tina looked like she could live with the uncertainty.

'Because he was too greedy,' Cobb said. 'He never threw the pouch back in the lake and so he couldn't spend any of the gold coins. He was a silly old man, wasn't he?'

Tina concurred. 'Why didn't he tie a piece of string to it,' she said, before returning to the straw and making sure she'd sucked up every last drop of lemonade.

Cobb almost fell off his chair laughing. When he'd recovered, he shifted his leg into a more comfortable position and turned to me. 'Robbie, I'm not half as smart as your daughter, but when I was not much older, I used to mix chalk and peppermint paste in a bathtub, cut it into discs with a bottle cap, dry it in the sun and sell those indigestion pills around every bar in Beaufort, South Carolina, for a dime a dozen. Do you think I did that and went on to build a pharmaceutical empire so that I could work until I dropped dead?'

'My mum's dead,' Tina said. 'Now I have Joanna who's like my mum, 'cept she's not.'

He smiled down at Tina. 'Sounds to me like you've got a mommy in heaven and one on earth too. One looking after you here, the other watching out for you from up there.' He let Tina stare up into the sky and ponder that while he turned to address me. 'You want to know why you're here, I expect?' He raised his hand. The young man left the side of the chair to walk a distance away and take up position by a tall holly bush, never taking his eyes of us. 'I'd like to know who ...' Cobb glanced down at Tina. I got the message. I finished my drink, gave my daughter the empty glass and sent her off in search of the nice lady with the lemonade jug.

'I'd like to know,' Cobb repeated, 'who killed Hercule Mercier.'

'Join the queue,' I felt like saying, but didn't. I wanted to know why he was so sure Hercule had been murdered. First of all, I reminded him what was on the death certificate. 'Alcohol and barbiturates, you'll know better than me that it's a classic combination.'

'Sure is, son,' he said. 'Next you'll be telling me Marilyn Monroe committed suicide.'

Okay, so I was dealing with a conspiracy theorist. There were a few of them around when it came to Hercule's demise. But why did Cobb care so much? Jill was highly suspicious of him, and his sister-in-law had only bolstered those suspicions. Maybe he was sounding me out, to see how much evidence I had. That wasn't going take him long.

Tina arrived back carrying a tumbler, and watering the grass with lemonade. Cobb took it, gave it to me and sent her off to get him one. She went without complaining. It was better than sitting around listening to us talk.

'I didn't like Hercule Mercier,' Cobb said. 'I'll admit that right now. He was Luciana's pet, her protégé. Still comes to visit her every time he's over here on business. She headhunted him from one of the big German outfits when he was still a youngster. When she knew she couldn't go on any longer, she decided to leave the running of the business entirely to him. Never mind leapfrogging me, that man was put ahead of our own daughter, God bless her. Luciana gave him carte blanche.'

'How did that make you feel?' I asked, like an amateur shrink.

'I was fine with it, eventually,' Cobb said, rather too tersely. 'I used to be a control freak, wouldn't delegate nothing to nobody. I always knew best. Luciana got tired of me sticking my nose in sometimes. Then Natalie died. Not long after that, Luciana got her bad news. The fight left me after that. I didn't have the stomach for the business any more. Suddenly I realised what was really important and so I retired. That was eleven years ago. I was sixty-one. I can't say I've regretted one minute of it, and do you know what? The company has gone from strength to strength without me.' He shifted himself in his seat again. His aide looked like he might come over to assist, but thought better of it.

'And now you are rich and retired the world is your oyster?' I said.

'No, sir. This is my oyster. I love Scotland. I used to spend summers here, and winters wherever I liked. Now I stay put. Never leave the place.'

I picked him up on that. 'I met your granddaughter last week.' I thought I saw a look of real hatred in his eye, just a flash and it was gone.

'You mean my *grandson*,' he said.

204

I remembered Findlay's list and embroidered the truth a little. 'She told me you were down in Edinburgh visiting her recently.' I didn't mention that it also happened to have been the weekend Hercule had died.

He squinted at me, serious, studying my face. 'Did *he* really tell you that?' Tina returned with Cobb's glass of lemonade. He thanked her, took a long drink and wiped his mouth. 'Tell me, Robbie, do you hunt?' he asked, the smile restored to his face. 'It's a great time of year for grouse and there's always plenty of deer. Too many, in fact.'

I had to decline. I'd never gone shooting on an estate. Through I had dealt with a few shootings on estates.

Cobb was determined to act the perfect host. 'Golf, then?' he said, and I couldn't deny having swung a club in the not too distant past.

He grinned. 'Why didn't you say? Golf is the main reason I settled in Scotland. There's no finer scenery and then of course there's the Scottish weather. Golf is all about the weather. It must be played under all conditions. Golf is all about consistency and control, and the weather is highly inconsistent and uncontrollable. You don't need different golf courses if the weather is never the same. I should know; I've played them all, all the great courses, with all the great players. I used to sponsor my own tournament. Which is why ...' With a great effort he levered himself out of the wickerwork chair, raised his walking cane above his head and waved it at, so far as I could see, no one in particular. 'I built myself my own golf course, each hole modelled on one of my favourites.'

Without any further signal, a golf buggy appeared from around a corner. When I say buggy, it looked more like the sort of thing the Pope would venture out in if he fancied a quick nine holes before Mass. It had two white leather bench seats, doors front and rear and a domed Perspex roof. Strapped to the back was a set of golf clubs in a green and gold bag. The buggy pulled up adjacent to us. The driver alighted to be replaced by the man in the suit. Cobb manoeuvred himself into the front passenger seat and Tina and I clambered into the rear. From there, through an archway in the high wall, it was a minute's drive to the first tee.

Cobb needed help to haul himself from the buggy. Once free he brushed away the hand of his aide. 'I had this one modelled on the fourteenth at Gleneagles King's Course. A nice hole to start off a round with, don't you think?'

It certainly was an early chance to put a par or better on your scorecard. A short par four, downhill with a very slight dog-leg left. Three hundred and ten yards made it just about driveable for a big hitter, but only if the ball was sent straight enough to split the series of bunkers slanting across the fairway at around the two-hundred-and-forty-yard mark.

'What's your handicap, Mr Munro?' Cobb asked gesturing towards the bag of clubs.

'Fourteen on a good day,' I said. 'A very good day.'

'Well, you ain't going to get a better one than this,' he said, and wasn't wrong. What little breeze there was came straight over my right shoulder and would help any drive in the direction of the yellow flag fluttering in the mid-distance.

I took the driver from the bag. It was brand new, graphite shaft with a head the size of a frying pan. After a few practice swishes, I teed up, squared myself to the hole and, though I say it myself, swung smoothly through the ball, sending it off into the azure with a satisfying ping from the titanium face. Aided by the wind, it carried over two hundred yards, setting off nicely towards the green until it took an unfriendly hop just short of the bunkers and dived into the sand.

Cobb allowed his aide to tee up a golf ball for him.

'With a little flair, ability and good fortune you can score well over one or two holes, but to win the game you need to be in control at all times,' he said, limping past me onto the tee. 'Three,' he said, and the man in the suit handed him, not a metal club, but a proper old-fashioned wooden club, the lacquer on the persimmon head polished to an extraordinarily high degree. With a few waggles he drew the club back to shoulder height and released. The club seemed to take an age to reach its target. When it did, the ball formed a shallow arc, travelled no more than one hundred yards, bounced and rolled down the hill landing twenty or so yards short of the sand.

I took two blows to extract myself from the steep sides of the bunker, and then only landed on the edge of the green. With the flick of a seven iron, Cobb pitched his ball low over the sand traps. It landed before the green and we watched as it bounced, rolled, and following the contours of the green, curled slowly around from right to left until it came to a halt a few feet from the hole.

'Control,' he said after I'd holed out for a bogey five and he'd knocked his putt in for a birdie. 'Life is all about control. It's necessary in golf, in business and in love.' He handed his putter to the man in the suit and strode off the green towards the buggy.

'Come with me, son,' he said. 'I'd like you to meet my wife.'

30

'How is Luciana?'

Not long after I arrived home from my visit with Braxton Cobb, Jill called seeking an update on how her money was being spent. As soon as she heard that I had some new information, she insisted on coming straight to see me.

I was serving Tina fish fingers, chips and beans when she arrived. We left my daughter in the kitchen eating her tea, while the two of us went for a stroll in the garden, Bouncer chaperoning. Fifteen thousand up on the deal, I felt I owed it to Jill not only to divulge what I'd learned in the Eternal City, but also from my visit to Braxton Cobb's country seat.

'Luciana's very ill,' I said. 'Her bedroom is like a hospital ward. She's linked up to a machine and there's tubes and wires and stuff going in and out.'

'Did you speak with her?'

'When I told her who I was and that I knew you, she was asking after Hercule.'

'Doesn't she know?'

She didn't. Her husband had kept the news of Hercule's death from her. 'Luciana's already extremely weak and in a lot of pain. Cobb thought the shock might be too much.'

'What else was she saying?'

'Not a lot, she has difficulty speaking. I was only there

a few minutes. I think Cobb was trying to make a point more than anything.'

'And that point would be?' Jill asked.

We had reached the top of the garden where any semblance of order turned into a chaos of withered long grass, straggly bushes and a small copse of spindly beech trees. Somewhere in there I'd made a den. During the summer, Tina used to have friends over, and they'd camp out, living rough in the wilds until juice and biscuit supplies started running low or something good came on telly.

'Cobb's heard the rumours. The ones linking him with Hercule's death. The ones put about by people like you, I suppose. He was making the point that he has no interest in Zanetti Biotechnic. He just wants to enjoy life as best he can and spend what time he has left with his dying wife. He never leaves her side. It was quite touching. He seems...'

'Seems what?'

'Entirely genuine.'

Jill grunted scornfully.

'Then, of course,' I said, unable to resist, 'we both know what a terrible judge of character I am when it comes to trusting people.'

Jill was either too deep in thought, or simply couldn't be bothered to come back at me. We about-turned, letting Bouncer continue onwards, sniffing about in the undergrowth.

'Did you find out why Cobb was booked in at The Newberry the weekend Hercule died?'

I was wondering when she'd ask me this. 'He'd arranged to visit his granddaughter.'

'How convenient!'

I didn't want to fuel Jill's suspicions any more, but I had to tell her. 'Did you know that Chiara and Braxton Cobb hadn't spoken in years?'

'I'd heard they weren't close.'

'There's more to it than that.'

'Chiara's a man!' Jill exclaimed, once I'd clarified matters.

'Well, she used to be. She still is in her grandfather's eyes. He doesn't approve, to put it mildly.'

'Wow. I never knew. Still, just makes it even more of a coincidence that he happened to come to Edinburgh that weekend, neglecting the wife whose side he allegedly never leaves.' Jill's face was drawn and pinched. A woman determined for revenge. I'd never seen her like this before. 'What did you learn from your trip to Rome?'

What I had to say about my conversation with Emanuela Zanetti only served to bolster Jill's views on Cobb's culpability. I thought I'd try and head her off at the pass. 'Suspicions are all very well, Jill, but—'

'But nothing, Robbie. I don't care what he says, Braxton Cobb hated being ousted from the Board of Zanetti. Everyone knows that.' She stopped on the slabbed path, to her left the drying green, on her right the vegetable patch. The former hadn't had its final winter cut and wouldn't until its first cut of spring. The latter was strewn with yellow leaves and grow-bags from Joanna's attempts to grow strawberries and courgettes, something for which the local bird and slug populations were forever grateful.

'At first, he felt aggrieved,' I conceded, 'but he says that when he realised what was important in life, he contented himself playing golf on his own private course and caring for his sick wife.'

Jill wasn't listening. She was talking more to herself

than to me, piecing everything together. 'Once Luciana is out of the way, Cobb thinks he can call the shots. He's a bully. No one on the board will stand up to him now that Hercule's not here.'

'So, let's get this straight,' I said. 'What you're saying is that in order to return and take control of the boardroom, Cobb, a seventy-two-year-old man with a bad leg and who walks with a stick, sneaked into Hercule's hotel room unnoticed and poisoned him?'

'Who knows how he did it?' Jill said. 'The fact is the Zanetti Board would never have voted Hercule out, not with his track record. He had to be got rid of some other way.'

No matter how much I tried to see things from Jill's angle, I just couldn't imagine friendly old storytelling Braxton Cobb slipping in unseen to Hercule's room and poisoning his champagne and oysters. Oysters? 'By the way,' I said, 'why didn't you tell me about the room service? And why would Hercule order champagne and oysters after all that had just happened?'

'What oysters?' Jill said.

'Findlay the butler took up room service after you'd left for the hairdresser. Didn't you see it when you came back?'

'I don't remember. When I found Hercule...' Jill covered her mouth with a hand and closed her eyes for a moment. 'When I saw him lying there I was in such a state I can't remember what I did, and then the police came.'

'Findlay says he brought champagne and oysters up to the room,' I said. 'He called it the Auld Alliance. Otherwise known as the lock-and-load.'

Bouncer came bounding out of the bushes and down the path. His coat was wet and his paws muddy. He jumped up at Jill, leaving mucky paw prints on her designer jeans. I chased him away.

'Robbie, what are you talking about?' Jill said, brushing mud from her legs.

'French champagne and Scottish oysters, the entente cordiale.'

'I got that,' she said. 'I'm talking about the lock-and-load.'

'It's what the Yanks call champagne and oysters. They're an aphrodisiac so ...'

Jill tilted her head back, looked up at the twilight sky and then at me. 'So, what you're saying is that Hercule had ordered champagne and oysters for me coming back?'

I'd hoped it was clear to Jill from the expression on my face that I really hadn't been trying to say anything of the sort.

'You know what this means?' she said, eagerly. 'The oysters. It would have been easy to poison them. Most barbiturates are water soluble and oysters are horrible slimy things. It would have been so simple for Braxton Cobb to walk in, all smiles and—'

'Kill Hercule?' I said. 'Then he wouldn't have minded killing you too. Don't you think that would have been a tad suspicious – you both dying in an apparent suicide pact?'

Jill had an answer for that too. 'Cobb must have known I wouldn't have eaten them.'

'Why would he? And why wouldn't you have eaten them?'

'I don't like oysters.'

'Then why would Hercule order a dozen? Do we even know if he ate one?' I asked.

Jill hadn't thought about that. 'That's your next line of enquiry,' she said. 'Find out if any of the oysters were eaten and where Cobb was when those oysters were being prepared and sent up.'

Tina appeared through the back door in her stocking feet and wearing her tomato sauce proudly like a novice after her first fox hunt. 'What are you doing?' she called to me.

'Just talking,' I said. 'Go back inside and put some shoes on.'

'Okay, what else have you got on Cobb?' Jill asked. From her tone of voice, she really believed we were getting somewhere with the Braxton Cobb as murderer scenario.

'How do I find out if the oysters were eaten?' I asked.

'Ask Findlay, of course.'

'Findlay's the butler, he probably took them up. If the oysters were poisoned who was in a better position to do it than him? Did he know you didn't like oysters? Jill, I'm afraid this is becoming weird. Face facts, you were going to be gone for two hours, champagne and oysters don't stay cold and fresh that long.'

'So, you're saying Hercule was going to drink the champagne and eat the oysters by himself when I was away?'

I put my hands on her shoulders. 'Yes, while you were away. No, not by himself.'

Jill frowned, puzzled.

'Oh, come on, Jill. Do I need to paint you a picture?'

'I could paint you a picture.' Tina had arrived unnoticed at our side wearing Joanna's wellies that were several sizes too big.

Jill wriggled free, took a step back. 'What are you suggesting?'

I sent Tina to find Bouncer and tie him up, so we could give him a wash before we let him in the house again. I waited until she'd scampered off.

'Let's look at the evidence, rationally and logically,' I said. 'When you left for the hairdresser that Friday afternoon, it gave Hercule two hours to himself. Except I don't think he intended to spend them by himself.'

Jill turned as though to walk away. I took her hand and pulled her back. She had to hear this. 'Why do you think there were empty champagne bottles in the room when you surprised him by arriving a day early? Why would he be lying on the bed in a dressing gown in the middle of the afternoon, pretending to read the notes of a speech he'd already given?'

'Pretending? You think ... You think he was having an affair. That there was another woman?' I didn't say it, but Hercule Mercier had been married twice before. He was rich, suave and sophisticated babe-magnet. He'd had no qualms at stealing my fiancée. The man was a walking affair.

Jill glared at me, on her tiptoes, pointing a finger in my face. 'I surprised him, remember? Where was this other woman? Hiding in the wardrobe?'

'No, Jill, you didn't surprise him,' I said. 'The person who surprised him was the person who had already brought your suitcases up to the room, which would have given Hercule just enough time to—'

Jill's slaps were getting harder. I think it was all the practice she was getting. I couldn't stop her leaving. I heard the engine of her car turning over as I walked to the back door and into the kitchen. I was clearing Tina's dirty dishes away into the sink when I heard Bouncer barking and a noise at the front door. Wiping my soapy hands on a towel, I walked down the hallway. 'Is that you, Jill?' I called.

'No,' a voice called back. 'It's me. Joanna.'

31

'And she kissed Dad twice, once there and once there,' Tina pointed to her cheeks in turn, 'and then she slapped him too.' We were sitting in the living room where Tina was providing my wife with a summary of what I'd been up to in her absence. We'd already covered the day I forgot to collect her from school, and had now moved onto my liaisons with other women. 'And he was dancing with a lady who was very sleepy on his shoulder, and we went to a fancy hotel and Uncle Malky said this beautiful lady was looking at him because he's more handsome than Dad, and she had big long legs and nice shoes, but she wasn't really looking at Uncle Malky, she was really looking at Dad, and so they went up to this big huge bedroom ...' Tina paused for the first time in a while, to catch her breath and throw her arms wide the better to demonstrate the vastness of the bedroom to which I and the beautiful woman had repaired. In doing so she bumped me, spilling some of my coffee. Fortunately, most of it landed on Bouncer who, hosed down and dried, was sitting at my feet. The dog yelped and moved to a safer location. 'And after that—'

'Joanna doesn't want to listen to all this,' I said, laughing, lifting Tina off Joanna's lap. 'Come on, time for your bath and then bed.'

'No, no, Robbie, do let her continue, please,' Joanna said.

'See, Dad?' Tina gave me a smug look. I soon wiped that off her face. 'Bath and bed or I'll tell Joanna what happened when you went to the toilet in the fancy hotel and what you found there. You remember what Joanna does for a living, don't you?'

Tina's face fell, and she trudged off towards the bathroom.

'How did you manage that?' Joanna asked.

'Do you know that fancy hotel she was talking about?'

'The one where you took the beautiful lady to the bedroom? Is that the same one where you also took Jill?' Joanna asked, smiling, well . . .sort of smiling.

'I can explain.'

'Plea in mitigation?'

'No, I'm confident I can provide a full defence.'

'You'd better.' Joanna put a clenched fist under my chin. 'What on earth happened to your head?'

'It's nothing. I tripped and fell on the stairs at Edinburgh Sheriff Court. You know what they're like, far too steep. But never mind that, how did you get on in The Hague? How fancy was *your* hotel? No expense spared by the Crown, I trust?'

'Hotel? Are you kidding? It was a glorified youth hostel and I had to share. Turned out the girl I was replacing had been taken into hospital with a burst appendix, so when I arrived the place was a tip and still full of her stuff. All her clothes were in the wardrobe, the bathroom was cluttered with make-up and all sorts. As for the drawers, they were full of fancy knickers and parachute gear.'

'Parachute gear?'

'You know, suspender belts, lingerie, all that kind of thing. She seemed to have a thing about frilly underwear, especially the colour red. Worst of all, my flatmate was a twenty-two-year-old paralegal who was looking for a new career as a glamour model. She'd had her boobs done, and I couldn't get a minute's peace for her prancing about topless looking at herself in the mirror.'

It sounded like hell.

Tina returned to say that the bath was running. After she'd been washed and put into her pyjamas, given her supper, read a bedtime story, tucked in, brought a glass of water, allowed back into the living room for a while to see Joanna again, removed from our bed where she'd accidentally strayed, taken back to her own bed for another very short story, followed by more tucking in, prayers and so on, I eventually managed to interpret my daughter's version of my visits to The Newberry.

'Firstly, the beautiful lady—'

'The one with the nice shoes?'

'Yeah, her. She used to be a man. Now she's a woman and happens to own the fancy hotel in question.'

'And the bedroom?' Joanna enquired.

'It was where Hercule died.'

'The same bedroom where you were with Jill when I called you that time?'

'Chiara...that's her name. She was asking for some information on Hercule's death. She knew I was advising Jill.'

'Robbie, to go to the bedroom with one woman when I'm in another country could be considered an accident, but two?'

'Actually, it was three. I went there with Fiona Faye too. We had dinner.'

'Let's get this straight. While I was away working, living like a nun—'

'And a nun took me to a bar for a drink. When I was

in Rome.' I might as well get it all out in the open at the one go. Joanna had the knack of finding out things that I'd thought were well hidden.

She screwed up her face in disbelief. 'You went to Rome?'

'Don't worry,' I said. 'It was business, someone else was paying for it all.'

'I'm guessing not one of your junkie clients or the Scottish Legal Aid Board.'

'No, it was Jill.'

'Jill? Why would she need you to go to Rome?'

'She's adamant that Hercule didn't commit suicide, despite what the medical evidence says. She sent me on a fact-finding mission.'

'Did she go too?'

'No, I went myself. It was just for one night.'

'And she paid for this? Stay in a fancy hotel there too, did you?'

'It was impossible finding anywhere cheap at such short notice.' Well, I was sure it would have been, if I'd bothered to try.

Joanna was serious now. 'Robbie, why haven't you told Jill to go for bereavement counselling of some sort? The woman's clearly in denial and highly vulnerable. She needs help. Goodness knows she can afford the best.'

'That's what I've been trying to do. I know Hercule killed himself. It's obvious. What I'm doing is humouring her, going through the motions. It's all therapeutic. Soon she'll come to her senses. It's just my way of letting her down gently.'

Joanna uncurled her legs. 'Well, considering the way she treated you, you probably earned a wee jaunt to Rome.' She leaned forward to give me a kiss as a seal of approval and then stopped and backed off. 'Okay, how much?'

'How much what?'

'How much are you screwing out of Jill for going on this crazy wild goose chase of hers?'

'What makes you think—'

'Robbie. How much?'

'Fifteen.'

'Fifteen.'

'Hundred?'

I shook my head.

'Fifteen thousand pounds! You've taken fifteen thousand pounds from that poor woman ...'

I took hold of Joanna and gave her a kiss. 'She's not poor, remember? And she practically forced the money on me.'

She pulled away. 'Oh, yeah, I can imagine how hard you must have fought back.'

I suggested she calm down, though in the history of husbands telling their wives to calm down I was unaware of any occasion when that had worked as a strategy.

'How can I calm down knowing that you've been stealing from a woman whose mind is unbalanced due to the death of a loved one?'

'Talking of loved ones,' I said. 'Did I mention how much I've missed you? Why didn't you call to say you were coming home today?'

Jill folded her arms and sat back, chin on her chest. 'It was supposed to be a surprise.'

'It was. The best surprise. Don't spoil it by worrying about Jill Green and her money. She'll miss fifteen thousand pounds like Donald Trump would miss fifteen thousand Mexican immigrants.' I drew Joanna closer and put an arm around her.

This time Joanna didn't resist. 'How's your dad's case going?' she asked. 'I've only heard snippets.'

Where to start? I couldn't help hearing the slurred words of Linda Duffy from the Fish Supper Ceilidh. 'I'd say anything for your dad.' Now wasn't the time to bring up my concerns. 'It's going as well as can be expected. He's due to go to court tomorrow to give a precognition-on-oath. The Crown already knows what he's going to say and it's ...' The words nearly caught in my throat. 'Supported by an independent witness. Long story short, I think he's in the clear.'

'That's a relief,' Joanna said.

'Tina's missed you, as you may have noticed from the fact that she wouldn't let go of you from the moment you returned.'

'I've missed her too. Did you mention anything to her about ...?'

'Calling you Mum? I've been trying. She'll come to grips with it, eventually. Perhaps not immediately.'

'It's all right. I'm not really that bothered ...' Joanna said, unconvincingly. 'I just thought it would be nice if ...'

I gave her a squeeze. 'It'll take time. She's just a wee girl.'

'I know she is, but, Robbie, we've been living here as a family for over a year. And, remember, we were together for a good while before that.'

I could sense things were starting to verge towards the emotional. 'Look at the time. It's nearly nine o'clock. How about I make you something to eat?'

Joanna got up of the couch 'No, thanks. I think I'll go to bed.'

'Good idea,' I said. 'Travel, it takes it out of you. You must be tired.'

Joanna looked down at me, took my hand and pulled me to my feet. 'No, not in the slightest.'

I can be slow on the uptake sometimes. But not always. We'd only just made it to the bedroom when there was a knock at the front door. I already had the shirt off my back and my trousers were round my ankles, so Joanna went to answer it.

'It's someone for you,' she said, when I met her in the hallway. 'Another of the many women in your life. Whoever she is, get rid of her,' Joanna whispered in my ear as she walked past me into the bedroom. 'I'm wearing parachute gear. It's red.'

The woman at the front door looked to be no more than early-twenties. She was very tall, and wearing an enormous overcoat that looked like it might be good for spending a cold night on the mountains. She had a strong face, a ruddy outdoor complexion and chestnut brown hair cut short and poking out from beneath a rather unflattering hand-knitted beanie. Gripped tightly in her right hand was a black canvas holdall. I was prepared to give her ten seconds to state her business before slamming the door in her face and charging back to the bedroom.

'Mr Munro?' she said. Her accent was not a local one. 'I saw you on television.'

Could it be true? Did I have my very own stalker?

'Do you know who I am?' she asked.

I hadn't a clue. 'Should I?'

'I don't know.'

'Well, if you tell me your name we'll soon find out, won't we?' I said. It was all becoming slightly surreal.

'I'm Emily Knox,' the young woman said. 'But I think I might really be Emily Foster.'

221

32

Joanna and I stayed up all Sunday night, but not for the reason I'd hoped.

Emily Knox, or Foster, had seen the *Night News* piece in which I appeared, and left Unst in a hurry to find me. It had taken a while, but she'd phoned around and eventually got my address from the police who kept a list of local lawyers' contact details. She'd brought a change of clothes with her, but no money for a hotel and so we agreed to put her up for the night, though not before we'd talked things over.

Emily had been four years old and something of a waif when she'd been abducted. That much I knew already. She had no recollection of the incident. Her first childhood memories were of growing up on a farm on the most northerly of the Shetland Isles, along with her mother and father, Bob and Betty Knox. She'd gone to the local school with twelve other pupils of various ages, left at the age of sixteen and now helped her parents run the family business of rearing sheep, inshore fishing for crab and lobster and growing ropes of mussels. She had a boyfriend who owned the neighbouring farm, and, by the way her eyes sparkled when she spoke of him, I strongly suspected there would one day be a unification of their respective lands.

We sat around the kitchen table. Emily hadn't eaten

since leaving home and I was getting stuck into some tea and buttered toast. The obvious question was asked by Joanna. 'What makes you think you're Emily Foster?'

'It was the television programme about the murder of three children in Linlithgow,' she said. 'When they showed the picture of the swing park, I had ... I don't know what you'd call it.'

'A flashback?' Joanna suggested.

'Yes, as soon as I saw it I thought I recognised it, but I didn't know why. I've never set foot out of Shetland.'

'These things happen,' I said. 'It's like déjà vu, no one can explain it.' For my dad's sake, the last person I wanted this young woman to be was Cammy Foster's not-so-dead sister.

'I know,' she said, chewing toast. Her fourth slice. 'It was such a strange feeling, it made the hairs on the back of my neck stand up, but I wouldn't have thought too much about it if my mum hadn't reacted the way she did. She was sitting beside me, and as soon as the story about the murders came on, she was out her seat and trying to switch the telly off. I told her not to and she went and got my dad. He came through and was quite angry, and ...well ...'

'And what?'

'My dad is never angry. Not ever. When I was fifteen we were mucking-out a stable, and I accidentally stuck a fork through his foot. He was laid up for a fortnight, but never once said a cross word to me. My dad's the kindest man in the world.'

'But he was angry this time?' Joanna asked.

'He roared at me to turn the telly off, and ordered me to get to my bedroom like I was a child. He apologised later, but by then I'd seen a picture of the policemen who caught the murderer.' She rammed in the final crust like she was stoking a furnace. Even after she had chewed and swallowed it was obvious she was having difficulty speaking. Her eyes went misty. 'One of them was my Uncle Jock.' Joanna budged her chair along and put an arm around her.

'Jock Knox?' I said.

She nodded. 'My dad's brother. He used to come and visit us every summer and at New Year. He's in a home now. Mum and Dad go down to see him sometimes. They never let me go. I have to stay and watch the farm.'

'Your dad's giving a precognition-on-oath tomorrow,' Joanna didn't need to remind me, after Emily had phoned home to say she was safe and we'd packed her off to bed. 'If Emily Foster is alive...' She didn't have to say any more.

At ten o'clock the next day, my dad was going to swear an oath that he'd snatched Ricky Hertz's cigarette from his mouth and thrown it away only for Hertz to pick it up again and carelessly drop it later while abducting and murdering the woman who was asleep in our spare room. That was a story that had already been corroborated by Linda Duffy. It was a story that had now been blown wide open by the dead girl's miraculous resurrection.

Fortunately, Joanna had the next couple of days off. She was able to take Tina to school, come back and keep Emily under wraps while I charged through to Edinburgh Sheriff Court to intercept my dad.

I arrived around nine twenty-five and was walking into the agents' room, to hang up my coat, when I met Fiona Faye on her way out.

'What are you here for?' she asked.

'I need another adjournment.'

'Well, there are two flights of stairs between here and Court 6. Knock yourself out. Literally.'

I followed her out of the door. 'I mean it, Fiona, he's not ready.'

'Nonsense, he's perfectly ready. What's the problem? I've got the affidavit from the girl who got away. Your dad just has to say his piece, we'll get the precognition typed up, have the case call again in a day or two so he can sign it in front of the sheriff, and then we'll send it up to the chaps at the Appeal Court. We'll have Ricky Hertz back behind bars before the week's out,' she said, setting off at a trot to the ground floor.

I didn't catch up with her until we'd reached the basement, where I'd expected to see my dad, hanging around in the lobby outside Court 6.

'You do know you're not allowed in, don't you?' Fiona said.

'It's all right, I'm just going to wait here and catch my dad for a quick word.'

'It'll need to be quick then,' she said. 'The thing starts in a couple of minutes.'

'Half nine? I thought it was ten o'clock like the last time?'

'No, they moved it forward so that the remand court isn't too late in starting.' She pulled open the door to the courtroom and walked inside.

I skipped in after her looking for my dad. Apart from Fiona, who'd taken a seat in the deserted public gallery, there was only the clerk, a bar officer, the shorthand writer and Ricky Hertz's solicitor. I couldn't remember his real name, only that he called himself the Jail Lawyer and trawled the prisons looking for claims to raise under prisoners' rights. It was low-paid, legal aid work that meant long hours visiting prisons. You could just about scrape a living if you could be bothered spending more time behind bars than most of your clients. More annoyingly for some, was his habit of signing up life prisoners, requisitioning their files from their previous defence lawyers and sifting through the paperwork, looking for any sign, imaginary or not, that might allow an appeal on the grounds of defective representation. It was the Jail Lawyer who had championed Ricky Hertz's case and brought it to the attention of the SCCRC. I had to admit he'd done remarkably well to get it this far.

I turned and bumped into my dad. 'Where have you been?'

'The toilet,' he said. 'I had a cup of tea earlier and I don't know how long this will take. You lawyers are good at dragging things out when you're being paid by the minute.'

I took a hold of him and manhandled him back out of the door. 'Come with me.'

'Where to?'

'The toilets.'

'I've just been.'

Keeping up my momentum, I shoved him across the lobby and into the Gents. There was one cubicle. I kicked it open to make sure it was empty. There was a ned sitting on the sink, rolling a joint. 'Beat it,' I said. He jumped down and left without a word. I caught a glimpse of my face in the mirror: unshaven, a sleepless night playing hoopla with my eyes and, to top it all, the stitched-up scar on my forehead. If I'd been him I'd have got out too.

'What's this all about, Robbie?' my dad said.

'You can't go in there and give a statement, Dad.'

'Why not?'

I looked him in the eye. 'You know why.'

'No, I don't. Everything's sorted. You said so yourself.'

'Well, everything has suddenly become unsorted,' I said.

A bar officer poked his head in. 'The sheriff's on the bench and wants to make a start.'

'Be right with you,' I called to him, and he retreated.

'Robbie, are you all right?' my dad said. 'You're looking a wee bit strange.' He tried to shove his way past me, but I didn't let him. 'Would you stop mucking about, Robbie? You heard the man, the court's starting. Let me get this over with.'

'I can't,' I said, 'there's been a change of plan.'

'I don't think so.' He took a hold of my upper arms, and tried to move me out of his way.

There was no time to get into a discussion, we'd only end up arguing and he'd never see things my way. If the sheriff was already on the bench, the bar officer would be back any second.

'Dad, remember that time you beat up Cammy Foster's dad?'

'What are you talking about?'

'Do you remember how you were in big trouble and Jock Knox helped you out?'

He released his grip on me. 'I've already told you, I'm not blaming Jock. I never was going to, and now there's no need.'

'And remember how you were always grateful to him?'

'Of course, I was, but why are you bringing this up now?'

'Because,' I said, pulling up the sleeve on my right arm and making a fist, 'I'm about to help you out of even bigger trouble.'

33

'Slipped and banged his head, did he?' Fiona Faye said, as we left Court 6. The hearing had been adjourned because my dad had sustained a facial injury. Although not requiring medical attention, it had left him shaken and unable to provide a precognition that day, or so I'd persuaded the presiding sheriff. 'You Munro boys sure are accident-prone.'

The Jail Lawyer was less understanding. 'If I find out this is a put-up job ...'

'What do you mean?' I asked. 'I've a good mind to tell my dad to sue this place. Blue light bulbs in the lavvies might stop the junkies finding a vein, but it also makes it impossible to see a puddle on the floor. No wonder he slipped.'

Jail Lawyer didn't reply, just pushed past us and headed up the stairs.

'How are your knuckles?' Fiona asked.

'Sore,' I replied, without thinking.

'You going to tell me why you did that?'

'No.'

'You'd better hope your dad won't report it.'

My dad hadn't been terribly happy at what had happened, that much he'd made very clear as I'd escorted him and his bleeding nose from the court building to an awaiting taxi, but he'd never rat on his own son. Even if he did, there were no witnesses. I hung around for a few minutes before setting off for the train myself. I didn't want to catch the same one as him. I was walking down George IV Bridge, past a café where J.K. Rowling was said to have written *Harry Potter*, and a few other cafés where it was alleged that she hadn't, when I met a familiar tweed suit barging through the other pedestrians on the narrow pavement. I had to put out a hand to stop him.

'It's you,' Prof. Bradley said, looking down at the hand in his chest, his remark as concise and scientifically accurate as were most of his medical opini#ons. 'Please don't say you want to ask me any more questions about dead people.'

'Why not? Everyone asks you questions about dead people,' I said. 'You're a pathologist. You live for dead people.'

'Seriously, Robbie, what is it?'

'Does it have to be something? Can't I just meet you in the street and say hello?'

'Hello, Robbie. Goodbye, Robbie.'

He would have walked on, had I not sidestepped into his way. 'But seeing as how you are here—'

'No.'

'You don't even know what I'm going to ask.'

'Yes, I do. You're going to ask me about that man Hercule what's-his-name.'

He was right. I was. 'No, I wasn't.'

'Oh, really?' He raised a disbelieving eyebrow.

'I was just wondering—'

'No. I've given you my opinion and I'm sticking to it.'

He shoved me aside, stepped to the kerb and waved at an approaching black taxi. It sailed past. 'By the way, how's your dad doing?' he asked, over his shoulder, eyes fixed on the road. 'I heard he'd got himself in a spot of bother over Ricky Hertz.'

'They're accusing him of fitting Hertz up for the murders,' I said.

'Well, if he did, good luck to him. Child murderers? Hang 'em, I say. Or, better still, let the parents have five minutes alone with them.' His next attempt at hailing a cab was more successful.

'Any chance of dropping me off at Waverley Station?' I asked, as the taxi slowed to a halt.

'Not headed that way. I'm going home.'

I knew the professor lived in Murrayfield. 'Haymarket's fine,' I said, pulling the door open. 'In fact, it's better.'

'I gave evidence at Hertz's trial,' Bradley said, trying to find the end of the seatbelt and eventually giving up. 'I carried out the post-mortem examinations of the children. Nasty. Both strangled and then, of course, there was all that stuff that was never mentioned at trial.'

'What stuff?'

'About the eyes.'

'Whose eyes?'

'The kids' eyes. They'd been removed, or, I should say, gouged out. The CID kept it strictly hush-hush so that Hertz might say something, and they could attribute a bit of special knowledge to him. He never said a word about it, and, since it hadn't been a cause of death, the Advocate Depute didn't think it necessary to lead it at the trial. It would just have meant upsetting the parents for nothing.'

I still wasn't sure why the professor was so certain of Hertz's guilt.

He explained. 'After he was convicted, they carried out

a psychiatric assessment. They usually do those before the trial nowadays. Anyway, I spoke to the shrink who did it. She's dealt with some real nut jobs over the years, folk who'd stick an axe in your head if you looked at them sideways. She said Hertz was a right weirdo. He never made eye contact at any time during the interview, to the extent that she was convinced he had ommetaphobia.

'What's that?'

'A fear of eyes. I thought you were a Latin scholar?'

It was true. My CV did proudly bear a band one standard grade in Latin. 'Phobias are Greek,' I said. 'If ommeta means eyes, it would be ocular or something like that in Latin, but, so what? He doesn't like to look people in the eye. I've noticed that for myself. It makes him a bit shifty, not a serial killer.'

Prof. B. held up a hand. 'Allow me to continue. When the shrink asked him about his views on children, all the usual stuff about whether he was sexually attracted to them, or bullied at school, he said he didn't like the way they *looked* at him.'

'Go on,' I said.

'What do you mean?'

'That's it? He said he didn't like the way kids looked at him? Hardly conclusive,' I said.

'I've just done telling you that the dead kids had had their eyes gouged out.'

I still didn't see it as a clincher on Hertz's guilt.

Prof. Bradley saw it differently. 'Maybe it's not enough for you lily-livered reasonable-doubters, but it's plenty good enough for me.' He snorted.

'What are you doing for lunch?' I asked.

'I have plans,' he said. 'They don't include you.'

'Shame. I was thinking about dropping into The

Newberry for a bite.'

The professor kept staring straight ahead. 'The Newberry? That some new sandwich bar is it?'

'No. *The* Newberry. It's a hotel, just off Charlotte Square.'

His face slowly broke into a smile, like someone had brought him a fresh one to carve up.

'Really? You can get us a table at The Newberry?'

Suddenly it was 'us'. I took my phone from my pocket. 'I could call ahead and let them know we're coming, but I'd hate to spoil your plans.'

'Plans? Oh, yes, plans. No, not at all, Robbie, my dear boy.' He wrapped an arm around my shoulders. 'Lunch with you is always a pleasure.'

34

'They seem to know you here.' Professor Bradley tucked a starched white napkin the size of a bed sheet down the front of his collar and allowed the waiter to place a bowl of lobster bisque before him. 'Come here often?'

'Only when I'm investigating murders that have been mistaken for suicides,' I said, once the waiter had left me a Caesar salad and drifted away.

'Hold on a minute, you told me you weren't going to ask about Hercule ...'

'Keep your voice down. This is where he died. He was their favourite guest.'

'He died here? In this hotel?'

'Yes, he was found dead in a room on the second floor.'

The professor sat back, spoon in hand. 'It's true what they say, then? There's no such thing as a free lunch.'

'Not at these prices, there's not,' I said.

Professor Bradley began buttering a piece of crusty bread. 'Okay, get it over with. Ask me.'

'If you were going to poison someone ...'

'I can think of one candidate,' he muttered.

'And all you were given was some barbiturates—'

'In what form?'

'Whatever form they come in.'

'They come in many forms. There are lots of different types of barbiturates. It's a general name for a wide range of drugs that suppress the central nervous system. There's always a chemist somewhere happy to string a few new molecules together.'

'Do they come in liquid form?'

'Could do. Most dissolve in water. There are tablets and capsules too. They come in all shapes and sizes.'

'And what do they taste like?'

'How the bloody hell should I know? Horrible, probably.'

'Do you think you would taste them if I put some in your soup?'

'I'm beginning to wish you would.'

The waiter came over to make sure everything was all right. It was, and he melted away.

'What about if they were crushed up or dissolved and put into oysters, would you notice the taste then?'

'I think that would depend on how fresh the oysters were. If they were fresh, I suppose you would, oysters are fairly bland.'

'What about in champagne?'

'Sorry, Robbie, I really, really don't know.'

'If you had to guess?'

'Not even if I had to guess.'

'Go on. Have a guess.'

'Yes, if you were sober, no if you were drunk. That do you?'

'Mr Munro, you are back again, I see.'

I turned to identify the source of the voice, though I didn't need to. Chiara De Rosa as elegant as ever, more formally dressed today in a white silk blouse and black skirt.

'I wonder if I might have a word,' she said, and, taking it for granted that she might, wandered over to the bar area.

I shovelled in a few forkfuls of lettuce, anchovies and croutons. 'You don't mind if I leave for a few minutes, do you?'

Prof. Bradley gave a light cough and leaned across the table. 'You do know, don't you? Your lady friend? Neatest chondrolaryngoplasty I've seen.'

'Neatest what?'

'Shaved trachea...Adam's apple.' The professor had scarcely looked up from his lobster bisque when Chiara approached, and yet he'd noticed what both Malky and I hadn't. 'You can bet she didn't get that done on the NHS,' he said out of the corner of his mouth. 'No wonder she's got a voice like honey on sandpaper.'

I got up and left him alone to his starter. He didn't have to look quite so pleased about me leaving. Over at the bar I pulled up the bar stool next to Chiara's. She really was a work of the surgeon's art.

'Lunch is on me,' she said.

'Lunch is on Jill Green,' I replied.

'Got you on a string, hasn't she?' Chiara nibbled casually on a Japanese cracker she'd taken from a small jade bowl on the counter top. 'I'd heard you'd been snooping around. How was Rome?'

'Rome was fine. Your great aunt certainly knows how to show a boy a good time – for a nun.'

'And my grandfather?'

'Doing fine. Still swinging a golf club.'

'Yes, well, Jesus might love him, but I think he's an idiot.' Chiara gently dusted salt off her fingertips. 'Still, I can blame the old bigot for a lot of things, but not for how much he loves my grandmother. Pathetic really. She was so strong once. Now she just wants to die. He should let her go instead of prolonging the indignity.'

'He wasn't so keen on Hercule, though, was he?' I said, glancing over to where Professor Bradley was spooning in the lobster bisque between mouthfuls of buttered baguette. 'Or on you, for that matter.'

Chiara said nothing. She carefully selected another cracker and popped it into her mouth. The barman came over and she ordered a glass of Prosecco. I was making do with water.

'Makes you wonder, doesn't it?' I said.

'What does?'

'Why a man who never leaves his wife, comes to Edinburgh, supposedly to see a person he never speaks to, all on the same day the person he doesn't like most in the world dies of suspected barbiturate poisoning?' Subtlety didn't feature largely on the Robbie Munro résumé.

'When you put it like that...'

'I do put it like that. So does Jill Green. Hercule either took his own life when Jill was at the hairdresser, or else someone slipped him poison. Did you know that Hercule had ordered room service champagne and oysters?'

Chiara called over the barman who retreated into the shadows and whispered into a phone behind the counter. In less than a minute Findlay the butler materialised.

'Findlay, the day Mr Mercier died, did you take champagne and oysters to his room?'

Findlay recalled having done so. 'One dozen oysters and a bottle of the Bollinger eighty-eight, ma'am.'

'Who took them away again?' I asked.

'Again, sir, it was I. After the police had left. They took a statement from me. They even counted the oysters. There were still twelve and one unopened bottle of champagne.'

With a smile and a nod from Chiara the butler was gone.

'Do you trust him?' I asked.

'If by that you mean do I trust Findlay sufficiently not to kill the guests, then, yes, implicitly.'

That left Braxton Cobb. The one person with a motive, the means and the opportunity. It was true what Fiona had told me. Find those three things and find the killer.

'It wasn't my grandfather,' Chiara said, reading my mind.

'Why not? He's the man with the motive according to your sainted aunt Emanuela. As for the means, he's not only connected to a pharmaceutical company, but his wife is terminally ill. Her room is like a hospital ward. There are all sorts of drugs lying about the place. It also looks like he had the opportunity.'

'Motive, certainly,' Chiara said, receiving a flute glass of fizzy white wine. 'Means, possibly.' She took a sip. 'But definitely not the opportunity.'

'He's got a bad leg, but he can still get about,' I said. He could have gone to Hercule's room and—'

'And what? Force-fed him an overdose of drugs?'

Chiara was right. I was starting to think like Jill. The man had killed himself. Just because she didn't like the idea, why should I start trying to blame other people? So what Braxton Cobb didn't approve of Hercule's business practices? It didn't make him a murderer.

'He wasn't here,' Chiara expanded. 'Oh, I know Findlay gave you a list of room reservations for that weekend, but what he didn't mention, because you didn't ask, was that my grandfather didn't actually stay here. He called off at the last minute when he thought my grandmother had taken a turn for the worse.'

Was she covering for the old man? I couldn't help myself. Maybe I had started thinking like Jill because of all the money she'd given me to find a culprit, and maybe it was because the sum total of my investigations had come to zip, but I had to ask the question. 'If the two of you don't get along, why did he arrange to come here in the first place?'

'Because I told him I was thinking of selling The Newberry. I knew he wouldn't like that.'

'Are you thinking of selling?'

'No, of course not.'

'Then why?'

'So Hercule could visit Luciana. She's very sick. He thought it might be the last time he ever saw her, and didn't want my grandfather hanging around, which he would have been. Whenever he went to see her, Braxton was always there telling Hercule what he should be doing, and how he was bringing shame on the company.'

'So, when Braxton called off, Hercule stayed here and killed himself. Is that what you're saying?'

'No, it's not. Not at all.' Chiara took another sip of fizz. 'I know Hercule would never do such a thing. He loved Luciana, but he was happy and too madly in love with someone else to take his own life.'

'I'm sure Jill would be pleased to know that.'

'No, she wouldn't.' Chiara downed the last of her Prosecco, placed the tall glass on the counter top and lowered herself from the bar stool. 'For you see, he was madly in love with me.'

35

I returned home straight after lunch.

'What happened?' Joanna asked, the minute I walked in the door.

Without going into any detail, I explained that my dad's hearing had been postponed. I didn't mention my lunch at The Newberry or the further investigations I'd been making on behalf of Jill. The mystery of the oysters and champagne had been solved. Chiara and Hercule were having an affair. Coming out of his hypo, Hercule had ordered the 'lock-and-load' to continue their liaison while Jill was away for a cut and tint. The man was a machine. Except, something had prevented him from making the call to Chiara to give her the all-clear, and due to Jill's surprise arrival, Chiara had assumed all bets were off. It didn't matter if the oysters were poisoned because no one had eaten any. We were back to square one. Either Hercule had killed himself or ...what? Death by Ninja?

I still had investigations to make, if Jill was to be kept happy, but no time right then to make them because my wife had been carrying out some investigations of her own.

'She *is* Emily Foster. I'm sure of it,' Joanna said, keeping me in the hallway. 'Emily Knox's birth wasn't registered until she was four years old.' By law, births in Scotland had to be registered within twenty-one days. It was a criminal offence to delay. 'Her dad, if that's what you want to call him, Robert Knox, appeared at Lerwick Sheriff Court in two thousand and one, charged with a contravention of section fifty-three of the Registration of Births, Deaths and Marriages (Scotland) Act 1965. It's not that unusual up there. There are a lot of farmers and crofters in out-of-the-way areas with more pressing things on their minds than filling in forms about the latest baby. And it's two ferry trips each way from Unst to the Registrar's Office in Lerwick. There are even some parents who refuse to register because they don't want their children registered as British. Anyway, he was fined the maximum, one thousand pounds. It's the only conviction on his record. It can't be a coincidence?'

'Joanna,' I said, putting an arm around her. 'This isn't something you can be involved in any more. I don't want you to feel duty-bound to make a report.'

'I'm not going to—'

'But you might feel obliged the more we explore things. It's better if you stay out of it. If there is any backlash at all then I should take it. It's my dad we're talking about.'

I went through to the living room. Emily was pacing up and down, deep in thought, daytime TV blazing away in a corner, unnoticed.

'We need to get out,' Joanna whispered in my ear.

I agreed. Emily didn't look like the sort of girl who spent a lot of time indoors. We told her we were going for a walk, and picked Tina up from school at three o'clock. There was only one place Emily wanted to go. Philip Avenue swing park. I wasn't keen, though the chances of someone recognising our visitor after seventeen, nearly eighteen, years weren't high.

'Is this the place? It's quite small, isn't it?' Emily said, after Tina had raced off to a set of swings, Joanna following to give her a push, but really to leave the two of us alone. She looked around some more and then shook her head. 'I don't remember it.' She walked into the centre and turned three hundred and sixty degrees. 'I don't remember any of it.'

'The last time anyone saw you was here, around nine o'clock on the night you went missing. After that, nothing. When the park was searched for clues the next day, they found quite a few cigarette butts. One of those was the same brand smoked by a man called Ricky Hertz. His fingerprint was on it. A weather report suggested he must have dropped it here sometime during the period you went missing.'

'He's the man who was found guilty of taking me away?'

'And of murdering you,' I said. 'Along with the murder of two other children. He made a confession.'

'He confessed to murdering me?'

'Not you, the murders of the two other children. He didn't need to confess to yours. Not when his confession was taken along with the evidence of the cigarette butt which he couldn't explain.'

Bouncer was tugging at the lead, desperate to be set free and join Tina whose excited shouts, as she soared higher and higher, were ringing around the play park.

We walked over to a red metal bench next to the wall and sat down. Unlike Ricky Hertz, Emily was not scared of looking me in the eye. 'You say that my real mother is dead and that no one has seen my dad for years, but, my brother, what's he like?'

'Cammy's all right,' I said. 'I don't know much about him other than he sells electronic gadgets. We used to play football for the same team, but that was years ago, around the time when you went missing. I saw him recently. Before that, I hadn't seen him for years. Not since your funeral.' Emily's face twisted, I could tell she didn't know whether to laugh or cry. 'You already know, he's got himself into some bother with the police.'

She nodded. 'I saw it on the news. You went and rescued him.'

'Something like that.'

'Why did he do it?'

'Hertz has appealed and been let out of prison. They think the police may have framed him for the murders, yours...that is, Emily Foster's included. Cammy decided to take the law into his own hands. He went to Hertz's flat with a replica pistol.'

'Why would he do that?'

'Two reasons,' I said. 'One, he's a bit of an idiot. Two, I don't think he knew it was a replica. He was caught red-handed and is now on police bail awaiting a court appearance in a few weeks' time.'

'What'll happen?'

'I'll tell the court he knew the gun was a replica and say that he only wanted to give Hertz a fright. He'll probably still get the jail, but, hopefully, they'll go easy on him in the circumstances. There was no actual harm done.'

'What should I do? Would it help if I came forward and told the truth?'

'It'll make no difference to Cammy if you come forward. Whether you are alive or dead, he shouldn't have done what he did. The fact that you are alive, and he was seeking revenge for your death, might actually make it worse.'

'But he'd be happy to know I'm alive?'

242

I knew Cammy would be delighted. So would Ricky Hertz's lawyers. Not so my dad or the Appeal Court.

Tina, who'd had enough swinging, had jumped off and was now clambering all over the climbing frame.

Joanna walked over and stood beside us. 'You two come to a decision about what to do?'

'I was asking Robbie if it wasn't better that the truth came out,' the young woman replied.

'That's not the sort of question you ask a lawyer,' Joanna said. 'Especially a defence lawyer.' Which I thought was rich coming from a member of the Crown Office and Procurator Fiscal's Office, the mob who'd prosecuted Hertz and had him convicted of at least one murder he hadn't committed.

I gave Joanna the end of Bouncer's lead and sent her away again. I had to agree with her. In this instance the last thing I wanted, for my dad's sake, was the truth coming out.

'The truth is all very well and good, Emily,' I said, 'but it doesn't always help for people to know it.'

'It's Cameron . . .' she said. 'I'd hate for him to spend the rest of his life thinking his sister is dead.'

'Then,' I said, 'you'd better weigh up which thing you'd hate the most.'

'What do you mean?'

I had thought Joanna might have discussed this topic with her while I'd been in Edinburgh that morning. She hadn't. 'The question you're going to have to ask yourself is whether you want to cheer up Cammy or ruin your adoptive parents' lives.'

The young woman looked puzzled. Why, I didn't know. It seemed perfectly obvious.

'Your real parents were a pair of wasters,' I said. 'Your

dad was a violent bully who was run out of town, and your mum was an alcoholic who couldn't look after herself far less a four-year-old. The fact you were taken away and cared for by another family, a real family, people who loved you and still love you like their own daughter, none of that will make any difference. Not to a court of law. The cold truth is that your Shetland parents were party to your abduction and have kept you for nearly eighteen years. I can't even begin to count the number of laws they've broken, and to make things worse, all that time a man has been serving life imprisonment because of your alleged death. Do you know how stupid that would make the Crown Office look? Do you think they'll recommend leniency for your parents? I promise you this, if you come out now with the truth, your parents are going to prison, and I doubt very much if they'll ever come out again unless it's inside a box.'

She looked surprised. Why? What had she been thinking about all day, pacing up and down my living room, wearing out the carpet – the price of whole haddock? Her face stiffened, she frowned and then burst into tears.

Joanna came marching over. 'That's enough, Robbie.' She handed me Bouncer's lead and, pulling me roughly to my feet, took my place on the bench next to Emily and put an arm around her.

I wandered off to see Tina. I'd learned from bitter experience that no good comes of trying to console a crying woman or arguing with my wife.

'What's wrong with Emily?' Tina asked, kamikaze-ing down the chute towards me, making me step out of the way quickly to avoid bruised shins.

'I think she misses her mum,' I said. 'You missed your mum, when she was away the last three weeks, didn't you?'

'My mum's dead.'

It was worth a try.

My phone buzzed. Malky. 'You punched him?'

'It was more of a wee jab,' I said, in mitigation.

Malky laughed. 'You actually punched Dad?'

'How is he?'

'Fine. He's taking the whole thing very well.'

'Is he?'

'No. Not at all.'

'Put him on, I have to tell him something.'

'He's not here right now,' Malky said. 'He's in your toilet looking at his injured nose. But, once you get back home I think you'll find he's got a few things he'd very much like to say to you.'

36

My dad and Malky had let themselves in and were waiting for me in the kitchen, the place where all important matters of state were discussed.

'What else could I do?' I said, getting my retaliation in first. The two of them were sitting at the table drinking cups of tea. I'd asked Joanna to keep Tina and Emily out of the way. My dad turned around when he heard my voice.

'What else could you *do*!' he roared.

'I was trying to help you, and you weren't taking my advice.'

'If that's what he does to you, Dad,' Malky said, 'just be thankful you're not one of his legal aid clients.'

'Practically took my head off!'

'It was a jab. Just enough to—'

'The thing will hardly stop bleeding,' he said, prodding his nose with a tissue.

'Then stop poking at it. It looks fine to me,' I said.

He dabbed his nose a few more times, examined the snow-white hanky, grunted and stuffed it back into his pocket. 'And now I've got to go back again and give my statement in front of three High Court judges.'

There'd been no time to arrange another precognition-on-oath hearing prior to Hertz's final appeal. It would have involved not only my dad giving his evidence before the sheriff, but for the shorthand notes to be extended and then a further court attendance so my dad could read over and sign the transcript in front of a sheriff. So, unusually, it had been decided to hear his evidence on the day of the appeal and then the judges would move seamlessly on to reaching a verdict on Hertz's conviction, and whether it had been safe or a miscarriage of justice.

It smacked of a foregone conclusion having been reached. The Appeal Court judges would already have had access to Linda Duffy's affidavit, and been tipped off as to what to expect my dad to say. In true Appeal Court style, they'd accept everything the ex-cop had to say as being gospel and conclude that even if the jury had heard about his DNA on the cigarette, my dad's explanation would have neutralised any advantage for the defence, and made no difference to the guilty verdict.

Little did they know that wee Emily Foster had neither been abducted nor murdered, but lifted by Jock Knox and dropped off somewhere on the Shetland archipelago, where she'd lived the life of a crofter for the past eighteen years. It certainly beat being left to roam the streets with only a violent father and an alcoholic mother to go home to.

I went over to the sink and filled the kettle. 'Then you're going to need a better story to tell them.'

'I've got a perfectly good story. And it's backed up by Linda Duffy!'

'I know,' I said, lifting some mugs down from a cupboard. 'She told me at the Ceilidh. *Your dad's a great guy. I'd say anything for that man.*'

It wasn't a great female impersonation, but, then, I hadn't had my Adam's apple shaved. Whatever, it caused my dad to explode out of his seat, the chair wobbled and tipped over, clattering on the stone floor. 'Are you calling me a liar?'

Calling police officers liars was part of my job description. On this occasion I thought it better to remain silent and let him calm down. It didn't work. He came rushing over to me, red-faced and moustache all a quiver.

Joanna appeared in the doorway carrying a whisky bottle and glass. 'Would you like a wee drink, Alex?' She stepped between us, allowing me to make a dignified retreat.

'Robbie got this for his birthday,' she said, tearing the foil from around the cork. 'I think it's quite a nice one.'

'I'm not wanting whisk ...' My dad took the bottle from her. 'Benromach fifteen-year-old?' He sniffed and gave his nose a rub. 'I suppose it might help ease the pain.'

There was only one way to find out. He took bottle and glass through to the living room with him.

Joanna waited until he had gone and closed the kitchen door. 'Really? You punched your own father?'

'What else was I supposed to do?'

'Not punch him,' was the best Joanna could come up with.

'Don't pretend you haven't thought about doing a lot worse to him,' I said.

'Thinking about it and doing it are two different things, Robbie. Why on earth would you do something like that?'

'I couldn't help it. He wouldn't listen, and I'd run out of ideas.'

'Run out of brains more like,' she said.

There was the sound of happy shouts from outside where Emily was playing with Tina and Bouncer. I looked out. It was the first time I'd seen the young woman smile since her arrival.

Malky, who was still sitting at the table drinking tea and enjoying every minute of my domestic crisis, laughed. 'Nice work, Joanna. Can you believe how easily Dad can be distracted by a bottle of whisky? I mean, one minute he's shouting at Robbie, and the next he's—' Something rattled off the kitchen window. Malky looked out. 'Oh, was that a football?'

'What are you going to do?' Joanna asked, after Malky had exited by the back door. She was about to find out. My dad returned, carrying a large glass of whisky that I was sure had been even larger when he poured it. 'What was that noise just now?'

'It's just Tina outside playing football with her pal,' Joanna said.

I walked over to him. 'Sorry for hitting you, Dad. I should have thought of some other way to have the hearing put off.'

'Aye, one that didn't involve me getting punched or you diving down a set of stairs would have been nice,' he said.

'What's he talking about, Robbie?' Joanna said. 'I thought you tripped?'

'Part of that wasn't true,' I said.

'Which part?'

'The tripping part.'

'You threw yourself down a flight of stairs to get an adjournment?'

That was sufficiently accurate not to require a reply.

'I've had it,' Joanna said. 'I don't want to know any more about this.'

'Then you could always stop eavesdropping,' I ventured.

She gave me a shove in the chest. 'If I hadn't been eavesdropping earlier you and your dad would be rolling around on the floor by now. But I'm only too happy to let the two of you sort it out yourselves, if that's what you want.' She was the next to leave by the back door.

I took my dad by the arm and led him to the kitchen table and we both sat down. 'We need to talk.'

He put a hand in his pocket, pulled out the silver box Tina had misappropriated and slid it across the table to me.

'Not about that,' I said.

'Yes, about this. Have you punished her yet?'

I hadn't.

'Why not?'

'Because she's only six. She's had a big row from you and a good talking-to from me. I think I'll let it go at that. Call it an admonition. I'm sure she'll not do it again,' I said.

He seemed grudgingly satisfied with that, but only, I was sure, because it was his granddaughter. With anyone else, my dad's view on petty thieves was only marginally more lenient than Lord Braxfield's: 'Hang a thief when he's young and he'll not steal when he's old.'

The ball ricocheted off the window again. My dad got up from the table, went over and peered out. 'Big pal for a six-year-old to have.'

'She's just visiting,' I said. 'Came all the way from Shetland. Your old pal Jock Knox was a Shetlander, wasn't he?'

He took a sip of whisky. 'That he was.'

'Maybe you'd like me to introduce you to his niece.'

He almost spilt his drink. Almost. Not quite. 'That's Jock's niece? What's she doing here?'

'She saw me on telly the other night talking about Ricky Hertz and saw a picture of Jock.'

'And she came all this way to see you? Well, well. Jock's

niece. She's a strapping big girl, I'll say that for her.' He took another drink from his whisky glass. 'It's a small world, eh?'

'No, Dad,' I said, 'it's a very big world. Big enough for Emily Foster to stay hidden for eighteen years.'

My dad took some time to absorb what I had just said, then he poured the remainder of the whisky down his throat, walked back to the table and sat down heavily. 'Shit.'

'My sentiments exactly,' I said.

He looked at the floor and shook his head. 'It was Jock. He took her and gave her to his brother to look after. Why didn't he tell me?'

'What would you have done if he had?'

'I don't know, but what am I going to do up at the High Court the day after tomorrow?'

'Don't worry. I've got a plan.'

'I thought you might have.'

'Yeah, I'd call it plan B, but for the fact it's the same plan I've had all along, so, strictly speaking, it's still plan A. You're going to have to grass on Jock Knox.'

'What about Linda Duffy?'

'She'll be fine,' I said. 'Her story will still stand. Big Jock must have taken the cigarette from Hertz's pack when he was arrested and planted it later at the scene.'

'And that would be me and Linda in the clear? What about Hertz?'

'Dad, Hertz had nothing to do with Emily's disappearance.'

'Aye, but there was another two weans before her.'

'He's going free, Dad. There's no corroboration once Emily's charge is scrubbed.'

'But he confessed.'

'Did he? Did Hertz actually tell you he'd killed those other two children?'

The expression of pain on my dad's face was more profound than when I'd punched him in it.

'Well, did he?'

'Not exactly.'

'How not exactly?'

'You know. Not in so many words.'

'Dad, confessions are all about words. If he didn't use words, what did he do? Admit his guilt through the medium of dance?'

He pulled the bottle across the table and poured himself more of my whisky. 'We'd tried everything to get Hertz to talk, but he wouldn't say a word. He just sat there looking smug.'

'Please don't tell me you verballed him,' I said, though why wouldn't he have? My dad was the man who'd taught Dougie Fleming everything he knew about police work, and Fleming with his legendary notebook was a master of literary fiction.

My dad looked at me in horror. 'Of course not. Hertz confessed.'

'That's a relief,' I said.

'Just not to me. To Jock.'

I didn't understand. 'I thought you were both present at the interview?'

'We were. It was when we were going to book him out, grounds no longer exist, that he whispered something in Jock's ear.'

'Whispered? Whispered what?'

'I don't know. That's why he was whispering, so only Jock would hear it. He thought he was so smart, but Jock remembered what he said and wrote it down in his notebook—'

'The confession?'

'Aye.'

'And you signed it?'

'Why wouldn't I?'

'Because you never heard him confess, that's why not!'

My dad looked at me as though I was hard of thinking. 'But Jock heard him. I worked with that man for over twenty years, and, let me tell you, he didn't have a dishonest bone in his body.'

'Dad, he stole a child!'

'I don't care. I'd have trusted him with my life.'

Was I really hearing this? I grabbed the bottle and poured myself a large one. Joanna, who was taking nothing to do with it all, just happened to be looking in the window at the time. She rapped on the glass. I waved her away and took a slug.

Joanna, who'd had enough of being happy to let the two of us sort it out ourselves, marched in through the back door. 'Okay, what's going on?'

'You don't want to know,' I said, which was easier than telling her that not only had a man spent the best part of eighteen years of a life sentence for the murder of a girl who was still very much alive, but also for the murder of two other girls based on his whispering sweet nothings into the ear of a dementia patient.

Joanna read my face and decided that she really didn't want to know. 'Emily is leaving. Her boyfriend is coming down and they're going back home together. If anyone asks, she was visiting her uncle. She's Emily Knox and she's going to stay that way.'

It was good to know, if not unexpected. Cammy Foster might be her brother, but really to her he was just a man; one who'd suffered the grief of having lost a little sister many years ago, it was true, but his happiness at learning that his sister was alive, was grossly outweighed by the prison sentences her parents would undoubtedly receive if the truth came out.

'Now that we know for certain that this is all Jock Knox's fault,' I said to my dad after Joanna had rejoined the others outside, 'there's absolutely nothing to stop you blaming him for planting that cigarette butt.'

'And let Hertz go free? I don't think so.'

'Dad, he's done eighteen years.'

'And so he should have. He's a murderer.'

'No, Dad, his conviction was based on fabricated evidence. He should never have gone to prison in the first place.'

'That's as maybe.' He poured himself another large measure. 'But come Wednesday, after I've given my evidence, he'll be going back inside to do the rest of it.'

37

I set off for work next morning, bleary-eyed and believing myself beyond even the restorative powers of one of Sandy's Americano-and-crispy-bacon-roll specials. Still, it was worth a try.

It had been another long sleepless night. I was sure Emily Foster would keep quiet. Joanna, who was speaking to me again, was not so certain, believing that once her parents were dead, the newspapers would pay big money for a girl back from the dead story and she might cash in. Or what if she told her boyfriend, swore him to secrecy and then they split up? Word might very well come out that we'd known about the situation and did nothing. Not a big problem for me. I had no obligation to do anything, but for Joanna, a representative of the COPFS, the idea that she had not divulged knowledge that could have prevented a miscarriage of justice was unthinkable.

I'd promised I would sort it. The way I saw things, if it was all Jock Knox's fault and Hertz was freed after appeal, it would make no difference if word of Emily's non-death leaked out in the future. And what could anyone prove about Joanna's knowledge, anyway? She had plausible deniability. That was why I'd done my best to keep her out of my discussions with Emily. There would be no inquiry. Not unless Hertz went back to prison. Only then, if the true facts came out, would there be a major investigation.

It meant that my dad couldn't be allowed to testify the story that so conveniently meshed with Linda Duffy's recollection of events. He had to grass on Jock Knox.

But the thing that had kept me awake most was the thought that Hertz *had* actually confessed the murders to Jock. If so, and my dad blamed his old police buddy, a child murderer would be on the loose again. Had eighteen years inside been enough to rehabilitate him?

'What's a matter you?' Sandy asked, from behind the counter, wiping his hands on a damp tea towel. Sandy liked to put on the Italian accent for the sake of the non-regular customers. 'You looka like you huvnae slept for a week.' It needed work.

He shoved a cardboard cup of coffee and a bacon roll in a greasy brown paper bag at me across the counter.

'Sandy,' I said, 'you wouldn't happen to know how I could get hold of Cammy Foster?'

He could. By the throat was his preferred option. 'Mind that time he came in here a few weeks ago? He never paid. Said he'd be back. Not a sign of him since. Chancer.'

I left. It was nine o'clock, and I had cases calling in court at ten. I was halfway to my office when I heard Sandy calling to me from the door of the café. I walked back to see what the problem was.

'Here,' he said, handing me a white paper bag.

'What is it?'

'Some empire biscuits. They're going soft, but it would be a shame to throw them out. I can't give them to real customers, so you can have them.' He produced something else: a business card. 'I forgot I had it,' he said, tucking it into the top pocket of my jacket. 'Cammy gave it me. Said he could sell me security cameras to watch the till in case anyone sneaked in when I was in the kitchen.'

At the moment Sandy's security system was a wee bell above the door that rang if anyone came in. 'If you're speaking to him, tell him I want my money!' he yelled, diving back into the café, while I continued the walk along the High Street, trying to drink my coffee and take bites from my bacon roll without dropping either them or the bag of biscuits.

At the office, Grace-Mary was lying in wait for me in reception. 'Look at the state of you,' she said, inspecting me like I was a suspect side of pork. 'You look like you've died and nobody's broke the news to you yet. And if you don't get that dressing changed you'll catch gangrene.'

'Nice to see you too,' I said. 'How's everything doing? I've brought some biscuits for your tea break.'

'Don't think you can butter me up with biscuits,' she said, taking the bag from me and having a squint at the contents. 'What you been doing recently? I've not seen hide nor hair of you. I'd almost forgotten you were running this law firm.'

'Then maybe this will help you remember,' I said, spreading Jill's two cheques across the reception desk. 'Bank these, will you?'

'Fifteen thousand?' Grace-Mary studied the cheques more carefully. 'From Jill Green? What did you do to earn this?'

'Fear not,' I said. 'There was no more hugging involved. My honour remains intact. I didn't have to sell my body.'

'If you did you were vastly overcharging.' She took the bank pay-in book from the drawer and began writing out a slip.

'Thanks for holding the fort while I've been busy,' I said. 'Give yourself a bonus this month.'

Grace-Mary looked up. 'A bonus? You not being around I can handle. Fifteen thousand pounds for doing

257

nothing, that's not normal, but a staff bonus too? Did they move April Fool's Day without telling me?'

'Well, if you don't want it ...'

'How much?'

'What do you think?' I asked.

'Five hundred?'

'It's a bonus, not a lottery win. How does two fifty sound?'

'Like tinnitus. Let's split the difference and call it three seven five, net of tax.'

'But that's—'

'Don't go hurting your brain with arithmetic at this time of the morning.' Grace-Mary stood and handed me some case files. 'Now quit hanging about here like a damp duffle coat. You've court in half an hour. What's the matter with you?'

'I've a lot on my mind,' I said.

'So? You've always got a lot on your mind. Your mind usually just ignores it and hopes whatever it is goes away.'

'This won't go away,' I said. 'It's more of an ethical dilemma.'

Grace-Mary looked at me as though there was a Christmas cracker somewhere missing a bad joke. 'Ah, well ... I suppose there's a first time for everything.'

She probably said more. I wasn't listening. I could not get it out of my head that in the eyes of the law Ricky Hertz was an innocent man. Whether he'd committed the murders or not, there was barely a scrap of evidence against him. How could I stand back and let an innocent man go to prison for the rest of his life? How could I forgive myself if he was released and another child was murdered?

'I'll not be back today,' I said, having filled my briefcase with the files for court that morning.

'Why not?' Grace-Mary asked. 'You've only got a few cases, you should be able to rattle through them by lunchtime, no trouble at all.'

'I've some business to attend to.' I laid Cammy Foster's business card down on the desk. 'Get him on the phone. Tell him I want to meet him in the Red Corner bar at one o'clock and that he's to bring some of his gadgets with him. Say that I think my wife's having an affair. He'll know what to do.'

'Robbie, no. Not Joanna.' Grace-Mary folded her arms and pursed her lips. 'Well, don't say I never warned you . . .'

'But you didn't warn me.'

'I must have. Holland? You know what they're like over there. It's all free love and cannabis scones with that lot.'

'Doesn't matter. She's not having an affair. I've no time to explain. Just pass the message on. He'll know what to do.'

The phone warbled. 'Messrs R. A. Munro and Co.,' Grace-Mary sang into the receiver. She listened for a moment and then clamped her hand over the mouthpiece, waited and then resumed the call. 'I'm afraid Mr Munro has left for court. Yes, certainly, I'll pass the message to him. Goodbye.' She hung up and then taking a wire basket full of mail from the desk made to do some filing.

'Well?' I said.

'Are you still here?'

'Yes, and I'd like to know who that was and what the message is.'

'It was Jill Green,' Grace-Mary said, yanking the drawer of a filing cabinet open. 'She's staying at some hotel or other in Edinburgh and wants to see you.'

'When?'

'She didn't say.'

'Then do a one four seven one and call her back. Say I'll try and be there just after six tonight.' That way I could be home at a reasonable hour and Joanna needn't know. I didn't want her to think I was still fleecing Jill for money, even though staff bonuses didn't fund themselves.

Yes, I thought the time was right for me to tell Jill the brutal truth. Hercule wasn't murdered. The reason he came to Edinburgh so often was to see Chiara. He was having an affair. Jill had caught them by surprise that Friday afternoon. When she'd gone to the hairdresser, Hercule had intended to resume where he'd left off assisted by a lock-and-load. The only person with a motive to kill Hercule was Jill if she'd known of his infidelity. I was quite convinced she hadn't a clue about it. Why else would she insist on me investigating Hercule's death, when, so far as the authorities were concerned, it was an open and shut case of suicide?

I'd said all along that Hercule had killed himself. Why, I didn't know, and, frankly, I didn't care. Maybe he felt guilty, torn between two lovers, and living a lie. Maybe he was depressed. Who knew all the reasons people killed themselves? The fact was that plenty did. With Jill out of the way I could concentrate on what to do about my dad.

'There are those who'd think it was you having an affair,' Grace-Mary said.

'Well, I'm not, so don't bother telling Joanna where I'm going or who I'm going to see.'

Grace-Mary slotted a few letters away and slammed the drawer shut.

'Don't worry,' she said. 'Some might think it. I know there couldn't possibly be two women in the world daft enough to want you.'

38

One o'clock. So far, so good. I'd finished court in record time, had the dressing on my forehead changed and nipped home to collect the silver box that I intended to smuggle back into Jill's toilet when I went out to see her.

Not for the first time I wondered what was in the box. More business cards? An emergency sewing kit? Worst case, some credit cards? Strange place to keep it – in the toilet. It was none of my business, so I thought I'd take a look. How had Jill opened it? She'd pressed a corner down to start with, I remembered that, but which one? And there'd been a sequence to it as well. Had she pushed the clasp up first of all, or sideways, or down? I gave up after a few attempts. The contents couldn't be anything too important. If so, Jill would have noticed it gone and reported the theft. Other than myself, the only people who'd been in Hercule's suite in Jill's absence were the hotel owner and Fiona Faye Q.C. I thought it unlikely either of those two would be suspects. Of course, Chiara knew that Tina had also been there, but I could hardly rat out my own daughter. There was no need for the world to know I was bringing up a criminal mastermind. I'd been fortunate so far; nonetheless, Jill had been back from Switzerland nearly a week and it would surely only be a matter of time before the box was missed. I had to replace it as soon as possible.

Cammy Foster was waiting for me at a table in the Red Corner Bar, sipping on a Jack Daniel's and Coke, a large aluminium briefcase on the floor by his side.

'It's always the husband who's last to know, isn't it?' he said, lifting the case onto the table and springing the locks on his case.

'If it is,' I said, 'I still don't know.'

'But your secretary—'

'I told her to say that because I didn't want to let her or anyone else find out what I wanted to speak to you about.'

'But I've brought all this stuff. Are you telling me that you don't want to buy anything?'

'Not buy,' I said, 'borrow.'

'Then that's too bad because I don't hire. I sell.'

'That a fact? When are you up in court for that business with you at Ricky Hertz's place?'

'Two weeks.'

'Who's your lawyer?'

'Well...I thought...You?'

'Then here's the deal. You give me a loan of some equipment today, and I'll handle your case. How's that sound?' He hesitated, took a deep breath in and released slowly. 'Okay, what do you need?' He swivelled the briefcase to face me, almost capsizing my ginger beer in the process. Inside there were rows of pens, some ornamental China dogs, a Coca-Cola can and a whole range of cufflinks, each item, I assumed, contained a camera or listening device. None of them looked very convincing to me. The pen was far too big and chunky, the Coke can was an old design, the China dogs were the sort of things no one in their right mind would give house room to, and the cufflinks were made from cheap plastic.

'What do you think?' he asked.

'Not much,' I said. 'I could pick up that lot in any joke shop. Where's the good stuff?'

'The good stuff is expensive,' he said.

'So's trying to keep you out of jail.'

He sighed. 'What do you need?'

'A wire. But one with no actual wires attached. At some point I might not be wearing anything else, so it'll need to be practically invisible.'

Cammy thought things over while he finished his drink. He put the glass down firmly. 'You're going back to see Ricky Hertz.'

'Shh. Not so loud.'

Cammy leaned in. 'What do you want to see him for?'

I wanted to ask him if he'd killed those other two children. The ones whose eyeless dead bodies had actually been found. If he really had whispered a confession to Big Jock Knox, Hertz might be the kind of person who liked to brag. According to my dad, he'd whispered to Jock when he thought he was about to be set free. If I could make him think the same, that his appeal was a stonewall success, would he do the same again? If I knew for certain he was guilty, I'd be happy for him to spend the rest of his days rotting in prison. If I didn't, what would I do? Over the years there had been many occasions when I'd felt like punching my old man, but when the moment arrived, I could hardly bring myself to do it. The blow I had landed in extremis had been weak. It was sheer luck that it had caused a minor nose bleed, enough to serve my purposes. There was absolutely no way I could send him to prison.

'Hertz isn't going to tell you anything,' Cammy said. 'He's not daft.'

'He might say something if he's sure I'm not wearing

a wire.' Hertz would know that if I told anyone he'd confessed to me they'd never believe it. If he was a bragger, what better opportunity for him?

Cammy reached inside his jacket and removed a large black wallet. He opened it. Inside were some devices that looked much more like the thing.

'These are state of the art,' he said. From a pocket in the wallet he slipped out a black disc, no larger than a penny piece, and a lot more hi-tech than the bug Dougie Fleming had had me wear. He held it out on the palm of his hand. 'I've got smaller, a lot smaller, but they're transmitters. You'd need to rig up a receiver somewhere. Hertz's flat is a concrete box and on the second floor. You'd lose the signal unless you could plank it somewhere in the same room or, maybe, right outside the door. The beauty of this little baby is that it also records. You'll only get thirty minutes tops out of it, but, if that's enough, this is the one for you.' He placed one hand on top of the other and gently turned the listening device over. 'It's got a sticky side. Just peel off the plastic and stick it somewhere out of sight. Press it to start and stop recording. Any ideas where you're going to put it? Hertz is thorough. You know that from the last time.'

'Oh, I've got an idea all right.' I had a place Hertz would never think of looking. The tricky part was going to be getting him to say something.

For all I knew, he had nothing to say.

39

The Moorings was pretty much deserted that Tuesday afternoon. Outside, a couple of neds were sharing a joint. One of them performed a one finger, one nostril, snot-blow as I walked by and pulled open the front door. Inside, a lot of broken glass lay scattered about the grey, concrete floor. I crunched over it, climbed the four flights of stairs to the second landing and knocked. It took an age for Hertz to answer.

'What do you want?' he asked through the two-inch gap the security chain would permit.

'A word.'

'Say it.'

'Not out here.'

He unlatched the chain, opened the door, grabbed the shoulder of my jacket and pulled me inside. 'What do you want?'

'You know who I am, don't you?'

'Aye, you're the lawyer of that clown with the toy gun,' he said. What had Professor Bradley called it? I couldn't remember the name, but it was eye phobia. It was amazingly off-putting trying to converse with someone who wouldn't look at you. No wonder he'd been convicted at trial. Eye contact with the cross-examining lawyer was the thing I was sure jurors looked for the most when deciding whether a person was telling the truth. That look them in the eye and deny it moment was why barefaced liars were so successful in the witness box.

'And you know who my dad is?' He didn't say anything, just stared over my head. 'He's giving evidence tomorrow at the High Court ahead of your final appeal hearing.'

He turned in the small hallway and I followed him to the same poorly furnished living room. On the floor beside the sofa was a mug half-full of cold coffee and an ashtray heaped with filter tips and cardboard roaches. Beside it a small white box with purple and yellow flashes at the corner and 'Subutex' in bold print across the middle. I knew all about Subutex; all lawyers with junkie clients did. It was a drug designed to ease the cravings for and effects of opioids. Subutex was often prescribed to heroin addicts by way of court-imposed drug treatment and testing orders, and, although meant for therapeutic purposes, like all drugs, was prone to abuse. Once crushed to a fine powder the tablets could be snorted or injected. Either way, improper use was dangerous, occasionally with fatal results. 'Subbies' might not be the connoisseur's drug of choice, in fact you'd have to be pretty desperate to go down that line, but, in its favour, it was readily available on the street, was a Class C drug and so unlikely to lead to court proceedings even if found in possession or supplying, and, for someone who'd spent the last eighteen years inside, and wasn't sure if they might shortly be returning there, they were a better hit than no hit at all. As I recalled from my dad's interview with Inspector Niblo, when it came to drugs, Ricky Hertz wasn't all that fussy.

He sat down, lifted a pack of cigarettes from the arm of the sofa and lit up. 'My lawyer says your old man thinks he's got it all nicely sewn up, him and that bird, Duffy. They're going to say that he took the cigarette out my

266

mouth and threw it away, and then I picked it up again and dropped it at the swing park when I'm supposed to have taken that wee lassie. My lawyer says no one's going to believe that shit.'

His lawyer was either delusional or a confirmed optimist.

'Your lawyer has done a good job so far,' I said, 'but that's not legal advice he's giving you now; that's wishful thinking. When was the last time you heard of a judge believing the word of a suspected child murderer over that of a cop?'

Hertz blew smoke at the low ceiling and tapped ash into the mug of cold coffee. 'They've let me out on bail. They wouldn't do that if they didn't think the fag end was planted.'

'That's because there was no explanation for my dad's DNA to be on the cigarette. It was highly suspicious. Anyone could see that. If a jury had heard about it at your trial, they'd have smelled a rat. But there is an explanation now. One that boots the DNA evidence into touch.'

Hertz stared at the glowing end of his cigarette, as though more interested in the smouldering tobacco than he was with what I was trying to tell him.

'My dad's an ex-cop with thirty-seven years' experience, and he's backed up by a young woman with no previous convictions. If they say he snatched the cigarette from you, and that's how his DNA got on it, then that's what happened.'

Hertz took a draw and snorted smoke down his nostrils.

I continued. 'Don't you see? What's the worst-case scenario if they accept what my dad says? An innocent man goes to jail. Happens all the time. Who cares? Weigh that alongside the worst-case scenario if they don't. The whole criminal justice system looks stupid, the Government has to pay you compensation and then it turns out, you are a child killer and you go and murder another one. As decisions go, it's not what the Appeal Court calls "a toughy".'

He dropped the rest of the cigarette into the coffee and gave it a little swirl. 'Awright,' he said, standing up, looking at the mug. 'What do you want? Why are you here?'

'I know the truth. I might be able to help you.'

'Why would you want to do that?'

'Because I know the cigarette dout was planted.'

'You'd grass on your old man?'

'I didn't say he planted it.'

'He must have.'

'You were interviewed for over five hours and they never let you smoke. That's right, isn't it?'

'Bastards,' he muttered.

'And after you confessed, you were—'

'I never confessed!'

'After they say you confessed, you were put in a cell. Did my dad bring you a smoke?'

He grabbed the front of my shirt. 'I telt you, I never confessed to nothing.'

'I'm trying to help,' I said.

He tugged at the shoulder of my jacket. 'You want to talk? Strip, and there better not be any more bugs on you. Get your clothes off.'

I stripped down to my socks and pants. He rifled through the pockets in my jacket and trousers, emptying the contents onto the sofa: hanky, wallet, some loose coins. He produced the silver box, held it up. 'What's in this?'

'I don't know,' I said. 'It belongs to a friend.'

268

He held the box to his ear and shook it. Something inside rattled. 'Yeah, right,' he said. 'A friend.' He tried to open it but had as much luck as me with the strange clasp. He threw it onto my jacket along with the rest of my clothes. 'Socks too.'

I pulled my socks off and added them to the pile. 'And the rest.'

I wasn't wearing anything else except my underwear and a splash of cologne. I pulled my boxers down and gave them a shake and pulled them up again. 'I'm keeping these on,' I said.

He was prepared to allow it. He bundled the rest of the clothes up, took them to the bedroom that was off the living room and closed the door firmly.

'Sit down,' he said. I did. 'Okay, what are you saying about me being given a smoke in the cells?'

Back when Hertz was arrested there'd been no smoking ban. Like other prisoners, his cigarettes wouldn't have been sealed up in a bag with the rest of his property, they'd have been kept out. Every now and again when they came to check on him, he'd have been allowed a smoke. Prisoner's weren't trusted with a flame, so one of the cops on duty would have taken a cigarette from the pack and lit it through the hatch in the cell door.

'If my dad gave you a smoke when you were in your cell, his DNA could have come off onto it at that time. You'd have been taken to court early morning on the strength of your confession alone.' I could see he was going to start protesting again. 'Let me finish. The cops didn't have corroboration of your confession at that time, but it was still enough to put you on a Petition for murdering the two kids, and holding you in custody while they made further enquiries.' He grunted, interested, but still not

269

looking me in the eye. I pressed home my point. 'A butt could have been picked off the floor of your cell later. There would have been a few lying around, and I noticed just now that you don't smoke them down to the filter.'

'It was planted, just not by your dad, is that it? Who by then? That other big bastard?'

'Could have been him. Could have been anyone. There would have been a change of shifts. After you'd been taken to court, a lot of cops were called out to search Philip Avenue swing park.'

'Why are you telling me this?'

'Why should either of us take a chance on who the Appeal Court believes?' I said. 'This way it's a win-win.' And my dad wouldn't need to blame his big pal Jock Knox.

'Why are you doing this? I thought you said the judges would believe your old man, whatever he came out with.'

'I'm doing this because you shouldn't have been found guilty,' I said.

'How's that then?'

'Because based on the actual evidence available you should never even have stood trial.' I rubbed the fresh bandage on my forehead. 'And, as for the others, how could you have lured two kids away all by yourself, killed them and dumped their bodies? You'd have needed help.'

'That's what my Q.C. said at the trial, but no one listened.'

'The two kids walking their dogs. Do you remember their names?'

A smirk writhed like a maggot at the corner of his mouth. He looked at me, eyes like flint, just for a second, then turned away, as though in pain. 'Naw, I don't remember.'

'Come on. You did nearly eighteen years for killing

them and you say you don't know their names? Christine and Jennifer – that was their first names. Two six-year-olds. How could you lure them away? Unless … Wait, now I remember. You like dogs, and dogs like you. You told my daughter that when we met you on Cockleroy. What were you doing up that hill? You've bail conditions not to go into Linlithgow.'

He reached down for his cigarettes, flipped the lid open with his thumb and put the pack to his mouth, drawing a cigarette out between his lips. 'They gave me a map with a boundary line on it. Cockleroy is outside it. I used to like walking up there in the Bathgate Hills. Nothing much else to do now. It's not like anyone's going to give me a job.' He lit his cigarette with a pink disposable lighter and chucked it onto the sofa along with the pack. 'Mothercare haven't exactly been battering my door down looking for new recruits.' He coughed up a laugh.

'A few years ago, they found the body of another kid up near Cockleroy, on the far side of the hill. It had been there a long time,' I said.

He sniffed. 'I know. The pigs came to Shotts and spoke to me about it. They did it proper. The whole interview was recorded on video that time. I told them nothing.'

'The child was strangled like Jennifer and Christine.'

'So? How else are you going to kill a kid?'

'I don't know,' I said. 'I'm no expert on the subject.'

He looked at my shoes and then out of the window. 'What is it you want me to say? You want me to tell you how I killed those two girls because they were looking at me like I was a piece of shit? Laughing at me? How I called their dog and it came to me? How I lured those rats across the road, down the path into the dark by the rugby park and strangled the little bitches?'

That was more or less exactly what I wanted him to say.

'Who'd believe you?' he snarled. 'And who do you think you are to come here and start telling me to lie to save your dad? That filth fitted me up like I was a corpse for a coffin and let me rot eighteen years for crimes he knew he couldn't prove. My lawyer is going to be interested in this little meeting. I'll be telling him all about it up at the High Court on Thursday, and there'll be no denying it. There's cameras in the lobby and outside, they'll have seen you come in here.'

I stood. 'Where are my clothes?'

He pinged his cigarette at me, sparks flew as it bounced off my bare chest. He picked it up again and sent it for a swim in the coffee mug, then went through to the bedroom. When he returned he threw my clothes at me, silently watching as I climbed back into them.

Hertz followed me to the door. I opened it and had one foot outside on the landing when he spoke. 'That your daughter you had with you on Cockleroy?'

I spun around to face his smirk. 'Say nothing about my daughter.'

He kept smirking, staring at my forehead. 'Green eyes. I've had blue eyes and I've had brown eyes, lots of brown eyes but not—'

I shoved both my hands in his chest and pushed him away. He recovered, stepped forward quickly again, arms held out by his side, chin jutting. 'I'm not going to hit you,' he said, laughing.

'Is that because I'm not a six-year-old girl who can't fight back?' I said. 'Enjoy the rest of your life inside, scumbag.'

As I made to leave, I raised my hand to the dressing

on my forehead. Hertz pulled me back by the shoulder. 'Think you're smart, don't you?' he said. 'Worse than that, you think I'm stupid.' He seized the dressing and tore it off my face. Stuck to the inside was a little black disc no larger than a penny. He peeled the bug from the dressing and snapped it between his fingers. 'Say hi to your dad from me. Jail's not so bad. It's the first eighteen years that's the worst.'

40

Tuesday evening, I was in the kitchen where there was a pile of dishes that needed doing before we embarked on preparing the evening meal. Joanna was washing, I was drying. Tina was sitting at the table doing homework, pencil in hand, tongue sticking out the side of her mouth in concentration.

'Why on earth would you do such a thing?' Joanna handed me a wet plate to dry. 'Two days before the appeal, you go to see Hertz at his bail address? Honestly, Robbie, if there's a wrong time and a place for something, you're always there, punctual and with bells on.'

Joanna wasn't the only woman unhappy with me. I'd had to postpone my meeting with Jill. I needed more time to think how I could limit the damage I'd caused my dad's predicament following my meeting with the child murderer.

'I thought he might be innocent,' I said.

'Robbie, you think everyone might be innocent. That's the trouble with you. You've been a defence lawyer too long. It's hard-wired.'

Although for professional reasons my wife was wilfully forgetting any knowledge of Emily Foster's return from the dead, I thought even she, a prosecutor, would accept that for Hertz to be convicted of the murder of someone who was, in fact, alive and well and running a small holding on the Northern Isles, was at least slightly unfair.

'Dad, what's five apples plus seven apples?' Tina called over, having realised she'd run out of fingers.

'A dozen.'

'What's a dozen?'

'Twelve.'

'Don't do her homework for her,' Joanna said. 'Tina, what's five and five?'

'Ten.'

'How many do you add to ten to make twelve?'

Tina thought about it. 'Two.'

'That's right,' Joanna said. 'So, five and seven is just five and five and two.'

'Eh?'

'Take your socks off and use your toes next time,' I said.

Tina turned her pencil around and started rubbing furiously at her jotter.

'And I suppose you feel it's your duty to right this terrible wrong,' Joanna said, plunging her hands once more into the bubbles and returning from the subject of fruit arithmetic to the one that most concerned me. 'How are you going to do that without landing your dad in prison? You know he'll never blame Jock Knox.'

'I don't want to right it. Hertz is guilty,' I said, stacking the plate.

Joanna handed me another. 'Make up your mind, won't you?'

'That was why I went to see him. So, I *could* make my mind up one way or another, and gather some evidence.'

The phone rang.

'And did you?' Joanna asked, after Tina had shot past us to answer it. 'Gather evidence, I mean.'

'Nothing I can use.'

'Then how can you be so sure he's guilty?'

'Something he said. A sort of confession.'

'Oh, good, another dubious confession. You do know that it doesn't matter how many times he confesses or how many people he confesses to, it's just one source of evidence? You still need corroboration to prove he killed those other two girls.'

'Yeah, but he confessed to me. That's different.'

'No, it's not. It's still uncorroborated.'

Legally true, but Hertz's comments had been enough to prove his guilt to the standard required by Robbie Munro, if not the law of Scotland.

Before I had a chance to say anything, Tina came bouncing through. 'Grandpa's having a barbecue and he says we've to go round. And he says Dad's to bring round a bag of that black wood stuff and tomato sauce and that Uncle Malky's there and he wants to know if we have any of Dad's special lemonade and if we have we've to bring some too.'

'We'll have to go,' Joanna said. 'He's panicking.'

'What makes you think that?'

'It's obvious. He wants your help, but doesn't want to make it look like he does so he decides to hold a barbecue and invites you round. Who does that in October?'

Like most men I found it almost impossible to resist the lure of smoke, fire and incinerated sausages, but I thought my wife might be reading too much into the invitation. For my dad, holding an impromptu barbecue wasn't all that unusual. Since building his own brick barbecue in the back garden, he was in the habit of staging them on the spur of the moment at all times of the year, and for any occasions that he deemed remotely special. When the three of us and Bouncer arrived, we discovered that this evening's event was to commemorate the leaving open of his freezer door, an incident that had resulted in a thawing of frozen foodstuffs and a small flood in the utility room.

That it was warmer in the freezer than in his back garden was not seen as a problem, nor that the sun had already set, and the light spilling out from the kitchen windows was supplemented by a series of table lamps plugged into an extension cable. It was all terribly exciting if you were six years old, which one of us was, and some of us still wanted to be.

My dad had gone to a fair bit of effort to make things look nice. He'd even had a bash at cutting the grass. The pinstripe effect was either unintentional or he was planning on racing chickens later. On a shoogly old wallpapering table, plates of bread rolls were laid out along with some knives and a selection of sauces, to which we added our tomato ketchup, part of Tina's five-a-day. The old man came out of the back door with some packs of meat and set them down beside the soon to be lit barbecue. 'The steaks are for me and Diane. There's plenty of sausages and a packet of beef burgers for you lot.'

'What's the vegetarian option?' Joanna asked. The answer was fish fingers. It wasn't that my dad didn't know fishes weren't vegetables, it was just that he thought vegetarianism was a fad that people would grow out of with enough encouragement and saw fish as a gateway food to beef burgers.

Diane Prentice had been given a slightly later starting time so that we could have the food on the go before she arrived, the lighting of a Munro barbecue being a ritual usually about as successful as that of the prophets of Baal on Mount Carmel. Not any more, though, Malky assured

277

us. He had a plan. First, you took a couple of old egg cartons, filled them with lump wood charcoal, poured on a bit of petrol, closed the cartons up again and introduced a lighted match to the proceedings.

Amazingly, for one of my brother's plans, it worked. One minor explosion later, we were in business, and as the last of the combusted hydrocarbon fumes dissipated, the Munro boys started lobbing sausages onto a blackened, crusty grill that my dad had half-heartedly cleaned with the aid of a wire brush on the basis that the flames would do the rest.

Diane arrived as the sausages were turning a healthy brown colour. They wouldn't be ready for a while yet. My dad slapped the steaks on and went over to welcome her before returning to the flames. While us men and Tina did all the work, Joanna chatted with Diane. I could hear them laughing about men who couldn't cook indoors, thinking they could if the cooking moved outdoors.

When Joanna went inside to make herself some roasted cheese, Diane sidled over to me.

'Alex seems to be bearing up well,' she said. 'I don't think he's looking forward to his court appearance much, though.'

I looked over at my dad. Tina was holding a sausage on a fork and he was squirting tomato ketchup on it. I saw him glance over in our direction and then look away again quickly. Joanna had called it correctly. He was worried, having second thoughts about what to say at court and wanting my help. I wasn't fooled by Diane's casual questioning.

'He says you think he should blame his old police buddy,' Diane said. Seeing that there were only two steaks, she'd graciously offered hers to Malky and he'd graciously accepted, until my dad had, rather ungraciously taken it off him again and given it back to Diane between two slices of crusty bread. She took a delicate nibble and wiped her lips. 'Do you think that's wise?'

I did. I always had. The trouble was my dad was going to use the cigarette-snatching story, as supported by Linda Duffy. If he did he'd be fine, and it would be Hertz going to prison, not him – but only for as long as Emily Foster agreed to play dead. After that, roles would be reversed.

'What I think is I'm going to get myself another beer,' I said.

Diane pulled me back. 'You're not trying to be difficult, are you, Robbie? This is your dad we're talking about. He'd do anything for you boys, I wouldn't like to think you were hanging him out to dry.'

'It's complicated,' I said.

'Try me. I'm a doctor.'

'What makes it so complicated,' I said, 'is that I don't know the truth. Not all of it. What I do know is that someone planted the evidence that convicted Ricky Hertz.'

'Hertz is innocent? That's not what Alex believes.'

'It's not what I believe either. The law, however, may have other ideas.'

Diane attempted another bite of sandwich and gave up. She was looking for somewhere to put her plate down when Malky swooped in.

'Are you not going to eat that?' he asked.

Diane laughed and handed him the plate. He took from her, giving me a look of triumph as though we were boys again and might end up fighting over it like a couple of cavemen.

'Alex says he's done nothing wrong,' she said. 'Will you please tell him what to do, Robbie? I think he'll listen to you now. I've never seen him like this before. You think he'll be all right because he's your dad and he always knows best.' Where did she get that notion from? 'But I can read the signs. I'm really scared he might do something silly.'

At that moment my dad was showing Tina how to get rid of hiccups by drinking a cup of juice upside down. I thought that was pretty silly, especially as he didn't bend readily at the waist. 'How do you mean, silly? You don't mean ... What? Kill himself?'

Malky had found an old tennis ball in the undergrowth and was dribbling it about, keeping the ball away from Bouncer who was chasing him all around the garden. When younger he could do the same against professional players, even while eating a steak sandwich.

'Who's killed themselves?' I hadn't noticed Joanna's approach. She was carrying half a slice of roasted cheese balanced on a piece of kitchen roll. 'Don't tell me, Robbie's asking you about Hercule,' she said, taking a bite of melted cheese and toast.

Diane looked confused. 'Hercule? Hercule Mercier? He's—'

'Yes,' I said, with a sigh. 'That's right. He's the guy Jill Green dumped me for.' I pulled Joanna close and gave her a kiss on her greasy lips. 'Best thing anyone ever did to me.'

'He's not tried to kill himself, though, has he?' Diane asked.

'He's done better than just try,' I said.

'He's dead? No. When did this happen?'

Tina had joined forces with Bouncer and together they tried to dispossess Malky. He passed the ball to me and we played a quick one two, which sent him off in another direction, leaving girl and dog in his wake.

'About four weeks ago,' I said. 'I suppose if you've got to go, barbiturates and vintage champagne at one of Scotland's most prestigious hotels is the way to do it.' I laughed. No one else did. My segue into a clearing of my throat was rather neat, I thought. I was the only one.

'It's not funny, Robbie,' Diane said.

Joanna signalled her displeasure more physically.

'Watch it,' I said, 'those ribs are still healing.'

'Sorry.' She didn't sound it. 'I'd forgotten about your trip down the stairs. When do your stitches come out?'

'The day after tomorrow.' I showed my bare forehead to Diane for her professional opinion. 'What do you think?'

'Very nice work,' she said. 'Now can you tell me more about Hercule Mercier? I can't believe it. I was at a conference just a few weeks ago and he was giving a talk.'

'Was that on a Friday, in Edinburgh?' I asked. It had been. It had taken place at the Scottish Parliament. Hercule had given a lecture on advances in medication for palliative care. According to Diane, it had turned into more of a sales pitch.

'The last private member's bill on assisted suicide was voted down by a margin of two-to-one, but, mark my words, it will be back, and with more support.' She seemed certain about that. 'Care costs are going through the roof. People are getting older. The Government will have a choice to make: either perform a screeching U-turn on one of its key policies and discontinue free care for the sick and elderly . . .'

'Or make sure there's not so many sick and elderly around?' Joanna said.

'It'll happen,' Diane said. 'Watch this space. It won't be like Switzerland. Not at first. They'll put controls in place, but it's the top of a very slippery slope. It started like that in Switzerland. Now the Swiss let you kill yourself even if you have nothing wrong with you. World weariness is enough. Hercule's company hope to corner the market over there with their new drug Euthanitol.'

'Go on,' I said.

'No, I'll leave it. It's a hobby horse of mine, and self-poisoning is not really an appropriate topic of conversation for a family barbecue.' Diane hadn't been to one of my dad's barbecues before. Self-poisoning, or at least avoiding it, was the reason I made him cook the sausages long enough so that he could write his name on a wall with them.

'The big problem trying to kill yourself pleasantly with barbiturates,' Diane said, helping herself to a glass of orange juice, 'is that they tend to make you extremely nauseous. Many people who take an overdose vomit it back up again.' She turned to Joanna whose next bite of roasted cheese was poised at her lips. 'Sorry.'

Joanna bit into the cheese and toast, smiling grimly at the same time.

Diane continued. 'That's why assisted suicides have to be give an anti-emetic about half an hour before; to stop them throwing up the stuff that's supposed to kill them. Doesn't always work, though. Until now.'

'Euthanitol?' I said.

'It's a new form of barbiturate that doesn't induce either nausea or vomiting. You take the pills and you're dead in a few hours. The more pills you take, the quicker you go. No mess. No fuss. You just slip away.'

'I don't suppose Hercule brought any samples over with him, did he?'

'Robbie, are you looking at your dad? That's not funny,' Joanna said.

I wasn't. I may have been looking in his general direction, but I was thinking of Hercule, in his hotel room, with too much to drink, two women on his mind and the easy way out at his fingertips.

'Only as part of a PowerPoint presentation,' Diane said. 'You can't come waltzing into the country with a drug like that. You'd be arrested.'

'You could smuggle them in,' I said.

Joanna wiped her fingers on the piece of kitchen roll. 'You can smuggle anything in, but why take the risk?'

My dad came over with a couple of burnt bangers on a roll. I could tell he'd been deliberately staying out of my way while Diane went to work on me. She wasn't finished. She took me by the arm and led me a few yards away.

'You are going to help Alex out of this jam, aren't you, Robbie?' she said. 'Help him help himself?' I remembered D.I. Niblo from the CCU saying something similar, except his intentions hadn't been quite so sincere. Perhaps I hesitated. 'Please, Robbie, you have to. You were talking about euthanasia a minute ago. You know Alex would never let himself go to prison. You know how other inmates would treat a former police officer.'

'This is my dad we're talking about,' I said. 'It's the other inmates who should be worried about being locked in with him.'

Diane didn't see the funny side. Possibly because there wasn't one. Did she really think I'd stand back and do nothing? I laid my hands on her shoulders. 'Don't worry. I'm on the case. He's not going to prison.'

'Promise?' she said. 'Promise you'll do your best to help? He might not show it at times, but your dad really trusts you.'

Anything I said to Diane would be relayed back to my dad, I knew that. I could hardly say that I'd already tried to help that very afternoon, only for things to backfire spectacularly. Hertz's appeal was the day after tomorrow, calling at ten o'clock. It meant I had just over thirty-six hours to put things right, and no idea how to do it.

'Don't worry,' I said. 'I know exactly what I'm doing.'

41

Wednesday was just like any other day. Sandy's, office, court, office again and home. I'd used up twenty-four of my thirty-six hours and still hadn't a clue what to do.

Joanna was aware of the situation. She made tea, checked Tina's homework and got her ready for bed, keeping my daughter as much out of my way as possible, giving me space to think.

Later that night after I'd read Tina her bedtime story, I was sitting in front of the TV, aware of the flickering pictures, but otherwise tuned out. That was until Cherry Lovell appeared for the mid-week edition of *Night News*. A picture of Ricky Hertz appeared on the screen. The old one from eighteen years ago. I sat up. The image disappeared, and we were in the studio, a backdrop of Edinburgh, a desk and chair for Cherry and a sofa on which Ricky Hertz and his solicitor sat. The Jail Lawyer had done a fine job. In the eyes of the law, Ricky Hertz was indeed an innocent man. He should never have stood trial, far less been found guilty of three murders. In my eyes, Hertz was as guilty as the Devil and hanging was too good for him. As for his own eyes, they wandered everywhere. If there was an Oscar for most shifty-looking character, Hertz had better start writing an acceptance speech.

Cherry turned to the Jail Lawyer. 'I realise you can't go

into detail at this stage, but how do you rate Mr Hertz's prospects at court tomorrow?'

Jail Lawyer smiled seriously. 'I'm sure the judges on the Appeal Court will consider the new evidence and come up with the correct decision.'

'And that is?' Cherry enquired.

'I'm innocent,' Hertz said, interrupting.

He looked like he might say more, but his solicitor was back in there before his client could do too much damage. 'What we have here is another example of the shambles in police procedures that existed before the Supreme Court's ruling in Cadder v HMA and the changes in the law that followed.'

'Remind us,' Cherry said, and the Jail Lawyer did. At some length.

Joanna came through with two mugs of tea, just as the interview was finishing and Cherry was moving on to a piece about the attainment gap between state and private schools in Scotland.

'What's Hertz's lawyer thinking about?' she said. 'Whoever's presenting the case on behalf of the SCCRC tomorrow will be furious.'

'Maybe he thinks he can turn the screw a little. Put some pressure on the Appeal Court.'

Joanna almost snorted tea down her nose. 'Yeah, like that's ever worked before.'

I knew what she meant. Hertz's lawyer was either brave or stupid. Just as with children, telling the Appeal Court what they must do was usually a sure way of achieving the complete opposite. Perhaps he was hoping the elderly ladies and gentlemen, who'd be on the bench in the morning, were already tucked up in bed.

'By the way, did you hear the phone ring when you were

reading Tina her story?' Joanna said. 'It was Jill Green. Apparently, you'd arranged to go and see her today, but you didn't. She sounded slightly tetchy.'

'I don't care. Did you tell her I had more important things on my mind than her conspiracy theories?'

'No, I thought I'd leave that for you to do, tomorrow. She's still at the same hotel and you'll be in Edinburgh with your dad, anyway.' Joanna put her mug of tea down and put an arm around me. 'I know you're worried about Alex. We all are. But be nice to Jill, after what she's been through.'

'And how do I nicely tell her that her boyfriend was having an affair with a transgender female, and, torn between two lovers, in a drunken state took an overdose?'

Joanna recoiled. 'How do you know he was having an affair?'

'I've not just been sitting back counting the money Jill's given me. I have been carrying out *some* enquiries.'

'You can't tell her,' was Joanna's definite opinion on the matter.

'But it's true.'

She shook her head. 'It doesn't matter. Bad enough that he's dead, worse that he was unfaithful as well.'

'Is it? Don't you think it would soften the blow?'

'Are you thinking something along the lines of, a "Good, the two-timing bastard's dead," reaction?'

Close enough.

Joanna picked up her mug again and took a drink. 'You really haven't a clue about women, have you, Robbie?'

'Is there an instruction booklet?'

She finished her tea and stood up. 'You wouldn't read it if there was.'

'Then what should I say?'

'Sometimes, Robbie,' she said, 'things are better left unsaid.'

42

Morning broke like a compound fracture. Tired, weary and caffeine-fuelled, I dragged myself onto the train and into Parliament House where the hearing of my dad's evidence, followed by closing remarks and the issuing of the final verdict in Ricky Hertz's appeal, were all to take place in Court 3.

I arrived early to speak to Fiona Faye, but couldn't track her down, and she wasn't answering her phone. Around half past nine I went out to meet my dad at the Mercat Cross on the east side of Parliament Square, scene of many a public execution. A few hundred years ago there wouldn't have been an appeal. After conviction Ricky Hertz would have been hanged, beheaded or broken on the wheel. From there we walked through the courtyard, beneath the statue of Charles II. My dad stopped to gaze up at it. The recently refurbished monument was the oldest equestrian lead statue in the UK. Supposedly depicting Charles II as Caesar, mounted on a horse, the statue was believed to have originally been intended as Oliver Cromwell until the restoration of the monarchy in 1660. The figure on horseback didn't look like either of them, and so what did it matter?

'How are you feeling?' I asked.

'So-so,' he said. 'I'll be glad when I get this over and done with.'

I gave him a slap on the back. 'You've given evidence before. You know what you're doing. This time there'll be no jury, just the lawyers and the judges, and, trust me, the judges are all on your side.' I took a deep breath. 'You're going to have to blame Jock. You know that, don't you? We can't go through the rest of our lives waiting for Emily Foster to be resurrected. Jock got you into this with his whispered confession and abduction of Emily, now he's going to get you out of it.'

'And what if I don't? You going to punch me again? I'll be ready for you this time.' He laughed and grabbed me in a bear hug. 'I know you mean well, Robbie. Big Jock meant well too. I'm not trashing his name just to save myself. I've done nothing wrong.'

A number of journalists and a TV crew bustled through the security checkpoint and began to set up in the square. A few interested tourists, who'd seen them arrive, began to gather to find out what the fuss was about. They were in for a long wait. Nothing happened quickly in the High Court of Justiciary. In the unlikely event that my dad was called to give evidence at the appointed hour of ten o'clock, he'd be a while. After that the court would hear final submissions, first from Hertz's legal representative demanding that the convictions be quashed, and then from Fiona Faye for the Crown in opposition. Thereafter the judges would retire to consider their verdict. During that time, Ricky Hertz's bail would be revoked, and he'd be held in the cells until the final decision was read out. I strongly suspected that in the expectation of what my dad's evidence was to be, that judgement had already been reached; however, the court would have to pretend to allow a decent length of time to pass before returning to the bench. I reckoned we were talking about two o'clock, at the very earliest.

I thought my dad looked pale. 'Have you had any breakfast?' He hadn't. 'Then you need to get some food inside you,' I said. The Lower Aisle Café, in the basement of St Giles' Cathedral, was only a few yards from where we were standing. It provided the best well-fired fruit scones in all of Edinburgh, everyone knew that.

'I'm not needing a scone,' he said. 'Take me into the court and I'll sit and wait.'

We walked up the three stone steps, through a stone archway and in through the main entrance. Once we'd passed the security check-in, we walked down a corridor, lined either side by advocates' wooden boxes stuffed with briefs, tied with pink string. At the crossroads we were about to turn left to Court 3, when I heard a voice from my right call to me. It was Fiona Faye, walking briskly across the Great Hall where Parliament used to sit before the Union with England in 1707.

Suddenly, it was becoming very real. My dad stopped. 'What should I say, Robbie?' Fiona Faye's high heels clicking on the wooden floor, like a ticking clock as she crossed the vastness of the hall towards us. I'd never seen my dad so vulnerable. What should I tell him? Blame Jock Knox and let Ricky Hertz go free, or stick with the cigarette-snatching story and hope for the best?

'Dad, you keep telling me that you did nothing wrong.'

'I didn't.'

'Then . . .' I said, though the words would scarcely come out. 'I want you to go in there, put your right hand up to God and tell the truth. Whatever that is.'

'All set?' Fiona asked, strolling up to us, horsehair wig atop her own perfectly styled coiffure, and tilted coquettishly to the right. She brushed an imaginary speck of dust from the sleeve of her pristine, black silk gown, and, keeping a fixed smile on my dad, beckoned me aside. 'We need to talk.'

'No kidding,' I said. 'I've been trying to get hold of you all morning.'

She gave me a gentle shove with her shoulder. 'Come on. Let's walk.'

Standing in the Great Hall is frowned upon. I had my dad take a seat on one of the wooden benches on the perimeter, while Fiona and I set off down the length of the Hall side by side.

'You haven't been doing anything stupid, have you, Robbie?' Fiona asked.

'Me?'

'Yes, you haven't been noising up the appellant at all? Not trying in any way to...I don't know...help things along a little?'

I laughed at the suggestion.

'Good,' Fiona said. 'It's just that Hertz's team are looking particularly smug today and I've been hearing some things which better not be true. What about your old man? Does he know his lines?'

That was something I'd been wondering for days. 'I'm not sure.'

'You've got to be sure. I need him to stick to the script.'

'What script?'

'*The* script. The one you prepared earlier, with the help of what's-her-name, the girl who got away. The two stories have got to mesh. It's good that you've kept it simple. It shouldn't be too difficult to piece together. It's not *Finnegans Wake*.'

'I didn't make any script up,' I said, as we reached the far end of the Hall, turned on our heels and started down the way we'd come, passing other couples also deep in conversation. 'My dad came up with it.'

'Then it's a neat job. Avoids any blame attaching to him, which I'm sure was the main objective, but also nicely neutralises the new DNA evidence.'

We walked the rest of the way in silence until we came to where my dad was seated and waiting impatiently.

'I'm heading for Court 3,' Fiona said to me. 'Best not to be seen conversing with the witness before he gives evidence.' My dad stood and looked at his watch. 'Is this thing going to start bang on ten or do I have time for a Jimmy?'

'Are you okay? You look a bit peaky,' Fiona said.

'I'm fine, love.' My dad managed a laugh. 'I've been in tighter scrapes than this. I mind the time once when—'

'I'm not talking to you, Mr Munro. I'm talking to your son,' Fiona said. She pointed down the corridor. 'The toilets are at the front door. Take your time.'

'It's not the truth,' I said, after he'd left.

Fiona turned and squinted at me. 'Sorry?'

'My dad's story. I don't believe it. It's not the truth.'

Pinching a lapel, she pulled me closer. 'Not the truth? Why are you telling me this? I don't care if it's not the truth. I don't care if he stumbled across the idea in the fiction section of his local library, if it all came to him in a dream or if he's had a team of scriptwriters working on it for weeks. Just don't *tell me* it's not the truth. I'm senior bleeding counsel.' She flattened my lapel with a few strokes of her hand, pushed me away and took a step back.

'I've told him to tell the actual truth.'

'You've what!'

'My dad says he's done nothing wrong.'

'I'm sure that's not the first time that a client has told you he's innocent.'

'He's not just a client. He's my dad. There are things you don't know, Fiona.'

'I'll bet there are, and I don't want to know them either.' She closed her eyes and took a couple of deep breaths. 'All right. I'm calm now. Tell me. What *is* the truth?'

I looked down the corridor at my dad's back as he strode towards the entrance lobby, and sighed. 'I've got absolutely no idea.'

43

I waited for my dad, and together we walked down the corridor, past Courts 1 one and 2, either side of us, before taking a left turn down the corridor serving Court 3. Beneath the high windows there were two wooden benches upholstered with green leather, cracked and worn over years of solicitors and counsel sitting waiting for cases to call. My dad couldn't remain at peace, and was pacing up and down. On the stroke of ten the macer came out, black suit, white shirt, white bow tie.

'Mr Munro?'

My dad and I answered in unison.

'Mr Alexander Munro?'

My dad walked towards him, but the macer put up a hand. 'Not yet, Mr Munro, I'm just checking you're here. It'll be a few minutes. We're still waiting for somebody.'

The somebody they were waiting for was Ricky Hertz. After another fifteen minutes, there was still no sign of him and we were told to go grab a coffee and come back at eleven.

It was the same position on our return. No one had seen Hertz since his appearance on TV the previous day. Although the programme had gone out in the evening, it had been recorded mid-afternoon so as to comply with Hertz's condition of bail that he remain at his address between the hours of 7pm and 7am. His solicitor had phoned the Moorings, and someone had knocked on Hertz's door, but elicited no answer.

'Looks like he's done a runner,' Fiona said, when she exited court three at noon, carefully removing her wig.

'What happens now?' my dad asked.

'I moved the court to hold that the appeal is abandoned due to lack of insistence,' Fiona said.

'And...?' I asked.

'The court is going to sit again at two o'clock. They're sending the police out to look for Hertz. If he hasn't been collared by then the appeal will be treated as abandoned, bail will be revoked and when he's found he'll be returned to finish his life sentence.'

My dad scratched his head. 'But what about me? When do I give my evidence?'

'No appellant, no appeal. There may be no need to trouble you further, Mr Munro,' Fiona said. 'We'll see how things are at two, who knows? Maybe Hertz will turn up with a good excuse for being late. Until then why don't you both go and have an early lunch?' She looked at me meaningfully. 'I'm sure you've got a lot to talk about.'

We walked out into Parliament Square, not sure whether to be pleased or not. Was it a stay of execution or had my dad been reprieved? We'd find out when court reconvened. Until then we had two hours to kill, and the pub wasn't an option. Not if my dad might still have to testify. In actual fact, there was no reason why he couldn't have been called to give evidence in the hope that Ricky Hertz would eventually appear, though that would have meant their lords and ladyships doing work that ultimately might not prove necessary. That wasn't how the High Court worked. As Fiona had said, no appellant, no appeal, and, until Ricky was found, proceedings were on hold.

'Robbie!' An arm waved at me over the head of the small crowd of interested spectators who had gathered outside, and Cherry Lovell bustled her way through to meet us, a TV crew trying to keep up.

I was vaguely aware of the sound of feet on the stone steps behind me. Someone tapped me on the shoulder, firmly. It was Ricky Hertz's solicitor, the Jail Lawyer.

'What did you say to my client?' he said, accusingly, lips tight, nostrils flared.

'What are you talking about?'

'Don't give me that.' Jail Lawyer straight-arm pushed me.

My dad stepped in between us and put one of his own arms across Jail Lawyer's shoulders. I knew how heavy that felt. 'Whoah there, son. What's all this about? You can't go around pushing folk like that.'

'Robbie?' Cherry called out. 'What happened in there? Can you and your dad do us an interview?'

'I know you went to see him.' Jail Lawyer wasn't for giving up, straining against the weight of my dad's arm. 'I know you went to see him and tried to get him to change his story.'

This seemed to be one of those times that Joanna had been talking about, when things were better left unsaid.

Jail Lawyer, restrained by my dad, jabbed a finger at me. 'You threatened him, that's why he's not come to court today. You're a disgrace. Call yourself a defence lawyer?'

'Let him go, Dad,' I said, fists as clenched as my teeth.

'Are we rolling?' Cherry shouted to her cameraman.

'You're sending that man to prison for the rest of his life. You know he's innocent. You know your old man fitted him up!' Jail Lawyer struggled against my dad, throwing his head about, the back of it striking my dad's chin. The old man's once alabaster complexion had lost its pallor and taken on a more natural ruddy hue that was now turning crimson. He let Jail Lawyer go. It was even money as to who was going to throw the first punch, me or my dad.

Cherry's cameraman seemed to favour me, and was moving in for a close-up.

'Stop this!' Fiona Faye came out of the door, under the stone arcade and down the steps, a security guard either side of her. One of them led Jail Lawyer away, the other took my dad by the arm and encouraged him in the opposite direction.

Fiona faced me. 'I can't leave you alone for a minute, can I?'

'Hertz's lawyer is a tad emotional about everything,' I said.

'He has every right to be.' Fiona glanced around at the crowd that had gathered, and at the ever encroaching TV camera. I followed her over to where my dad and the security guard were standing in the narrow gap between St Giles' Cathedral and the Signet Library. She sent the guard away with orders to waylay the TV crew, and the three of us walked onto the cobbles of West Parliament Square. It started to rain as we crossed the square and over the High Street into the Lawnmarket court building.

'Ricky Hertz is dead,' Fiona said. 'Just after you left, the police called to say that they'd gone to his hostel and put the door in. He was in bed. Looks like an overdose. The last time anyone saw him was just before seven when he came back from the TV studio. He'd got the train to Falkirk Grahamston. The television people had given him expenses, enough to cover travel and something to eat. It looks like he spent the money on drugs and took too many of them. No appellant, no appeal.'

'Does this mean I can go home?' my dad said.

'You can, if you like,' I said, 'or we could stay in Edinburgh and celebrate.' Was celebrate the right word? A man was dead. A child murderer was dead. Yes, celebrate was the right word. 'I was thinking we could all go to The Newberry.' My dad was thinking more about the train back to Linlithgow and the Red Corner Bar. 'Well, I'm going,' I said. 'I have to return something.' I put my hand in my pocket, removed the little silver box and showed it to him.

'If you don't mind,' he said, 'I'd rather not be there when my granddaughter is revealed as a thief.'

'How about you, Fiona?' I asked, after my dad had set off down the News Steps towards Waverley Station. 'A spot of lunch down at The Newberry?'

Fiona screwed up her face. 'Tempting though the offer is, I'll give it a miss. There'll still be some tidying up to do about this Hertz appeal. Maybe the next time.'

But I didn't think there would be a next time. Not for lunch at The Newberry. Not when, as I returned the silver box to my pocket, I realised it no longer rattled.

44

I could have walked from the Old Town to the New Town in twenty minutes. It would have given me time to think things over. However, it was still raining and I'm lazy, and I had everything pieced together by the time the taxi reached the foot of the Mound. That was how long it took me to google a certain drug on my phone.

There wasn't all that much information on Euthanitol. It was new and still in the test stages, but according to one pharmaceutical website was set to be the preferred choice for those seeking assisted suicide, and greatly preferred to secobarbital or pentobarbital, which both had the upsetting side-effects described by Diane Prentice.

The drug came in a handy soluble tablet form, each containing five grams of a synthesised barbiturate. Ten grams was the recommended fatal dose, although more might be required for those who had been receiving palliative care and built up a tolerance to certain similar medications.

Roadworks at the far end of Queen Street caused a delay. I alighted there and walked the rest of the way to The Newberry, where, as ever, Findlay the butler was waiting to receive me. I asked him to check if Jill was in the hotel. She was. He phoned up to the James Clerk Maxwell suite and she came down to meet me in the guest lounge.

'Here to scrounge another free lunch?' she asked.

I wasn't feeling all that hungry. Not any more. I had pieced everything together except for how to explain it to Jill. We repaired to the library for some privacy. There were no other guests present, just a maid in black dress and white apron silently polishing the woodwork. We sat down opposite one another in two green-leather, Chesterfield armchairs, either side of a large fireplace. Along the mahogany mantelpiece, delicate porcelain pieces were arranged, and above it an oil portrait of Sir Arthur Conan Doyle stared sternly down at us from an ornate gold frame.

'I've been expecting to hear from you for days now,' Jill said, 'but apparently you've had more important matters to deal with. I've had to delay my return to Switzerland twice because of it, so I'd like to know, before I leave tomorrow, what, if anything, have you discovered about Hercule's death?'

It was one of those moments like when after presenting your case in court and the sheriff asks if you think he's stupid. I knew what to say. I just didn't know how to say it to avoid a scene.

'Well?' she asked, eyebrows arched. 'Found that missing motive, yet? As if it isn't obvious.'

I decided to play along. 'Now that Hercule's dead, who's running the company?'

'Marianne Villeneuve is acting CEO. I expect she'll be given the post on a permanent basis.'

'And is she likely to steer a different course from Hercule?'

Jill shifted slightly in her seat. 'I doubt it. She's under-studied Hercule for years.'

'So, Braxton Cobb killing Hercule on any point of principle regarding the future ethical direction of the company would have been a waste of time?' She didn't answer. I tried another question. 'Who inherits Hercule's estate? I take it he was very rich?'

He was. He also had three children from two previous marriages. They'd inherit everything, apart from a small allowance for Jill. I guessed it was small by Hercule's standards, not mine.

'You're not suggesting . . .'

'No,' I said, 'I'm not suggesting his children killed him. That's because I don't think they or anyone else had a motive for murder.'

'So, we're back to suicide? How convenient.' Jill crossed her legs at the ankle, tucked them under the chair and leaned forward at me. Unlike Ricky Hertz she had absolutely no trouble staring me in the eye. 'You've never really tried to investigate Hercule's death, have you, Robbie? Four weeks, fifteen thousand pounds and one all-expenses-paid trip to Rome later, and we're no further forward. You don't have so much as a single clue. Even your means, motive, opportunity theory has been tossed out of the window.'

Findlay arrived as quietly and smoothly as though on well-oiled casters. He enquired as to whether we desired anything. Jill ordered coffee. The only thing I wanted was to break the truth of Hercule's death to Jill and leave; however, it wasn't something I could just come out with.

'What's your role in Zanetti?' I asked. 'You told me before that you were a junior vice-president. What does that actually entail?'

Jill sat back in the chair, hands folded in her lap. 'I work as part of a team to promote different ranges of non-prescription drugs, some cosmetics and various new types of beauty treatments . . .'

'Then you're not at the cutting edge of pharmaceuticals?'

She seemed to take that as an insult. 'My department had the biggest growth in manufacturing turnover during the last quarter.'

'I'm not being critical. I don't care what you do.'

'Then why ask?'

'Have you heard of Euthanitol?'

'No, I can't say I have. What is it? A sedative?'

'It's a new barbiturate-based drug Zanetti is developing for clinics that provide assisted suicide services. I think that's what killed Hercule.' I took a deep breath. 'I think he brought a small supply with him here to The Newberry.'

Findlay arrived with Jill's coffee on a tray. He pulled over a low table and set out a white China cup and saucer, a cafetière of coffee, a small jug of cream and a side plate with some amaretti biscuits.

'What would be the point of doing that?' Jill sneered, after the butler had glided off again across the hardwood floor. 'To kill himself? Is that what you think? He came all this way to Scotland so he could do illegally what he could do perfectly legally in his home country? How many times do I have to tell you? Hercule was not suicidal. He was happy.'

'Maybe so,' I said, 'but Luciana Zanetti definitely isn't happy. She's dying painfully and slowly. It's not how a lady with so much dignity would want to go. What better candidate for assisted suicide?'

Jill poured cream over the back of a teaspoon into the blackness of the coffee and watched it bloom. 'Braxton Cobb would never allow...' Her voice tailed off. She picked up one of the tiny biscuits and bit it in half. Crumbs fell onto her lap, but she didn't notice, eyes glazed, seemingly staring at something over my right shoulder. She was getting there. Slowly.

I helped her along. 'Why do you think Luciana's granddaughter invited Cobb here to The Newberry that weekend? It was so that Hercule could go see Luciana, say goodbye and slip her the drug. I think Luciana was expecting him. I think she still is.'

Jill didn't reply, her eyes fixed on the far wall, half an amaretti biscuit at her lips.

That's how I assumed it had all been planned. The staff at the Perthshire mansion were used to Hercule's visits. This time there'd be no Braxton Cobb hovering in the background. No one would think anything of it. An old sick lady who'd finally given up the ghost? Slipped away. There wouldn't even be a post-mortem.

'When Braxton Cobb called off his trip to The Newberry, Hercule had to postpone his visit. Don't you see, Jill? He still had the Euthanitol, here in his hotel room. That's what killed him.'

Jill gave herself a little shake, popped the rest of the biscuit in her mouth and raised the coffee cup to her lips. It was an age before she spoke. 'Hercule wouldn't do that. He'd need a special licence to import the drug. There would be a record of it. Someone at Zanetti would have informed the police as soon as they heard Hercule was poisoned by barbiturates.'

'That's the point I'm trying to make,' I said. 'I don't think anyone knew Hercule had brought them over.'

'Of course, someone would know.'

'Not if he smuggled them into the country.'

Jill was having more difficulty comprehending than I thought she might. To help her understand, I took the little silver box from my jacket pocket and laid it on the table next to her cup and saucer. 'Did this belong to Hercule?'

She picked it up, brow furrowed. 'Yes, but what

happened to the clasp? It's broken. Did you do this?'

I could have told her the results of my internet search on Euthanitol. Reminded her that Hercule was a pharmacist, and that he'd have known it would take more than the normal dose to kill someone like Luciana who'd have built up a tolerance to similar medication. Two would have been enough for most other people. Hercule had smuggled four to be on the safe side. I could have told her the tablets were white, round and chunky, like glucose tablets. That they would have dissolved nicely when mixed with orange juice, especially if forced down the throat of a person having a hypoglycaemic attack and unable to resist. Unlike Ricky Hertz. But then, Hertz wasn't fussy when it came to drugs. Give him a box of pills and he'd happily take a risk for a hit. I could have said all that. But there were times when things were better left unsaid.

Jill flipped the lid open and looked inside. The silver box was empty. As empty as the eye sockets of Ricky Hertz's child victims.

She was still staring at it as I took one of the amaretti biscuits from the plate and crunched it on my way out of the door.

45

There was a lot of work to catch up with back at the office. Before that I'd had to pay a visit to the surgery for the removal of my stitches, and, when I returned home that evening, I discovered the Munro household gearing up for a party.

My dad was there, not so fresh from the Red Corner bar, and Malky arrived later once he'd finished his Thursday night football phone-in, bringing with him a few bottles of special lemonade.

Tina, who'd been allowed up late because of the special occasion, though she hadn't a clue what it was all about, was in her pyjamas and dressing gown and sitting on Joanna's lap on the sofa. Bouncer was curled up beside them.

When we were all gathered, my dad poured himself a glass of Benromach fifteen-year-old just the way he liked it: lots and in a glass. He raised his drink and put his other arm around me. 'Here's to Robbie. The best ... One of the two best sons a man could ever hope for. A son who never stopped fighting for his dad. A son who ...' He pointed to the scar on my head. 'Who did that for me.'

He looked like he might cry or at least try to. I pulled away from him. He was drunk. That could be the only reason for the compliments he was sloshing around like my birthday whisky.

'What's the matter?' he asked me.

'Nothing, I'm fine.' I took the beer bottle that Malky was holding out to me, cracked it open and took a slug.

'No, there is something the matter.' My dad handed his whisky glass down to Joanna for her to hold and took a grip of my upper arms. 'Tell me what it is. Come on. Tell your dad.'

'Okay,' I said, after another gulp of beer. 'I'll tell you what it is. I don't know the truth. You never told me what really happened. How did that cigarette butt end up in Philip Avenue swing park?'

He snorted. 'What does it matter?' He let go of me, reached down and relieved Joanna of his whisky glass, the two had been parted long enough. 'I told you from the start that I'd done nothing wrong. Won't you take the word of your own father on that?'

He was right. He was stubborn, but he was right. I had to admire him, covering for Jock Knox. Not letting his old buddy's reputation be sullied even if the former ex-cop would have never been the wiser.

I clinked my beer bottle with his glass and he hugged me again.

'We should have been doing this in style,' Malky said. 'Robbie could have treated us all to a night out at The Newberry.' He managed to wink, nudge me with his elbow and made a clicking noise out of the side of his mouth all at the same time. 'Seeing how he's so friendly with the owner. Did you know that, Joanna? About Robbie and—'

'That reminds me,' I said, and went and found my suit jacket. From it I took my wallet and removed a business card. 'You remember Chiara?'

Malky smiled lecherously. 'How could I forget those legs?'

'Well, this is her phone number,' I said. 'I'm sure she'd love to hear from you.'

306

Malky seemed pretty sure she would too. He took the card and gave it a flick with a finger. 'You know what? I think I might take a drive through tomorrow night after five-a-sides and surprise her.'

She might not be the only one to get a surprise. But maybe this was one surprise Chiara at least could do without. I snatched back the card before he had a chance to slip it into his pocket. 'On second thoughts, Malky,' I said, 'maybe she's not the right girl for you.'

My dad finished his whisky and started looking around for the bottle which by now Joanna had hidden.

'I think you've had enough, Alex,' she said, lowering Tina off her lap, and standing up.

My dad flapped a hand at her. 'Nonsense, lassie, I'm celebrating.'

My wife gave me a knowing look, and tilted her head at the kitchen.

'Come on, Dad, I'll make you a cup of tea,' I said. 'And how about some toast as well? I think you'd feel better with some food inside you.' Tina ran over and grabbed hold of my leg. I released her grip on me.

'Off you go with Joanna. She can read you your bedtime story tonight,' I said. 'I need to make Gramps his supper.'

Joanna scooped Tina up, wriggling, into her arms. 'You, young lady, are coming with me.'

'Aw, Mum, can I not stay up for a wee bit longer?'

Joanna froze. She looked over the top of Tina's head at me. She blinked and tried to talk, but could only squeak, 'Robbie...'

I shook my head. Some things were better left un-said.

'Tina, do as your mum tells you,' I said. 'Mums always know best.'

Tina cuddled into Joanna and the two of them left the room.

Meantime the whisky-finder general had located the bottle of Benromach behind the curtains. He poured himself another glass and sat down on the sofa recently vacated by Joanna and Tina, if not Bouncer. Malky joined them. I went through to the kitchen, returning with a mug of tea for my dad and a plate of buttered toast. The Munro boys really knew how to party.

By this time my dad had moved from the sofa into an armchair by the side of the fire. His eyes were closed. If left alone he'd drop off to sleep. I placed the mug of tea in the hearth, and taking the plate of toast with me sat down beside Malky. For the first evening in a long time I was going to sleep soundly.

'Switch the telly on,' Malky said.

I found the remote under a cushion. The Scottish news was underway, a newsreader announcing the headlines. One in particular caused me to sit up.

'Convicted child killer, Richard, better known as Ricky, Hertz was today found dead at an address in Falkirk ...'

'What's that?' my dad said, spluttering awake. 'Is this about Hertz? Turn the volume up.'

'...the body of Hertz, whose appeal against his conviction for murdering schoolgirls Jennifer Smart, Christine Tomlin and four-year-old Emily Foster in 2001, was due to be heard today, was found by police after he'd failed to attend court. There are believed to be no suspicious circumstances.'

No suspicious circumstances being journalese for suicide.

Ignoring the mug of tea, my dad lifted the whisky glass from the arm of the chair, held it up to the light and stared deep into the golden richness of the sherried single malt. 'Good riddance to him,' he said, and putting the glass to his mouth poured the contents down his throat. 'The murdering wee bastard should have been drowned at birth...' He wiped his moustache with the back of a hand, and reached down the side of his chair, fumbling for the whisky bottle. 'Would have saved me all the bother of stitching him up.'

The Best Defence Series

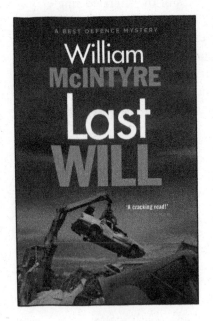

The trial of Robbie Munro's life: one month to prove he's fit to be a father. No problem – apart from the small matter of a double-murder in which his dodgy landlord is implicated.

'*Last Will* has a great lead in lawyer Robbie Munro and a cast of reprobates to keep you guessing, laughing and on the edge of your seat – a cracking read.'

Gregor Fisher

Robbie Munro is back home, living with his dad and his new-found daughter when one of his more dubious clients leaves him a mysterious box. The contents will change his life forever...

'Clear and crisp writing.'
ʰe Scotsman

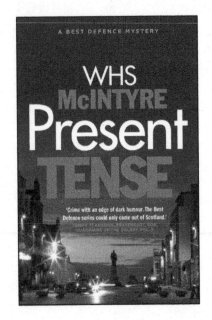

The Best Defence Series

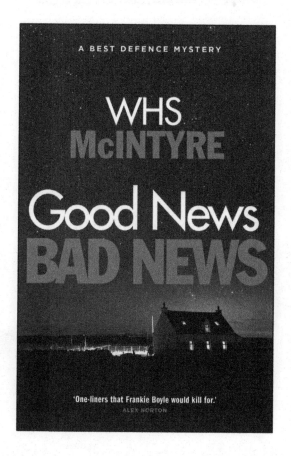

A BEST DEFENCE MYSTERY

WHS McINTYRE

Good News
BAD NEWS

'One-liners that Frankie Boyle would kill for.'
ALEX NORTON

Robbie takes on a new client, only to find she's the granddaughter of a Sheriff who hates him.
His old clients are causing a few problems too, not to mention his shady former landlord. The more Robbie tries to fix things, the more trouble he's in.

'A page-turner of the highest quality.' Alex Norton

www.sandstonepress.com

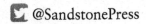 facebook.com/SandstonePress/

@SandstonePress